Poisoning the Nest

Natalie Muller

BLACK COCKIE PRESS

Poisoning the Nest.

Published by Black Cockie Press

Copyright Natalie Muller 2019

Cover design Natalie Muller 2019

Distributed by IngramSpark

Printed by IngramSpark

ISBN:978-0-6481366-6-8

Dedication

This book would not be here today without the love and support of many people.

Here is a big thank you to all those who read multiple drafts, offering advice and feedback. A big thank you to those who believed in my vision and helped with research and resources. A thank you for lending an ear to my endless discussions and brainstorming.

Table of Contents

The Age of Heroes

In the ancient times, before the gods withdrew from the earth and left humanity to fend for itself, there was the age of heroes. For though the world had been purged of the Titans' monsters, the realm of men was not at peace. Brother fought brother and rivalries among the great houses of Greece, threatened to plunge the world into chaos. His brother and sister gods, pressed Zeus to provide a worthy challenge for their offspring. A challenge that would place their children among immortals, for the sons and daughters of gods, should not be condemned to a mere mortal life. It was at this time that Gaia, the earth herself, cried out to Zeus, her miraculous grandson. Pleading with him, to relieve her of the burden of so many men, who scampered across her surface. At once Zeus saw the answer, a solution that would satisfy all those who came begging at his throne, clutching his knees and grasping his chin: A war. Not just any war, but the greatest, fiercest, longest war the world had ever known. It would be a war to end all wars, a war which would grant immortality to its combatants. Ranking them alongside the great monster slayers of old, Theseus, Perseus, Jason and of course Heracles.

And the greatest of those heroes, that the war would produce, the man whose name would become synonymous with this war, would be the redheaded son of Thetis. A man whose life shall culminate in a great pursuit. One, which will be spoken of, over a hundred generations from now. He knows, as he runs, that his actions will seal his fate and yet he presses on. Running down the man, whose death, will cause his own. He is Achilles, death in battle will make him immortal.

He is a man running. A man so caked in dust, he looks like a statue. He is an armed man running. His arms and legs ache with fatigue, yet he cannot stop. He can feel the sweat running down his face, bleeding tracks of living colour back into it, as the dust turns to mud. He cannot stop. On his heels, another man, clad as he is, pursues him. His chest is burning. Every *breath he takes is painful. Above him, tower the walls of the city, around which he runs. Three times, he will run around these walls, before he halts his flight. He is man-killing Hector and today his fate will be decided.*

It was one of those clear crisp mountain days, where winter seems to have placed itself on hold for a few hours, granting a brief reprieve to the inhabitants of the towns clinging to the ridges overlooking the valleys. At this time of year, the cloudless sky looked cobalt blue, above the sapphire mountains and valleys. It was a day for activity, as gardeners taking advantage of the mild conditions pruned fruit trees and ornamentals. The century old custom, of imposing gardens of European favourites on the thin fragile soils of the sandstone ridges, first begun when homesick colonists and convicts alike stepped off their ships in Sydney harbour. Another blue jewel in this unfamiliar land. Here the mountain ridges bore the brunt of the southerly winds causing the wanton eucalypts to dance a wild jig, but tearing down far more staid oaks and pines. Today there was no wind. Today the gardeners' waste material ascended to the heavens in orderly columns, while slow combustion stoves fuelled by local eucalyptus, perfumed the air, so that one at once recognised the smell of home and warmth.

The man wasn't sure what had brought him to this exact spot. It was not the most convenient spot for what he had in mind, not with all the sightseers flocking around the viewing platform like a noisy gaggle of geese. Pointing and exclaiming, some holding guide books, trying to name the cliffs, which rose from the valley floor like ridges along a dragon's backbone. Women in white dresses, clung to the rope at the edge, as they looked down to the valley floor, invisible beneath the thick canopy of eucalyptus, coach wood and sassafras.

Sitting down on a bench, the man placed both his hands over

the handle of his walking stick. Leaning forward he rested his forehead against his hands, closing his eyes. Perhaps, if he wished hard enough, they would all go away. He was too old to believe in wishes anymore. He felt so old, like he had lived more lifetimes than he could count, yet at the same time it had not been enough. The same way, that one can sleep for eight or nine hours and still wake up feeling exhausted. Hell, he would be thankful for three or four hours, of uninterrupted sleep.

Raising his head, he rested his chin against his hands, watching the tourists walk to and fro.

"Mummy, that man is crying!"

Turning to look, the man saw a small boy, having broken away from the crowd gazing at the view. He stood staring at the man, as if he were far more interesting a sight than the mountains that the boy had in fact come to see. Turning away, the man swiped at the tears with the back of his hand. Helpless to stop their flow, he squared his jaw and stared back at the boy, making further ineffectual swipes at his face. Until the boy had seen him, he hadn't even noticed that he was crying. Things like this happened all too often these days.

"George, come here! Leave that poor man alone," called one of the women, standing by the edge.

The boy turned his head towards the voice with a look of irritation, acknowledging that it was his mother who had spoken to him, but remained fixed to the spot.

"George, don't make me come over there!"

Hearing this too common threat, the boy turned and ran back to his mother. The man watched, returning the child's gaze as he twisted his head round to watch the crying man. The man once again attempted to dry his face, before accepting the futility of such action, resting his forehead against his hands, watching as big salty tears dripped from his nose, and splashed onto the dry sand between his feet.

As the afternoon drew to a close, the constant stream of sightseers dwindled and the warmth of the day died, bringing with it hardness, as the temperature dropped rapidly. With no cloud cover, the temperature would fall below freezing tonight, and tomorrow morning would wake to a thick layer of frost. The man shivered in his coat, as he watched the sun disappear behind Narrow Neck. Already the moon shone in the darkening sky.

Alone now, the man rose from the bench he had occupied, all afternoon. His movements were slow and uncertain. He leant on his walking stick, dragging his left leg, which had grown stiff and sore with cold and hours seated in the same position. As he made his way, across the viewing platform, to the ropes strung above the drop.

The two dozen steps from bench to the edge had exhausted him. He leant against the ropes, looking over into the gathering gloom, which hid the forest from sight. This was it, the end. He had travelled this far and would go no further. He had walked these forests as a boy, not so many years ago, though it felt like centuries. It was fitting that he should return to them. Here, he could find the peace, which no green and pleasant countryside had given him.

Behind him, he heard the sound of a cab roaring down the road. The wheels scattered gravel, as the driver brought the car to a sudden halt. Mustering all his energy, the man swung his left leg over the rope. He paused a moment, gathering his strength, one leg planted on the ground, the other dangling over the valley floor, waiting.

"Jack!"

Chapter One

Sitting in the back of his cab, Archibald Kelly was grateful for the elasticity of his conscience. Not that he had been in danger of stretching it out of shape in the past few years, but knowing of its elastic proportions was of use at, times like this. He had not sought Sally Jenkins out. She had hired his cab. It was she, not him who suggested he sit with her in the cab, as the storm that had been lowering over the town all afternoon, broke. It was she, who seeing his unusually subdued mood, had offered to, in her own terms, cheer him up. He had not resisted when Sally, with the adroitness of her profession, opened his flies and took him in her mouth. In all honesty, he was on the receiving end of an act of charity. It would be selfish and ungrateful, to deny Sally the chance to help the needy. At most, he was guilty of a sinful act, but not with his full consent, a lesser offence than if it had been premeditated. A few Hail Mary's and a couple of extra shillings on the plate on Sunday would clean it away.

Outside the cab, the horses shook in their harness, sending a tremor through the cab. A similar tremor shook its driver.

Sally shifted her position, lying against Arch's chest, her head rising and falling with his breathing. "When was the last time we did this, Arch?"

Looking at Sally, Arch brushed her disordered hair out of her face. Her hair was dry and brittle, a casualty of her carelessness with curling tongs. "It must be 'bout five years."

Shifting, to lie propped up on her forearms, Sally picked something from off the tip of her tongue. "Yeah, I got sick of picking your red hairs out of m' teeth."

"Is that why we stopped?" Listening to the rain drumming on the roof of the cab, Arch closed his eyes and pushed the memories Sally's words revived, back into the shadows.

"That, and you went off and became respectable." Clearly wishing to indulge in the luxury of nostalgia, Sally's words continued, oblivious to Arch's disinterested coolness. "You were pretty wild back then. I once thought you wanted to marry me."

Arch stirred, beneath the weight of Sally's body, trying to shake off the numbness that had settled on his limbs. "You wouldn't have married me if I'd asked."

Sally narrowed her eyes, giving Arch a look of exacting frankness. The softness of nostalgia evaporating, as the toughness of her profession, reasserted itself. "You wouldn't have asked, because we didn't love each other. Besides, neither of us are the marrying type."

"I've always been fond of you." Arch ran his the backs of his fingers down the side of Sally's face, smudging her face powder.

"Yes, I know, I'm your favourite tart." Sally pushed herself up, and brushed Arch's legs off the seat, settling herself in their place. Fumbling in her handbag, Sally reapplied her lipstick, using the cab window for a mirror. Outside the rain had stopped, the only drops to be felt now, were those falling like fat tears, from the leaves of the tree they had parked beneath.

Pulling himself up into a seated position, Arch rearranged himself, tucking his shirt tails into his trousers. Sally watched, as he pulled a comb from his pocket and tidied his hair, setting his hat carefully on top.

Watching Arch transform, settling his face again into the visage of a good bloke, the man about town, Sally felt the urge to delay the change. To say one last thing, before they both became their public selves again. "I was really sorry to hear about your dad."

"Thanks." Arch ran his fingers over his moustache and goatee beard, flashing Sally a tight sad smile, as he turned away. Opening the door, Arch stepped out of the cab, with all the fastidiousness of a girl, as he sought to keep his boots clear of the mud. Climbing back into the driver's seat, he signalled to his horses and set the cab back on the road.

***

Stepping into the kitchen, Dottie Kelly flicked the switch of the electric light, in a movement that was rapidly becoming second nature. Picking potatoes out of the bin under the sink, she began to wash and peel them. Marvelling at how much easier the job had become, now that she was freed from the kerosene lighting of their previous home. Still that home had its charms, not the least of which, was that it was not her husband's childhood home. Or the fact that it had not required significant repairs, to bring it into the twentieth century. This house had eaten the whole of the deposit, she and Jack had saved for a house of their own. They had envisioned a rather grander house, than old Pat Kelly's little weatherboard house, up on Bathurst road. Jack had fancied something more in line with the big brick houses, with their rambling gardens one sees in Leura. Though they both knew that Jack's budget would not stretch that far. Not before he made solicitor, at the very least. They had got the repairs done cheap, thanks to Dottie's uncle Alfred, recently arrived from Mudgee, with her aunt Martha and daughter Mary. Her mother, Lottie, always said that Martha's husband Alfred, was the family's social experiment, marrying down, all be it not too many rungs. While Lottie herself represented the other great experiment, marrying Irish.

Placing her pan of potatoes on the heat, Dottie was glad that their budget had stretched to a new stove. There were somethings that she would not countenance, and cooking on a poor stove, was one of them. Clearing away the babies' dinner, Dottie lay the table for three, as it was a certainty that Jack would bring his brother Arch home. It had become a habit since their father's death, to eat an evening meal together, establishing a ritual that would never have been possible, while their father was alive. Jack had escaped the family home into marriage, almost as soon as she, a few months younger than him, had turned eighteen. Their third anniversary, was coming up in a matter of weeks. As for Arch, she knew he had a wild streak, one could not grow up in a town this small, and not know that. Though he kept it hidden fairly well. They would be down at the billiard hall now, playing a game to avoid coming home to this house. Even with most of the old furniture gone, Arch had claimed much of it for his cottage by the stables, the house still didn't feel like theirs. Already three months in, and over fifty pounds worth of renovations, she and Jack had begun talking of selling it. He had already escaped it twice, first to go to school in Parramatta, living with his aunt and then later upon his return, into marriage. Now he was back again, his father's death pulling him backwards into the home he had thought he'd left behind. The back bedroom that had once been his, she noticed he had so far refused to enter, that it had become a guest room for the moment, allowed his refusal to be explainable, logical. Why enter an empty room. But Dottie had seen enough of his behaviour in this house, to know it was more than convenience, or lack of need, that made Jack's eyes slide quickly past the door. She had seen the mortified look on his face, when Arch told him the house was his.

In the front room the clock chimed the half hour. Opening up the icebox, Dottie took out the pork chops she had bought for dinner. Placing them into the hot skillet, she turned to the pantry and took out a jar of sauerkraut, another of apple sauce. Returning to the stove, Dottie drained the potatoes and began to mash them, whisking in butter and cream. Turning the meat, she put the kettle back on the heat, to make a fresh pot for the dinner table. As she was taking the dinner plates from the plate warmer,

Dottie heard the sound of footsteps on the front veranda. By the time the footsteps and the bodies that belonged to them, reached the kitchen door, dinner lay upon the table.

Looking up at her husband standing by the door, Dottie could see the flush of the cold walk home, still upon his cheeks. She liked seeing him like this, full of animal health and vitality, forgetful of the worries and cares that had burdened him of late. In the electric light, his green eyes glittered.

Crossing the room, Jack bent down and kissed Dottie on the cheek. A cool greeting for all its intimacy, and nothing like the types of kisses they had shared, only a few months earlier. Taking his seat at the table, Jack reached for the salt. Silently, Dottie and Arch joined him.

"Did you have a good game?" said Dottie, to no one in particular.

"He took three shilling off me," said Arch, gesturing towards his brother with his knife.

"Really, I'll have one of them," said Dottie, as Jack fished in his pocket for the shiny silver coin.

"Are the children asleep?" Jack tossed off the words, he knew were expected of him, focusing his attention on the plate of food before him.

"Yes, they both went down about six." Dottie put the silver coin into the kitty, which stood on the table, beside the teapot.

Listening to Dottie's words Jack nodded. He ate quickly, slicing the meat with unnecessary ferocity. Loading his fork with meat and mashed potato, he filled his mouth from neither greed nor pleasure, but for the silence within which, eating allowed him to shroud himself.

"How was your day, Arch?"

"That big storm came on just as the Sydney train came into the station. It was fierce, even with m' coat, I got soaked going down to the guest houses. The tips were good, but it took me all afternoon to dry out," said Arch, gesturing as wildly with his knife and fork, as if his hands were free.

"Have you got football this weekend, Jack?"

Every Saturday in winter, for the first two years that she knew him, Dottie had stood in the cold, watching Jack play rugby. His fine muscular legs, in their long socks, and his shock of ginger hair, making him unmissable on the field. Among the under 21's, Jack had been the source of much female admiration. Dottie was herself, the source of much envy, as breathless with victory, Jack would appear at the barrier and kiss her, with more enthusiasm than society allowed. Next year, when Alfie was older, she would be back at that barrier, watching the game. Encouraging the children to cheer their father on, as he chased and tackled grown men into the mud, over possession of a leather ball. It was completely stupid, and utterly futile, but at least it would be a return to normality.

"No, we got knocked out by Lithgow last week."

"If you're free. I'm going down to Aunt Bette's to pick up my new cab. Do you want to come?"

"I'll think about it," said Jack, buttering a slice of bread.

Finishing his dinner, Jack pushed his plate aside, and rose from his seat. "Where's the paper?"

"In the front room on the tea-table," said Dottie, laying down her knife and fork. "Would you like me to bring you tea?"

Jack frowned and turned away, leaving the room. Dottie listened to his footsteps along the hall and the sound of the front room door, being shut.

Dottie looked down at her plate.

"He'll be right, Dot," said Arch, resuming his meal. "It's the shock of everything. We didn't expect Dad to go just like that."

"No, 'course not."

Chewing through the silence, Arch looked at Dottie. Never since Arch had known her, had Dottie actually looked so young.

Always possessed of a confidence and self-assurance, which had made her seem so much older than her years. Stripped of that, by Jack's behaviour, sitting with her head bowed over her dinner, she appeared for the first time as she actually was, a girl disappointed and frustrated in her desires. The image of married life that had seduced Dottie and his brother, had begun to crumble, as hard reality began to press in on them, revealing them more as children playing house, than responsible adults.

Pushing his empty plate away from himself, Arch broke the silence. "That was a lovely dinner, Dot. You don't mind if I go out and have a smoke?"

"Be my guest," said Dottie, clearing away the dinner plates.

Pulling his boots on, Arch stepped out onto the back veranda and lit his pipe. The cool night air, was a shock after the warmth of the house. Looking at the darkened garden, he could tell where every shrub, tree and flowerbed was with his eyes closed. He knew where the daffodils would emerge, as they had every spring, thicker than the year before, as they multiplied silently and stealthily beneath the lawn. He used to pick them as a boy, filling his arms with golden faces to present to his mother. And she would smile down at him, from a face so like his brother's, wreathed in coppery gold, placing his offering in the crystal vase, she had been given as a wedding present.

Arch sighed, blowing a stream of smoke towards the daffodil bed. He wasn't sure if there was a word for how he was feeling, how he had been feeling for months. Sad was too strong a word, he wasn't sad, perhaps melancholy. But that sounded too posh a word to attach to himself; it was the kind of word Jack would use. Perhaps it could be best expressed in one of those, guttural German words, Dot occasionally came out with, Weltschmerz. He thought of the way she looked, when she came out with these words, her eyes would narrow, she would draw her chin towards herself, her lip would curl, making her look like a small terrier and then from the depth of her throat, would come this strange barking language. She didn't know many German words, just ones which seemed to have no translation in English, as if her Teutonic blood felt more than could be expressed, in her native tongue. Whatever the word for what he felt was, it was damned unpleasant to feel.

"Mind if I join you?" Jack, stepped out onto the veranda. Reaching into his jacket pocket, he pulled out his cigarette case, and slipped a ready rolled cigarette between his lips, tucking the silver case away in his pocket in a practiced move.

Arch looked up at the clear night sky, which showed no hint of the afternoon's storm. It would be another fine day tomorrow, another day of carting tourists up and down Katoomba Street, to see the sights. It was shaping up to be a good season, lots of tourists, fine weather, punctuated by the odd storm to send them scurrying for cabs.

"I miss living here with Dad, you know," said Arch, watching as Jack lit his cigarette, the engraved silver lighter a wedding present from his father-in-law.

Try as he might, Jack struggled, to remember anything positive about the house. For him it had always been, the site of raised voices, broken objects and dodged blows. The idea that he and Dottie, were expected to live and raise their family here, a place where family had never existed, baffled him. He thought vaguely of the block of land, with a view of the valley, Aunt Betty had bought for them. The house they wanted, the house they had been saving to build, seemed further off than ever.

Jack drew on his cigarette, exhaling the smoke in a long steady stream.

"When is that new cab you've been boasting about arriving?"

"I'm going down to Parramatta, to pick it up from Aunt Bette, Friday evening. I'll spend Saturday visiting with her, drive it back up Sunday."

"Do you know how to drive it?"

"Of course I do, you cheeky bastard. So, you want to come with me?"

"Yeah, that'd be good," said Jack, as his brother turned, entering the kitchen.

Sitting back down on the step, Jack finished his cigarette. Another six months, a year at most, and it would not seem indecent to sell, to get away. Arch would never forgive him for selling the house. He could rent it out. Jack fiddled with the lighter in his pocket, taking it out, he watched the frail flame flicker in the evening breeze. Burn it down. Burn down the whole place, like a pile of scrap wood. And take all the blame, the guilt and fear, with it.

Closing the lighter with a sigh, Jack ground his cigarette beneath his shoe. Rising, he followed his brother back into the house.

***

Long after Arch had gone home, to his cottage by the stables, on the other side of the railway tracks, Jack sat in his front room watching, as the fire died down in the grate. Down the hall, he could hear Dottie climbing out of the bath. Any minute now, she would appear at the door, telling him that the bath was free. Alfie was three months old now, yet it had been ages, since he and Dottie had made love. It had been ages, since he wanted to.

"The bath is free," said Dottie, peering into the dark front room.

"I'll be there in a minute."

Stepping into the front room, Dottie pulled the towel from her head, and began to rub her long, dark brown hair dry, before the fire.

Jack, looked at Dottie bent over, before him. Reaching out to lay his hand on the small of her back, Jack allowed his hand to follow the curve of her backside, down to the edge of the towel and the bare thighs below.

Feeling the hand against her leg, Dottie stopped drying her hair. Tossing the hair towel into the arm chair opposite, brushing the damp strands away from her face.

Removing his hand, Jack stood, covering his confusion by rubbing his hands together.

"Can't let the water go cold."

"Jack, I'll wait for you."

Looking at Dottie silhouetted against the dying fire, Jack shook his head. "It's been a long day Love, I'm tired."

Chapter Two

Aunt Betty, was the only member of their extended family, Arch and Jack had ever met. Though their father's family boasted more aunts, uncles and cousins than anyone could remember, Patrick Kelly's dubious immigration status, meant that they remained a world away. The only proofs of their existence, were the letters which sailed across the world, from Dublin, to arrive months later in Katoomba. The transparent leaves, were barely thick enough, to carry the precious ink of familial love, to their exiled brother. Their father's exile, left them for family, only their mother's elder sister, Aunt Betty. A woman of no little notoriety. Aunt Betty, like her sister Edith had married young. Unlike her sister, Betty's husband was not a member of The Brotherhood on the run from the British. Hoping to disappear, into the great expanses of the first English speaking country to which, he could gain passage. Her husband, was instead a Rake, from one of the older Sydney families. Who, having inherited a city block of commercial buildings in George street and a large house in Parramatta, had set about to drink and gamble his fortune away, as quickly as possible. Fortunately for Aunt Betty, her husband after only a few months of marriage, found himself on the business end of a grocer's blade, in a dispute in a Kings Cross Two Up school. Aunt Betty took possession of the fortune, her husband had spent his short life, attempting to rid himself of. Possessed now of a fortune, a name and a tragic history, which could open the best doors in Sydney, Aunt Betty proved that she was as much a gambler, as her husband had been. Turning her back on a life as a socialite, in an act which not only shocked Sydney society, but also her highly conservative brother-in-law, she took advantage of Sydney University's liberalisation of enrolments, enrolling to read Classics.

When Arch was ten and Jack only three, their mother was killed in a railway accident. After his wife had died, Patrick Kelly had cut off contact with his sister in-law, his grief making him sullen and withdrawn. For Jack, this meant that Aunt Betty, was nothing more than a name on Birthday and Christmas cards, which unfailingly contained a ten shilling note. At least that was the case, until the year Jack turned eight.

Over the years since his mother's death, Arch had learnt that there was a pattern to his father's bouts of drunkenness. Anniversaries and birthdays were danger times, when after the housekeeper had gone home, their father would sit all night by the fire, drinking whisky. Growing maudlin and touchy, alternately embracing or growling at Jack when he approached, making it impossible for his young son to know which reaction to expect. Though in recent months, Patrick had grown less sentimental and more easily roused to anger, at the sight of his youngest son. At eight, Jack with his strawberry blonde hair, green eyes and cheeky grin, drew a striking resemblance to his mother. A resemblance which, provoked in Patrick a desperate ache of grief and loss, which none of his dalliances with the working girls could cure, as well as a bitter resentment, towards the existence of his youngest son.

Sitting home by the fire, Arch knew that this anniversary was going to be a bad one. It had been five years now since his mother had died. Five long years, of putting his father to bed on nights like this, steering him in the direction of his bedroom and pulling his boots off. Of listening to his father's drunken ranting, or stepping over him in the hall of a morning, on occasions when he proved too intractable, for Arch to put him to bed. As he had entered the world of men and their talk, he had heard how his father had fallen in the esteem of his peers and even, his own cabbies. They spoke in harsh whispers, about his drinking, making dark allusions to what happened that misty day in August, five years earlier. Arch had heard the rumours that travelled about the town. That his mother was weak in the head. That the accident was only one on paper, and it was only the good standing of her husband, with Sergeant Moran that had made it so. Thus granting Edith Kelly, a proper funeral service, and a grave in the Catholic section of the cemetery. It had been the sudden death of the housekeeper Mrs O'Dwyer, earlier that year, which had finally derailed the delicate balance, which had been maintained in the house, for over four years. Faced with the difficulties of finding a new housekeeper, or a new wife, to care for his children, Patrick became immobilised by indecision. In the past few months, Patrick had taken to drinking at the pub, where unlike at home, the beer would make him grow bellicose and aggressive. As his father's drinking had worsened, the talk about his situation had become more overt, sending Patrick deeper into the bottom of his glass for solace.

Sitting and waiting for his father to return, more than anything else Arch felt alone, frightened, and as hurt as ever at his mother's absence. The worst of it was, that he in part shared his father's anger, his sense of betrayal that his mother had died and left him to deal with his father alone. If he didn't cry, it was less from the fact that he was fifteen and felt he oughtn't, than he knew he would need all his strength for the fight he could see had been brewing all week. His father's savage asides and the resentful way he looked at Jack, told Arch that the anniversary that approached was going to be, not difficult as it usually was, but dangerous for himself and his brother.

At the sound of footsteps on the garden path, Arch steeled himself against his father's return. Rising from his seat by the fire, Arch walked into the hallway determined to provide at least some obstacle to his father, if not to divert his attention entirely.

After his long vigil, he felt strangely calm, as his father opened the door.

Patrick Kelly, felt the room sway as he stepped into the warm bright house, after the wintery night. One thought had lodged itself in his mind this night and no amount of beer had managed to dislodge it, though the reason for it had fled long before the last bell. All that remained in the beery haze that surrounded him, was that the boy in the back bedroom, was to blame for his misery. That all would be well, if he could be got rid of. Blinking against the light and warmth, Patrick could see that his way was blocked. Swinging blindly at Arch, Patrick caught him a glancing blow with his big gold signet ring, splitting his son's left eyebrow. It wasn't the first time he had hit his son in the past five years, and as Arch had grown bigger, the backhanders and slaps had grown harder.

Immediately Arch struck back, but as a slim and lightly built fifteen year old, his blows were ineffectual, against a man of six foot three who spent all day driving the big cab, with its two heavy draught horses. Even drunk, Patrick Kelly's fighting instincts did not fail him, his blows landed on his son, with savage accuracy, sending him reeling against the hat stand.

For a moment, Arch felt as if he were choking. His nose and mouth filled with blood. Lying dazed amongst the hats, coats and canes of the fallen hat stand, Arch opened his mouth and felt the blood, run hot and sticky down his chin, dripping onto his woollen jumper.

Picking himself up, Arch, found his hand closing, around the handle of the silver headed weighted cane, his father had given him to protect himself with on the cabs. By now, Patrick Kelly, moving with the unbalanced sway of a heavily drunk man, had moved past Arch, heading in the direction of Jack's room. Scrambling to his feet, Arch raised the weighted silver head of the cane above his head, bringing it down hard on the back of his father's head. Patrick Kelly, staggered and fell, knocked out cold.

Stepping across his father's body, Arch pushed open the door to his brother's room. In the darkness, he groped across the room to the bed, stretching out his hands until he came to the lamp. Taking matches from his pocket, Arch lit the lamp to see an empty bed.

"Jack," whispered Arch, looking about the room. "Jack, we've got to go."

Slowly, the door of the wardrobe opened and Jack peered out. "Where are we going?"

"Away, we're going away until Dad calms down. Come on, get your coat we have to go." Crossing the room, Arch lifted Jack out of the wardrobe and pulled his coat on. "Slippers, and teddy. We are going to have an adventure."

Standing by the door, Jack looked down at the prone figure of their father. "Is Dad alright?"

"He's having a sleep, that's all," said Arch, grabbing a pillow from the bed and placing it under their father's head.

Satisfied with this explanation, Jack pulled the blanket from his bed, draping it over their father. He had seen his father asleep on the floor, after a night of drinking often enough, when he had woken up of a morning. Stepping past his snoring form, to have the breakfast Arch made for him, before he went off to school.

"Come on, we've gotta go," said Arch, pulling on his coat and dabbing ineffectually at his face with his handkerchief. "He'll be fine, Jack. We can't miss the train."

At that moment Patrick Kelly, groaned, belched a long yeasty burp, rolled over and began to snore. Satisfied now that their father was only sleeping, Jack took Arch's hand and followed him out into the night.

***

Opening her eyes, to pitch darkness Elizabeth Ebsworth, wondered whether she had dreamt the knocking that had woken her. Lifting her head, she strained to hear any noise in the quiet house. Suddenly there it was again, a banging on the front door of her house. Sitting up in bed she bristled with outrage, how dare the bosses send their goons round, to try and frighten her in the night. If they really thought, she was the type of woman to be scared off so easily, they had another thing coming. Reaching into her bedside table, Elizabeth, reached for the pistol that had once been her husband's. She had never had cause to use it before, though Earnest had spent quite a few afternoons, before their marriage, teaching her to shoot. He had been reckless beyond words, and at seventeen, the wild child youngest son of her employers, seemed to fulfil all her desires. Closing her hand around the smooth polished wood of the handle, Elizabeth steadied her mind, bringing it back to the moment.

Again the banging on the door reached her, this time followed by a shout, in the cracked and tired voice of a teenage boy, "Aunty Bette."

Slamming the drawer shut, Elizabeth snatched up her dressing gown, flying down stairs. Arriving at the door before the butler, who had by now, also been woken by the noise.

Opening the door, Elizabeth saw two faces she had not seen in five long years. The cheerful three year old, now a boy of eight, leant against his brother asleep on his feet, his overcoat buttoned over his pyjamas. While the lively ten year old, she once knew, stared back at her from a pale face, smeared in blood and a dusting of painful looking acne.

"We ran away. Will you take us in?"

Sitting in one of Aunt Betty's plush armchairs, Arch watched his aunt fill a bowl with hot water, adding it to the other things sitting before him, on the little low table beside his chair.

"The doctor will be here soon, but I can clean up the worst of the blood."

Sitting down on an ottoman next to Arch, Aunt Betty dipped a wad of cotton into the hot water, dabbing at the dried blood on her nephew's face. "I wish you had told me that it had got so bad with your father."

Arch watched, as his aunt dabbed at his face, her face a study of tactfully suppressed disapproval. Turning his gaze to rest on the water bowl, which grew darker and more opaque, each time his aunt dipped her cotton in it. He felt strangely distanced from what was happening. Almost, as if he was standing back from himself, receding to a deep part, away from the surface of his being. Torn between a desire to defend his father, and his current need for his aunt's help, Arch said, "It's not always like this, just when he gets down about Mum."

The words felt thick in his mouth and were hard to form. He could feel his eyelids growing heavy, despite his best efforts to keep them open, his vision grew dark, as he slumped forward into a faint.

***

It was early November, when Arch found himself again on the train. Sitting with his head resting against the glass, feeling it cool against his temple, his eyes watching the scenery flash past in an unfocused blur. After nearly three months stay with his aunt, he was once again returning home, taking with him nothing, but a fresh scar which cut across his left eyebrow and a gold eye tooth, to replace the one his father had broken.

After an initial week of rest and recovery with their aunt, she had begun to speak about making their stay permanent. The news that he was not returning home, struck him as hard, as the blow that had broken his tooth. In seeking sanctuary for Jack, it had not occurred to Arch, that his aunt might see him, as equally in need of her protection. Aunt Betty spoke of sending him back to school, even though he was only months shy of his sixteenth birthday, making him impossibly old to be starting high school. Besides he enjoyed working on the cabs, enjoyed the respect he had earned from the other men, he could not give that up and become a schoolboy again. To her credit, Aunt Betty had made it as an offer, a suggestion, respecting the maturity and strength he had shown, in seeking her help to begin with.

As the letters flew back and forth, from Aunt Betty's solicitor and his father, Arch had time to think. Time to relax the tightly wound nerves, that had kept him alert to the smallest fluctuation in his father's mood, ready to react accordingly. Time to sleep deeply, without worrying about the safety of his brother, asleep in the back room. It was a luxury to think and live simply for himself, allowing another to worry about the wellbeing of his family for a change.

When at last, after weeks of negotiations, Patrick Kelly was sat at the big table in the dining room of Aunt Betty's house, Arch knew he had come to a decision. The proud and powerful man his father had been, was now replaced by a man Arch hardly recognised, remorse was etched into every line of his face, as humbled, he fidgeted in his Sunday best. Seated away from the table, he could see the hostility in the way his father and Aunt looked at each other, a buried current of resentment and anger, of which this was merely the latest outbreak. By his aunt's side sat her solicitor, a dry twig of a man, whose voice droned like cicadas in summer, as he explained the terms of the agreement. Jack would become Aunt Betty's ward. In light of recent events, she would permit limited, supervised, contact with his father. Arch could see his aunt's distain for his father, expressed in the turn of her head and the rush of air she expelled through her nostrils, it was a positively equine show of contempt. Looking at his father, Arch saw him shrink down into his suit, shame colouring his face and closing his eyes.

At long last it was Arch's turn, as all eyes turned to him, he rose, joining the adults at the table.

"Because you are older, Archie, I'm offering you a choice. Would you like to stay here, or to return to live with your father?"

Looking at his aunt, Arch knew that her offer was genuine, she had too much integrity to play tug of war over a child. Turning to look at his father, he could see that Patrick had already resigned himself, to the loss of both his sons. That upon returning home empty handed, his father would crawl into the bottom of a whisky bottle, and never emerge.

"I'll stay with Dad," he had said, watching a flicker of self-respect return to his father's face. "I like working on the cabs. Dad needs someone to help him."

Watching as the solicitor wrote his decision onto the document, Arch added, "But I want to spend Christmas holidays here with Aunt Bette and Jack."

Out of the corner of his eyes, Arch saw his father nod his consent, the shadow of a smile on his lips.

***

Sitting alone in the train carriage, Arch raised his hand to his face as much to shade his eyes from the glaring sun, as to hide the tears that he felt building behind them. Jack had become near hysterical, as they said goodbye at Parramatta train station, making him question his decision to leave. He had failed to keep his family together, something that he had sworn he would always try to do. Filling the space left by his mother, attempting to cover up the gaping hole, her absence had torn in all their lives. He had tried, beyond all reasonable hope, to limit the damage of their father's drinking. Had tried to give his brother enough love, so that he would never feel he was going without. And where had it got him in the end? A broken tooth, a scar and three months rest at Aunt Betty's for nervous exhaustion. Although there was no doubt that he wanted to go back home, Arch realised now that his dreams of returning to the family life he had known before his mother died, were finally, irrevocably finished.

Chapter Three

Although he would never say so, Arch always looked forward to his visits to Aunt Betty's place. For over ten years he had been making an annual visit, first to spend time with Jack, and once his brother had returned to Katoomba, he went alone, for his annual holiday. Of all his family, it was Aunt Betty whom he loved the most, more so even than his mother, for his feelings for his aunt were more pure; untainted by anger or betrayal. To love Jack had made him responsible beyond his years, and though he never resented Jack, he found in Aunt Betty a person towards whom he could be open, without risking it being seen as weakness.

Aunt Betty's house had been built by her husband's family, nearly sixty years earlier, when their fortune had been tied to the brick factory, they had established on the outskirts of Sydney. The house, grand for its time, stood on several acres of manicured gardens and orchard, to the west of the Catholic Cathedral with a commanding view of Parramatta. As the family's fortunes grew, and money moved to more fashionable investments, so too did the family move to the more fashionable real estate of the Eastern suburbs. Leaving the grand old house to aged relatives, who eventually passed it on to Aunt Betty's husband, and ultimately to Aunt Betty.

It was in the dining room of this grand house, with its French doors offering a view of the garden and cathedral beyond, flooded with early morning light, that Jack and Arch sat waiting for their aunt, to come down to breakfast. Sitting opposite Jack at the breakfast table, dressed in the quilted dressing gowns that Aunt Betty kept for them, Arch reached across the table towards the tea pot.

"You never were a morning person, were you Archie," came

the loud ringing voice, as a tall and stately figure, whose silk dressing gown swirled about her, entered the dining room. Always one for an entrance, but despising ceremony, Elizabeth took her seat at the head of the table and helped herself to the pot of coffee, pouring herself her usual morning drink. Something which neither Arch nor Jack, had been able to accustom themselves to, despite all their visits, sticking to the tea pot halfway down the table.

"Neither are you Aunty. Though, I suspect that has more to do with you being up past midnight most nights."

"Jack however, has always been an early riser, even in the dead of winter," said Elizabeth, turning to her younger nephew, who sat screened by the newspaper, one sleeve hovering dangerously close to his tea cup.

"I had to get up for footy practice in the morning, before school," said Jack, from behind the paper, throwing his words away with pointed disinterest.

Turning towards Arch with raised eyebrows, Elizabeth gave him an inquiring look. Arch sighed silently and shook his head. The newspaper shook, as its reader made a greater pretence of reading. "I know what you are doing."

"We're not doing anything, read your paper," said Arch, pacifying the reader, as he filled his tea cup. "What were you doing last night? You were still busy when I went to bed,"

"I was writing a few letters, in preparation for my trip to Melbourne, on Monday." Elizabeth buttered a slice of toast and loaded it with marmalade.

"Are you visiting that Goldstein woman, the suffragette?" Arch, helped himself to sausages and eggs laid out on the table.

"My friend Vida, yes." Elizabeth had never been impressed by the male of the species attempts to diminish a woman's contribution to a conversation by forgetting relevant facts. Though looking at Arch, and the candid way that he spoke, she was willing to give him the benefit of the doubt. In fact she doubted Arch had such a devious bone in his body, at least he had never given her cause to suspect he did. "Since our government has seen fit to involve us in a war in Europe, we must coordinate our response."

"For or against?" asked Jack, from behind the newspaper.

"Against, of course. The arguments that this country is somehow lacking, because our men have not fought in a war, makes a mockery of all we have achieved. It was bad enough when we sent men to South Africa, but we were colonies then. To do the same as a sovereign nation..."

"It is just too much. Isn't it?"

"Don't mock," said Elizabeth, waving a buttery knife in Arch's direction. Her ginger curls, faded now and streaked with white, like the pelt of a tabby cat, trembled as they worked themselves free of the combs holding them in place.

Seeing that he had pushed too far, Arch changed the subject. "Was delivery of my new car easy?"

"Utterly uneventful, I had it put into the garage beside my town car. We'll go out and have a look after breakfast."

"I'm going into town after breakfast. Dottie wants a few things that she can't get at home." Jack folded the paper and pushed aside his plate.

"Do you want to take my driver?"

"No, I'll take my bike. I don't know how long I will be. I wouldn't want to put you out."

"It's in the garage, on the wall under an oilcloth." Elizabeth, reached for a second slice of toast, gesturing with her buttery knife as she spoke, as if drawing a diagram in the air for Jack to follow. "Enjoy your day

***

Walking about the high street of Parramatta, Jack had tried to find things that he had heard Dottie wishing she could find, in stores at home. The last thing he wanted to do was return to Aunt Betty's empty handed, after a trip into town. Besides returning home with boxes of presents for Dottie should prove enough of a distraction, and with their anniversary next weekend, she would not think his buying her presents amiss.

Jack looked at the great ape like face, of the German beneath his spiked helmet. Reaching into his pocket, he pulled a boiled lolly out of its paper bag, and slipped it into his mouth. The creature, for it could not rightly be described as a man, was surrounded by the bodies of slain women and children, the bayonet in his hand dripped red. It was a stupid poster; no one could believe that the people who produced Beethoven, Bach and Marx could have degenerated into ape men, within the space of three months. By the side of the poster of the German was another, here a strong, athletic AIF man called out for help, encouraging others like him to come and join him in his adventure. An adventure, moreover, which it was your patriotic duty to join, to aid England in her time of need.

It would be over by Christmas, so they said. If not Christmas, then shortly after. He could finish his articles once he got back, and then he would be in a position to set up on his own. Hector Johnson, had made it abundantly clear that he had no intention of keeping Jack on, once he had finished his articles. Intending to take another clerk, rather than split his income and his business, with a fellow solicitor. The fact that he had failed to turn in his Articles these past few months, had earned him impatient reprimands, as eager for a new, cheaper clerk, Hector Johnson looked for ways to get rid of him. If that happened, a returned serviceman should command more respect in finding a new position, over an article clerk with six months left on his Articles. He and Dottie would be able to sell the house, that albatross around his neck, once he returned and no one would murmur a word of complaint. Not even Arch, would be able to complain or find fault with his actions, once he returned. Not like now, when his every move seemed scrutinised, and blame for events which he could not even remember was loaded on him. Blame made worse, by the fact that some how he felt that it was true. He had been meant to make his mother happy, meant to make their lives all right again, but it hadn't got better. Their lives had got worse and it was his fault.

Rolling the peppermint around his mouth one last time, Jack crunched down on the boiled sugar, in a habit his aunt said would break his teeth, if the rugby didn't do that first. Taking one last look at the tall, brave, AIF man in the window, Jack pushed the door open and entered the recruitment office.

***

"She's a beauty isn't she Aunty." Arch, ran his hand across the shining red paintwork on the bonnet of his new cab. "I'd been telling Dad for years that we should move into motorcars. That sooner or later, someone else will bring motors up for hire and we would be left behind. But he wouldn't listen, even once I had taken over the business he wouldn't let me. So long as it was Kelly and Son cabs he ruled."

"It's yours now." Elizabeth opened the cab door and slid in sitting behind the wheel.

Arch opened the passenger side door and slid in, sinking into the new upholstery, breathing in the smell of new leather. Cocooned in a world of gleaming metal and soft leather, Arch closed his eyes and sighed. At last in his own element, he felt able to confide what had been gnawing at him for weeks now.

"I'm worried about Jack."

Elizabeth leant back in the seat and waited for Arch to

continue. Her hands, with their shining bands of blue, green, purple and red glittered in the light streaming through the garage doors and the windshield of the cab.

"I didn't tell you this at the time, but when Dad died, one of the last things he said to Jack, was that it was his fault Mum died. All that time and the miserable old bastard, still blamed Jack. He was three. Mum left him with that horrible old housekeeper we used to have, Mrs O'Dwyer, Moran's sister-in-law. Do you remember her, she was losing her mind and kept demanding to know who we were, when we went into the kitchen. You have no idea how happy I was when she finally kicked the bucket. Well, Mum left Jack with her. She must have been really suffering to do that, don't you think?"

Elizabeth looked at Arch, as he struggled to contain the grief and hurt that rose up in him. His big vigorous frame, a match now for his father's after years of driving the big cab, slumped forward in his seat. He had always tried to carry too much, to take on far more than it was reasonable for him to do. And when he had faltered, under the great load he had assigned himself, his guilt was palpable. How easy it had been for his father to assuage his own guilt by forcing, more through neglect than design, his eldest son to shoulder the greater part of his responsibility. From what she had seen of Patrick in recent years, it did not surprise her that dying, he should have tried to shift the great weight of guilt and grief onto Jack.

"Edith was ill. I tried to persuade your father to let me take her away for a while. Give her a change, a rest, until her mood improved. It had worked before. But he was stubborn and Edith was worse than she had been before, worse than I had imagined."

Elizabeth could feel her words probing her own feelings of failure. Feelings, which frequently rose to surface at this time of the year, forcing her to indulge them with a morbid curiosity, the way that your tongue will search out a broken tooth compulsively despite knowing it will cut and hurt. Reaching across the seat, Elizabeth grasped Arch's hand, squeezing it tightly.

Arch breathed deeply several times, his long strong fingers wrapping themselves around his aunt's hand, until it was completely covered. Turning to look at her, his rose brown eyes glittered wetly in the sunlight. "It was eighteen years this past Thursday."

"We can go into the cathedral for Vigil Mass tonight. Light a candle for her."

Arch nodded gently, releasing his aunt's hand.

***

Returning to his aunt's house that afternoon, Jack kept his visit to the recruiting office folded up within himself, as he held his papers in his pocket. Having taken such a momentous step, he felt no need to confess his decision to anyone, least of all his aunt and brother.

"Did Dot really ask you to buy all this stuff?" Arch had decided to pack Jack's purchases straight into the motor car, in order to save time in the morning. It had been a while since he had driven, and though he had spent the afternoon freshening up his skills along the quiet streets surrounding Aunt Betty's house, he still didn't relish the trip. A confidant and assertive driver, Arch knew that the road over the mountains always attracted the usual loonies, who tore up the road and lost their grip on the sharp turns and steep slopes. Added to the recent storms and the delays that the washed out road could cause, slowing the traffic to a crawl or worse a standstill, Arch knew that the drive back up the mountains to Katoomba meant a long day tomorrow and he wanted to start early.

"No, but it's our anniversary next Saturday and we don't come into town very often." Jack slipped into the driver's seat, as his brother packed the trunk.

"Get your grubby mitts off my motor."

"Can I have a go driving tomorrow?" Jack stretched out and pressed his feet against the peddles, gripping the wheel like the racing car drivers he had seen in the paper.

"No."

"Is Aunt Betty still angry I didn't take up her offer to study law?"

Arch slammed the trunk shut and walked around to the driver's seat, where Jack sat.

"No, what makes you ask that?"

"Nothing, I just know how proud she is of her coloured paper from Sydney University. I wouldn't want her to think less of me because I didn't want one."

"She doesn't. I think she would like it if you were the solicitor rather than the clerk, you'd be finished your Articles by now if you had kept up with them. You really must finish them. It's only a few months."

Jack opened the driver's side door and climbed out of the car. Closing the door carefully, he wandered out of the garage, away from the glow of the electric lights and into the dark garden. He could feel the chill of the night, as he gazed across the lawn and along the trickle of water, which a few miles east became the river. Seeing in his mind's eye Sydney harbour, and beyond the heads, the great expanse of the Pacific. Reaching into his jacket pocket, Jack fingered the folds of his recruitment papers.

"No, I have other plans."

The Call to Arms

Paris Prince of Troy, had come from across the sea, travelling up the river to the inland city of Sparta. He came with a mission, to take home the beautiful queen Helen of Sparta and make her his wife. It was the will of the great goddess, to whom he had awarded the golden apple. Though he could not, even now, tell if it had been a dream. As he lay in the grove on Mt Ida, three immortal beauties had appeared, demanding that he choose which of them was the fairest.

He had tried to resist the pull to Sparta, resist the desire that grew within him day by day, hour by hour, to take what had been promised him. It had been an exquisite form of torture trying to deny what he knew to be his destiny. Now that he had taken the defining step, as he sailed his ships up the river, and caught his first glimpse of Sparta shining in the dying rays of the spring sun, he knew what he had to do.

News of the abduction of the Queen of Sparta had travelled rapidly to the court of Mycenae. At a word from his brother Menelaus, the wronged king of Sparta, Agamemnon pledged his men, his arms and his kingdom to join in war with Troy. Those Trojans would learn, in the bitterest way possible, what it meant to challenge the might of Greece.

And so, word went out across all the kingdoms, "Agamemnon shall go to war with Troy. He calls for his brother kings to join him at Aulis."

Many heard the call, gathering their men and ships to join the fleet, a thousand ships in all. It would be the largest force ever to brave the wine dark sea. Others ignored it and continued to sow their crops, little trusting Agamemnon's word, that they should return in time for harvest. While some saw their chance to gain advancement, not on the battlefields of Troy, nor in the deserted fields of their neighbours, but in the empty beds of the soon to be widowed wives.

Chapter Four

Standing in her kitchen Dottie Kelly rubbed butter, flour and sugar together, enjoying the sensuousness of silky flour and greasy butter, as it passed between her fingers and thumbs. It was her anniversary and she had spent the afternoon cooking. She was a good cook; it had been her father's idea for her to learn how to cook, as something to do after he had pulled her out of school.

While no one could accuse Harold Joyce of not being a good Catholic, when the nuns started putting ideas into his only child's head about joining them, he put his foot down. At twelve Dottie had found herself back where she had been at five, standing by the cook, watching what she was doing.

Dottie had adapted herself to this change with remarkable ease. Freed from her scratchy convent uniform and the mindless routine of lessons and lectures, that the nuns called an education, she devoted herself to learning how to cook. Devouring every cook book her parents could buy for her, in compensation for the loss of her lessons. Added to her newfound passion for cooking, a talent for gardening and budgeting, meant that by the time Dottie was fifteen her mother had given her full control over the household, a role which allowed her to set herself above her former school mates. School girls who still giggled at the new boy working the counter at Medicotts, where they bought sweets and soft drinks, making him blush and fumble their change. Not that Dottie was immune, to the charms of nervous boys with faces that flushed as red as their spots, when you looked at them. But like all the girls about town, she knew that part of the attraction of Medicotts was its proximity to the cab rank, where old Pat Kelly's cabs waited for tourist from the train from Sydney.

Here, either arriving or departing, one might catch a look at Arch Kelly, Old Pat's eldest son, driving his cab with its magnificent chestnut draught horses. The perfect shade to complement the driver's auburn hair, which poked out from under his cap and adorned his face, in an immaculate Vandyke and moustache. Not that he ever seemed to pay any attention to his teenage admirers, much to their chagrin.

Charlotte Joyce, relieved from the burden of domestic duties, found she was free to sit on the many church committees with which she involved herself. Free to play whist, once a week with her friends who lived in north Leura, in the streets surrounding the Chateau Napier hotel, over in Hun town. And to correspond with her extensive family back home in Mudgee. Charlotte Joyce had never adapted well to domestic duties. Growing up in a family of nine children, a nanny and three domestic staff on her father's vineyard in Mudgee, it had never occurred to her that she might have to learn skills which extended beyond the parlour. Nor for that matter had it occurred to her parents, who seeing her talent for music had sent her for five years to live with cousins in Ingolstadt to study music and languages. As a result upon her return to Mudgee, although incapable of keeping house, she was fluent in German, French and Italian. She could also play the piano with greater skill and finesse, than the pianist come all the way from England, to perform for the edification of the poor colonials in the Bathurst Town Hall. At twenty two, Miss Charlotte Spies found herself to be the most eligible young lady in the district, admired as much for her dark brown hair and flashing brown eyes, as for her genteel manners and noble bearing.

However, it was Harold Joyce, a wine buyer for the big hotels in Katoomba and Leura, who won the girl known locally as Die Schöne Mudgeenerin. Harold Joyce wanted more than anything, a large family. An orphan who had built himself up into a successful merchant, Harold had made himself into the kind of man whom many would envy. Well thought of, socially secure, financially stable, Harold knew he had much to offer a wife. All without mentioning his admirable taste in clothing, or his noble bearing which in the absence of a real family, often lead people to mistake him for a member of some of the finest families in Sydney, a mistake he allowed them to believe. So much so that he was at times associated with the Macarthurs, the Coxs and the Ebsworths and to a lesser degree the Wentworths and the Macquaries.

Harold committed to his dream of a large family, and inspired by the stories he had heard about huge German families, decided that a Teutonic Rhine maiden would be his best bet for a wife. Moreover, a wife with a large family herself, might just offer him the family connections and sense of belonging he had craved all his life.

By the time of the Bathurst piano recital, Harold had been courting Charlotte for four months and though she had responded warmly to his wooing, he had yet to coax a definite answer from the dark eyed beauty. Charlotte, who had only been back in the country for six months, had scores of suitors, but had yet to find one who met her exacting standards. When Harold proposed and Charlotte had begged time to think, he had feared the worst. The Bathurst concert was his last attempt to persuade her to his favour.

Even to Harold's untrained ear, the much lauded English pianist was a disappointment, so much so that sitting at supper after the concert, he was sure he had spoilt any chance of hearing a positive reply to his proposal.

"Imagine coming all the way from England to play piano when one doesn't play even half as well as you do, my dear Charlotte. The organisers of his tour must think we are all savages in this country to be dazzled by such poor playing. It wasn't even interesting repertoire, an all British program. Even I can hear the difference between that and the music you brought back from overseas," said Harold, by way of apology, as they ate their dinner. His face a study of resigned disappointment, as he considered the loss of his charming companion.

To Charlotte, some acknowledgement from a suitor that they valued her as more than a mere trophy, was what she had been waiting to hear. Reaching across the table, in a gesture he at first mistook for consolation, she took Harold's hand in her own.

"Harold, did you bring it?"

"It has never left my person." Harold reached into his pocket and drew out the velvet ring box.

Relieved to be liberated from domestic tasks, Charlotte Joyce marvelled at her daughter's skills, hoping that her daughter might also excel in that other area where nature had failed her. Her inability to have the large family she and her husband had planned, made Charlotte feel like a lap dog some days, beautiful and beloved, but essentially useless. For Charlotte loved babies and children, most of her charity work was directed at improving the lives, of poor and neglected children. She was a woman who could not bear to think, of a child going without food or a warm coat, and idly standing by. The frequent recipients of her greatest generosity though were her dozens of nieces and nephews, with seven brothers and a sister, she was always knitting or sewing some item of clothing or small toy for her extended family. Never was a birthday forgotten or a Christmas unmarked, by some small gift from Aunty Lottie, in Katoomba. So when Dottie made her a grandmother not once, but twice, in the space of two years, she was overjoyed and relieved, that her daughter did not suffer from the same complications that had marred her own pregnancies. All but one of which had failed to run to term. Dottie seemed able to give birth, as easily as a cat.

Feeling that the butter and flour mixture between her fingers, had taken on the texture of damp sand, Dottie brushed off her hands and added eggs to the pastry. On the hob, the potatoes were boiling in their pot, waiting to be fished out, sliced and thrown into a pan of fat and roasted, alongside the shoulder of pork, which had been slowly roasting in the oven all afternoon. Soon she would have the apple pie in the oven and custard cooking on the hob.

***

"If you can get a week off work in November, Dad said he would like to take us all out to Mudgee. He'd like to take you out shooting. Granddad can always do with the rabbits being cleared out of the vineyard."

"I'll think about it," said Jack, picking at his food.

"Are you not enjoying it? There's more apple sauce if you want it."

"No, it's fine," said Jack, continuing to move his roast meat and potatoes around his plate, as if trying to disguise the fact that he wasn't eating.

"Do you want some more wine?" said Dottie, reaching across the table to refill Jack's glass. "I think it's getting better with age. Granddad said it was his best vintage in years."

"Its fine, it's all fine," said Jack, reaching for his glass and emptying it without tasting. Mindlessly refilling the glass, Jack wondered how much longer he could keep up his charade.

"Is anything wrong? I have apple pie in the oven, if you would you rather that?"

Dottie, made to rise from her place. Jack noticed the cut crystal drop earrings she had worn on their wedding day. They caught the light from the electric lamp, as she turned towards the kitchen, and reflected it against her neck. For the first time in months, he felt the urge to reach across the table and touch her, to press his mouth greedily to her pale skin and feel every inch of her pressed up against him. The feeling was strong and so unexpected, that Jack had to close his eyes for a moment.

"No, stay here," said Jack laying his cutlery down and taking a sip from his glass.

Dottie settled herself back into her chair.

"Dottie, I enlisted in the army while I was down in Parramatta, last weekend. I'll be leaving tomorrow for Kensington race course, to start basic training."

Dottie heard Jack's words, but for several terrifying moments they were nothing, but sounds with no meaning attached. Her whole body felt suddenly numb, not cold but numb like when you sit in the same position and your leg falls asleep. She could see the whole of her life, as she had envisaged it, rent by Jack's words, and yet the meaning still had not dawned upon her. Enlisted. Leaving. These were not words that were meant to come out of your husband's mouth. Signed up for university, perhaps. Had an exciting new job offer, certainly. But not enlisted in the army. Opposite her Jack sat waiting, his face wearing a puzzled expression, confused by her reaction. Looking at him Dottie knew that she had to respond, she had to find words soon, to express emotions that she couldn't even register herself. As a result when she finally found her voice, it came out as a shriek.

"Just like that you joined up. You signed up without even telling me."

"I'm telling you now," said Jack, the earlier tenderness he had felt for his wife evaporating.

"That's not good enough Jack. What about me and the children, did you even think of us."

Looking at the carving knife lying on the serving plate, Jack wished he had waited until the table was clear, to tell Dottie what he had done.

"You'll be getting two thirds of my pay, that's enough to take care of you and the children."

"And how much will they be giving you? I've seen the bits of paper they hand out, two pound twelve shillings and nine pence. That's nothing. Hector Johnson gives you five pound a week."

"We have savings, you can use those. Besides the war can't last that long. I'll be back before you know it. This is something I have to do, you understand that, don't you Dottie?"

Dottie rose from the table, beginning to clear away the dinner she had laid.

"What are you doing, I'm not finished."

Jack held back his plate, as Dottie gasped hold of it.

"Oh, so you like it when I make dinner and a nice home for you. And you like the children I give you, but not enough to discuss with me when you plan to turn that home upside down."

Dottie scowled at Jack, giving him a look that would have frightened a Roman legion as it advanced on the Rhine. Jack no longer saw his little wife, who cooked, cleaned and brought up his children, the woman who stood before him was ancient, wrapped in furs and robes, the black forests, and mountains of Bavaria were reflected in her eyes.

"I have every right to sign up, there is a war going on," said Jack, releasing his plate.

Taking the plate, Dottie threw it to the floor, followed by hers and the serving dish.

"Take it easy Dottie, that was a wedding present," said Jack, looking down at the pile of shattered crockery and the remains of the roast dinner.

"Suddenly you care about our wedding. Go, Jack. Go, fight and have an adventure. Perhaps you'll be ready for marriage when you come back."

"Dottie, don't be like that," said Jack, moving to embrace his wife.

Dismissing his attempted embrace, Dottie strode across the room. Jack heard the bedroom door slam shut. Looking down at the mess on the floor, he went to fetch a bucket from the laundry. Returning he bent down and began to pick up the joint and the potatoes. Followed by the broken china, listening to it slither and fragment further as it slipped from his hands and fell into the bucket. Turning to the dresser, he took down the remaining four plates of the dinner service and dropped them one by one, onto the floorboards, watching as they broke and scattered fragments across the room.

Once all the plates were broken, Jack picked up his hat and coat and walked out the front door.

***

Dottie could feel the early morning light, pressing against her eye lids, but still she resisted opening her eyes. She did not want to make the empty space, in the bed next to her, a reality, not yet. Though, the absence of her husband from their bed, had disturbed her sleep almost as much as their argument the previous night had. Three years of sharing her bed, made the odd lonely night she had spent in that time, as difficult to accommodate to as sleeping with another had been in the first place. Three years of marriage had been ruined in one night and a pile of broken crockery. If she opened her eyes, she would have to get out of bed. Her bed, the bed she shared with her husband, the husband who had decided that his marriage vows stood for nothing and that she had no claim over any of his actions. Pulling the quilt over her head to block out the sunlight, Dottie knew that it would only be minutes before one of the children woke. Just a few more minutes, she thought, begging the sleep that had already released her, to return and obliterate the mess that her waking life had become.

But such thoughts were futile, as Alfie began to cry, forcing her out of bed and across the hall to the nursery. Lifting her son from his crib, Dottie took him back to her bedroom and laid him on her bed, to change his nappy. Taking care to avoid looking at Jack's side of the bed, Dottie lifted up her son, opening the front of her nightdress. Sitting on the edge of the bed, she began to feed him.

Dottie looked down at the green eyes that stared up at her as he fed. Their trust and love, more complete than anything she had ever known, before her children came into her life. "Not even you could keep him here, my little love."

Half his usual pay, less than half of what he brought home now. How would they survive on less than half his pay? Not that Jack ever noticed what she did with the five pounds he presented her every week. There would be no more prime cuts from the butchers, she would have to queue with the working men's wives, for cut priced sausages and offal. The thought was sickening, not to mention humiliating, to stand at the end of the day with those gossiping uncouth women, just to make ends meet. She would have to let go of Molly, the girl from the Gully, who came to help with the washing and cleaning most days. She had only just promised Molly a raise of sixpence a week, since Alfie was going through so many nappies these days. The savings for the children's futures would have to stop, so too would the donations to the church every Sunday.

Then there were the electric lights that had recently been installed, it wouldn't be possible to pay for them on an army wage. To lose them was a galling thought, as they made it so much easier to do things of an evening; perhaps she could keep them on if she took in some sort of work. As if she didn't have enough work to do, with the children, as it was.

Dottie could feel the anger mounting in her chest, as all the practicalities of Jack's decision, entered her mind. Perhaps another woman would be distraught and sobbing, at the thought of her husband marching off to war. Perhaps she was supposed to be distraught, was that what he had expected when he dropped his news on their dinner, like a bomb. Had she failed to be submissive and delicate enough, to keep him interested in staying home. Had she somehow failed to be the wife he wanted, because she was strong and capable, and did not need his help to do her sums? Though why he would wish for a lapdog of a wife, all of a sudden, was beyond her. It had been her keen mind and practical nature, which had attracted him in the first place. She knew that she could not be what nature had not intended her to be. Jack had entered their union with his full consent; he had pestered her until she agreed to step out with him. The brash, flame haired young man, fresh from school in Sydney, the star player of the local rugby team and with the help of her father, soon to become Hector Johnson's new article clerk. He had seen her at church, sitting up the front with her parents, at ten o'clock Mass. He sitting down the back, by the door with his father and brother, the pew Mr Patrick Kelly had claimed, in his mind as his own. So much so, that he would arrive early to church to retain possession of it, his sons arriving later, clearly embarrassed by their father's behaviour. He had introduced himself after Mass one Easter, a good time for such things, as the festive mood allowed for a relaxation of the reserve which existed between families, who were acquainted only by a nod of a head across the aisle once a week.

He had introduced himself to her, and she had allowed him to chat, a rare thing for her in the presence of her parents. For Dottie always felt more reserved in social situations. This day, however, she allowed herself to flirt with the audacious young man, even though his cheeks were still not clear of acne, and his voice boomed and broke, in that uneven way of teenage boys.

From that day, until the day he proposed, Jack had pursued

her with great enthusiasm. To think that he had now grown tired of her seemed impossible. And yet there was a pile of shattered crockery in the dining room to prove just that. The willow pattern plates they had been given by one of her oldest friends. Plates she had coveted in the store for weeks, until they had disappeared from the window display, only to turn up amongst her wedding gifts. She wondered where Jack had gone to last night. Had he gone to Arch's and complained of a fight, without sharing the cause. More than likely, he had gone to the train station and caught the last train to Sydney. That had been his plan, to sneak off without telling anyone, or at least to leave, while blocking his ears to all words of complaint.

Laying Alfie back in his crib, Dottie entered the dining room looking at the mess on the floor. All six plates had not only been broken, but had been trampled into splinters. Taking the dust pan and broom from by the fireplace, Dottie knelt down and swept up the shattered china, tipping it into the bucket Jack had abandoned there the night before. Picking up the bucket, she carried it across the yard and emptied it into the rubbish pit by the outhouse.

***

Sitting at the bar of The Harp and Fiddle, Arch nursed his beer. It had been a long day for a so called day of rest. One of his best horses had come down with colic, and he had spent all day at the stables, working with her. By evening, whatever had upset his mare had passed and Arch, though not a drinking man, felt he deserved a night at the pub.

Arch had just ordered his second beer, when he heard himself hailed from across the bar.

"Arch, long time no see."

Arch turned to see Charlie Sumner, seated across the room.

No longer was he the dapper larrikin, Arch remembered from their youth, Charlie Sumner was now dressed in a faded and patched blue jacket and dusty charcoal trousers, which had once been black. His battered hat sat on the table as he nursed his beer, his eyes glancing round the bar from time to time, hoping to meet with a friendly face. Arch picked up his beer, and moved across the crowded pub, to join the one time cabbie.

"So how is life treating you these days?" Arch took a sip, settling himself into a seat.

"Not bad, apple trees don't give the same sort of lip as tourists."

"Ah, Charlie, I couldn't do it. I'm sociable, unlike you, you miserable bastard, stuck out in Shipley with only cockies and kangaroos to keep you company." Arch reached into his jacket pocket and fished out his pipe and matches.

"There is the Missus, she's a good sort," said Charlie, draining his glass.

"You want another?"

"I shouldn't, but if you're buying. I'll partake again."

Arch signalled to the barman to bring another round. "So, what brings you into town?"

"Had to bring the Missus in to see the Doc tomorrow. She's expecting our first in December," said Charlie, as the barman placed a fresh schooner on the table. "What about you?"

"What about me?"

"Well, is there anyone I should know about, any wedding bells on the horizon?"

"No, but you'll be the first to know if anything happens in that department. I owe you a turn as best man, don't I?" Arch elbowed his mate with a grin, making him slop his beer as he laughed.

"So, what about this war?" Charlie returned his glass to the table.

"Bad business, but it's not our problem. Let the Poms and the Frogs deal with them." Arch blew a stream of smoke from his nostrils, for added emphasis.

"Be careful where you say things like that." Charlie gave a wry smile, as half a dozen heads turned in their direction, nodding agreement with Arch's words. "Say that stuff anywhere but The Harp and Fiddle and you'll get yourself into trouble."

"When the Pommie bastards leave Ireland and stop persecuting our people, then maybe." Arch pounded the table making the glasses dance. "As it is I have one life and I'm rather attached to it a present, so I don't feel much like giving it up for an Englishman's squabble."

"It's a bad business all right. I've already lost a couple of the boys who do jobs for me about the farm. Because, you know they'll take everyone they can get, whether they need them or not. You know Fletcher, the horse breeder down in Megalong, well his boy signed up, headed for the Light Horse apparently."

"It's a bastard of a business. You won't catch me swearing to fight for an English king and leaving m' business in the hands of idiots. Could you imagine Smithy trying to manage the books, he can barely manage to make change from a ten shilling note. You should have seen him when some bloke handed over a five quid note once. It was a good thing I was there. I've considered hanging a sign around his neck, saying 'Correct fares only. No change given.'"

"Why do you keep him on?"

"He's good with the horses. I don't send him out much, only when there is no one else. Besides, he has a sick mother and three younger than him to support. I couldn't chuck him out knowing that."

"You're soft, Mate. You always have been one for hard luck stories, bedraggled animals and damsels in distress. I gather your brother doesn't share your sentiments about fighting for King and Country."

Arch gave his friend a questioning look.

"Well, I heard it from Stephen Jefferies, at the paper shop that your brother was seen leaving on the last train down to Sydney last night. Didn't he tell you?"

"No, come to think of it, I haven't seen him since Friday. One of m' horses was crook; I've been looking after her all day. I think I'd better go and find out what that brother of mine, has gone and done." Arch drained his glass and rose from his chair. "Any way, it's been good seeing you again Charlie. We should do it more often."

"Yeah Mate, always good to have a catch up."

Charlie watched, as Arch's tall figure, was absorbed by the crowd and disappeared from view.

***

"My George signed up last week," said Mrs Richardson, a large bosomed woman, whose tweed overcoat made her look like a speckled hen. Standing in line at The Crown bakery, Mrs Richardson enjoyed her daily gossip with the other shoppers.

"You must be terribly proud." Mrs Jones watched as Mrs Richardson swelled beneath her tweed. "I'm sure if I had sons I should be proud to see them sign up."

Mrs Richardson, unable to detect the sarcasm in Mrs Jones' voice, bestowed a smile of one whose opinion has been upheld, upon her fellow shopper, as she stepped up to the counter to place her order. Mrs Jones, watching the back of Mrs Richardson, found herself thanking the Lord he had seen fit to send her only daughters. Six girls, she and Mr Jones had hoped for a son, but today for the first time she could see the wisdom of the Lord in giving her only daughters. Besides Jones was such a common name there was no great chance of it dying out.

"You cannot imagine how well I will sleep knowing that George will be fighting the Hun and keeping us safe," said Mrs Richardson, as the baker wrapped her order.

"Yes, I can imagine what a relief that must be." Mrs Jones stepped up to the counter, to speak to the baker.

"I heard one of the Kelly boys has signed up too," said Mrs Richardson, seeing Mrs Jones' confusion added, "Pat Kelly, the cabbie's boys."

"I don't believe that, not one of Patrick Kelly's boys. Don't you remember how he used to rage against all things English?" Though she had the good sense not to add, as any good Highland Scot should, "Not that I could disagree with him."

Mrs Jones' Highland accent, was still as austere as ever, even after a quarter of a century in her new home. She had met her husband in Sydney, both fresh off the boat, ready to start a life in a new land. Mr Jones had been drawn to Katoomba to work in the mines, while Mrs Jones had found a wilderness to match her Highlands and a home in which she ruled rather than served, as the immigration posters had offered. Once the mines had closed, Mr Jones had taken a job at Clarence and Mrs Jones, who refused to move again, having sworn that one move, was all a body could take, remained in Katoomba with their girls and only ever saw him late at night or on weekends. Though in truth all she really wanted to see of him was his pay packet. With six unmarried girls under twenty, her husband's pay packet, was more important than his presence.

"You can never tell how your children will turn out. Seems old Patrick Kelly managed to produce one good son," said Mrs Richardson, as she placed her loaves into her basket.

Watching Mrs Richardson leave, Mrs Jones rolled her eyes at the baker, who smiled into his cash register, as he made change. He was a small man with thick arms, from kneading dough and a dusty complexion, partly from the flour and partly the unsociable hours to which his work tied him.

"I trust you won't be heading out to sign up, Mr Beaton?"

"Not on your life, I've got three littlies at home and another on the way," adding in a low voice, so that Mrs Jones had to lean in to hear him. "I had a brother in the AIF; they sent him to fight Boers in South Africa. He has never been right since. 'E's out bush somewhere, travelling about, sleeping rough, working stock yards and shearing sheds when he can. You're lucky to have girls, they don't cause that sort of worry."

Gathering Armies

Among those lured to Aulis, by the promise of fame and glory was Achilles, son of Peleus and the goddess Thetis. In turn, he would be used to lure another to Aulis. The becalmed winds, which stilled the ships in the harbour, could only be the work of a god, for only a god could be so constant and capricious. When it was announced that only the sacrifice of Agamemnon's daughter would satisfy the offended deity. The Great King sent word to his wife, ordering her to join him at Aulis, so that they could celebrate his eldest daughter, Iphigenia's, betrothal to Achilles. Realising too late, what Agamemnon truly planned, Clytemnestra was unable to save her daughter from her husband's knife.

Returning home, without her beautiful girl, Clytemnestra cursed her husband's self-interested actions. She cursed him and all his endeavours, as the Greek fleet sailed out of the heads at last. Enjoying a favourable westerly wind, which drove the fleet closer with every minute, to the glory that awaited them in Troy.

Chapter Five

On first impressions it looked like the house of a person whose life was falling apart. In the far corner of the front room, under one of the windows, a desk heaped with papers, files and books squatted on three legs. Its forth, lost long before its present owner had found it, replaced by a pile of bricks, giving it a slight lean forwards to the left. Its surface, what could be seen of it, was a mosaic of spilled ink and scorch rings from hot teapots. Beside the desk, stood precarious piles of books and newspapers, piles which ran along the wall to the door. Where a book case, evidently bought to house the balanced literature, lay on its side, abandoned there and now serving as a further surface to house piles of books. Against the wall, on the other side of the door stood a hamper of clean clothes, delivered days earlier by the laundry, but which had still not made it to the bedroom. The wardrobe itself, stood open and empty, apart from one black suit and a winter overcoat. Its job taken by a series of hampers in the bedroom, containing clean clothes, while dirty ones lay piled about the bedroom, waiting to be hurriedly gathered together, the night before laundry day. The walls of the front room were stained with a mixture of wood, kerosene and tobacco smokes, giving the walls a flat grey colour, and causing the room to look dark, even in midsummer when the sunlight streamed in the westerly windows. Against the opposite wall to the books and desk, lay a tangled clutter of harnesses and polishing materials. Dominating the room was a large brown leather lounge. The leather of which, in contrast to the neglect of much of the rest of the room was polished to a supple sheen. On the floor before the lounge, lay a pile of used crockery, and a large silver teapot.

Lying on the lounge, looking up at the clock striking ten on the mantel piece, above the empty fire place, lay Arch. The dark had closed in around him, as he lay on the lounge, eventually enclosing him in near complete darkness, broken only by the glow from his pipe and the occasional flare of a match. He had been lying on the lounge since he had returned from work that evening, smoking pipe after pipe and drinking tea which grew increasingly strong and cold as the evening wore on. One could be tempted to say that he was thinking, though thinking was too positive a word, to apply to what Arch had spent the evening doing. No, lying in the dark Arch had been feeling, allowing the many conflicting emotions he had been experiencing in recent months to wash over him, an ever shifting array of colour and light. For Arch dare not attempt to pull out one single emotion and examine it in any detail, contenting himself to skirt around the edges, of his complicated mass of feeling. Were he to reach in and pull free a single feeling and examine it like a jewel in the light, he would see and put into words that which he had so far kept at bay, by rendering it inarticulate.

Deep down Arch knew that words would break him; they would break the carefully constructed facade with which he clothed himself, stripping him of all the protections he had won for himself over the years. Did he really need to put into words that he no longer felt he could trust anyone, first his mother's death, then his father's abuse and now Jack's departure, had all served to prove that other people could not be relied upon. Yet, that he felt betrayed by them, only served to remind him of how much he had needed to trust them. How much he wished he could trust another person. Sally was right, he could have asked her to marry him all those years ago, but he knew what he felt for her could not be called love, lust yes, but lust was easy, an animal instinct. The consummation of lust was merely the meeting of two willing animals. That was all he and Sally had shared.

Sally had been one of the girls who hung about the edges of

the Katoomba Push, a group of loafers who hung about causing mischief and mayhem, when not at work as apprentices, factory hands or day labourers. Although one of the youngest members, Arch had through wit and charm, managed to rise through the pecking order of the Push with remarkable ease and rapidity. That he always had money, and didn't need to roll drunks to get it, solidified his place at the heart of the Push. It also made him popular with the girls who hung about them. Rough girls, the girls who worked hard scrubbing floors in big hotels, standing over hot coppers, boiling with other people's clothes. The girls whose mothers could not remember which of the men who had come and gone had begot them, leaving yet another mouth to feed.

Sally, a scullery maid at The Carrington, was the youngest, but one, of seven children. Having seen the lives of her mother, brothers and sisters, she had made her mind up to live differently. Not that she had much say in the matter, for when Sally was born, the possibility of passing her off as another of the mysterious, but fruitful Mister Jenkins offspring, hit a snag, when Sally emerged into the world with the golden complexion and tapered eyelids of her Chinese father.

Growing up, Sally had watched the men who came to visit her mother, look her over, judging her age and the possibilities she offered. Her older sisters had all gone on to marry men who once visited their mother, rough men who left them with many children and little money. She often spent what little money she had, on potions from Medicotts, to make her sisters regular again. They would come to her in secret, accosting her on her way home from work, their faces drawn and thin. Sally was amazed at how greater poverty and worry, had erased all sense of individuality from her sisters, to the point that she could hardly tell one from the other. Their words were always the same, their hands like claws grasping at her dress, beseeching and at the same time threatening. Their fear showed in their eyes and emanated from their bodies like a foul odour, so palpable, Sally had to resist the urge to block her nose. Sally would agree to buy what they asked, would have agreed to anything to free herself from their desperate clawing need, that threatened to pull her down with them should she refuse. As the months turned into years, and her age crept up and up, Sally could see herself being trapped like her sisters. Sold off to men, for the promise of gin or a few pounds, married off, once the children came and her worth diminished. Already she could see the desire in the eyes of the men who came to her mother, wondering if she could be exchanged for the used flesh they had paid for.

At fifteen, Sally decided to take her fate into her own hands and join the sparkling silk clad women who emerged every night to shimmer, like moths underneath the electrified lights, and drink with wealthy and lonely men. The women who were known jokingly about town as the Mountain Devils. To do this though, she would have to pass muster with Madame Fleurie.

Madam Fleurie was a woman about whom gossip loved to linger, she was at various times throughout her life, said to be a Russian princess, the love child of a French countess, and the Mistress of a very senior member of the Royal family. All of which Madame Fleurie would encourage with her stories and discreetly dropped hints, which were always followed, by her throaty giggle and nasal confessions that she had said too much. Pressing her perfectly manicured fingers, to her delicately painted lips, to prevent more from spilling out. In truth, if truth can be applied to a woman like Madame Fleurie, she was a girl from Cannes who thanks to some very rich and very lonely men had by the time she was twenty five, become one of the most famous courtesans of that city. The highlife ended, with the ruin, both financial and social, of her most significant gentleman. She had tried to repair the damage his departure made to her finances, but with debt collectors on her doorstep every other morning; she knew that there was only one option. She had to leave. Being a pragmatic woman, she took all her moveable valuables and walked out of her old life and onto a ship travelling east, living a vagabond life, in only the best hotels for the next ten years. Until fate deposited her in Katoomba, and recognising a tourist town when she saw one, Madame Fleurie, whose arrival coincided with the opening of The Carrington Hotel, was only too aware of the opportunities such an establishment could bring. It was this woman, Sally Jenkins now stood before, seeking admittance to her select few.

"You, little skin and bones, want to be one of my girls, do you? You do know what my girls do, don't you?" Sally nodded, watching the sensual movements of Madame Fleurie's body and face, like those of a pampered house cat. Within her mature, but still beautiful face, Madame's eyes fixed her with a grey predatory gaze, watching the trembling mouse before her, sizing her up, calculating the perfect moment to pounce. "My girls are entertainers, companions. When I was in Japan, I met geisha, highly accomplished women. Any tart can spread her legs, but only an accomplished woman can entertain a gentleman beforehand. The men my girls see are very wealthy, very powerful, and very discerning. You will be expected to keep your mouth shut, about who your clients are, but I suspect that you already know how to keep secrets, non?"

Madame Fleurie leant forward in her chair, a satisfied smirk crossing her lips, at Sally's stiff nod of agreement. Reaching out, she ran a bejewelled finger down the left side of Sally's face and down the front of her worn dress, pausing to cup her small firm breast in her palm. Sally felt her breath deepen and shudder in her chest, catching in her throat, as she tried to swallow her nervousness. Slowly the hand withdrew and joined its partner on the heavily brocaded lap. Sally watched as the slumbering cat slowly shifted, the room crackled with energy, though the cat barely moved. At a moment when most small rodents would seize the opportunity to flee, as their hunter made the rapid, but not instant shift from observer to participant, Sally stood her ground.

The grey eyes hardened, as red lips parted to reveal a mouth glittering with gold and discoloured porcelain, again came the purring throaty voice. "You are very pretty, or you will be once you put some flesh on your bones. Unlike the other girls I have seen, you are more interesting, more exotic. You remind me of a Chinese business man I once knew in Singapore. Yes, I will take you. For three years, you will work for me as my maid, while you learn all that is needed to entertain men. You can read, can't you? Good, you will learn how to dance, to converse, to flirt, to dress and carry yourself.

"One more thing, I do not sell virgins, my girls know what to do to please a man. So I want you to find a nice clean boy and find out what he likes. Do you understand me?"

Sally nodded. Never had a mouse been more grateful to be gobbled up, than she felt right now.

For Sally, the Push offered the only respite she had, from home and work. Here at least the boys who watched her, were content with her flirting and attention. Too inexperienced, and frightened of their mothers to bring a girl home pregnant, they watched the girls, but rarely advanced beyond the odd comment or if particularly daring a lunge at their skirts. Archibald Kelly however, was different. He was tall and skinny for sixteen, with hair like hell fire. While the other boys of the Push preened and paraded, hoping to look tough and threatening, all the while knowing that dinner would be on the plate when they returned home of a night, Arch was the real deal, as hard and rough as a piece of granite. He had joined the Push not long after his return from Parramatta. His abrupt disappearance from the town and the fight with his father, had fed talk that he had been sent down to a reformatory in Sydney. Talk that his silence on the subject only encouraged. Sally Jenkins had been looking for a boy like Arch for some time. This was the boy Sally knew could give her what she wanted.

He had been casually, almost cynically selected to meet Sally's needs, and when the time came, he had just as casually discarded her. Knowing that his respite from life, running with the Push had to cease with Jack's return, he had cast it off and resumed the mantle of responsibility that is brother's return, had handed him.

It was Jack's complete disregard for his responsibilities, which had annoyed him most about his brother signing up. Not the politics or the stupidity of it, but the fact that he had run away from a life that he had built, that he had said he wanted. Was it really possible to grow tired of a home and family in three short years?

Not that such self-destructive impulses were foreign to him either, how else could he explain his running a SP book on and off these past five years, or the amount of time he spent in the Two Up school above Ian Ashcroft's Butchers shop. It wasn't the money though, which drove him to the gambling dens, he never wagered more than a few shillings when he visited. The money from his bookmaking, usually went to his cabbies, or to working girls going through a dry spell. He did this, not to assuage his conscious as is the usual explanation for such largess with ill-gotten gains, nor to show his generosity and detract from the exploitation of running a gambling ring, for his charity was anonymously given, but because he liked the risk. The risk of a police raid, of being hauled to the court and forced to pay a fine. The risk that people would find out that beneath the good and responsible man he had always appeared to be, he was in fact a devil, that he was no more than the treacherous, ungrateful son his father repeatedly accused him of being. It had been that thrill that sent him running with the Push and had primed him to be the perfect choice for Sally Jenkins. The more external voices spoke of him as the hard working dutiful son, the more he wanted to be found out and show how little he should be admired. He had betrayed his father by bringing his aunt into their lives, he had raised his fists towards his father, an act which had stopped his father beating him, but had only intensified their arguments.

Then again sometimes his actions had been to punish his father, as he did the day he gambled the day's takings away in the School, continuing until every penny was gone, after an argument about Jack's engagement and the fact that their father wished to withhold his consent. In the end their father's consent was unnecessary, Aunt Betty was Jack's legal guardian and she did not see the need for him to wait until he was twenty one. Despite her suffragette beliefs, Aunt Betty could be as great a romantic as she was when she had embarked on her own marriage, all those years ago. Besides, unlike her husband, Jack had proved himself to be a steady and hardworking type, even if he lacked in ambition.

His father used to say, when he found out about one of Arch's more reckless exploits, that it was his mother in him. Not that his father was a model of restraint and moral fortitude. It was the only time that Patrick would ever directly mention his wife, and the words were a warning and a threat. So it did not now surprise Arch to see his brother, who was so much more their mother's son, demolish all that was good in his life.

Lying in the dark as the mantle clock struck half past ten, Arch thought about the fare he was to collect from the 11 pm train. Mr Alexander had been a regular fare for the past ten years. Once a month, sometimes more, he would weekend in a cottage he owned down along Cliff drive. A producer for the Tivoli in Sydney, he had on more than one occasion presented Arch with tickets. Tickets which in turn, Arch had sent to his brother or had given away to friends. At eighteen, when he had first accepted the fare, he had not understood his colleagues' aversion to accepting the well-dressed gentleman with his rather dandified younger companion, especially since he paid over and above whatever Arch asked for. Every few months the companion changed, though all were handsome immaculately dressed men, with what Arch assumed, was a theatrical manner. Though for the past few years his companion had changed, no longer a dandified actor, but a quiet and intense young man whom Mister Alexander called Charlie. Charlie with the rough hands and powerful physique of a working man, a carpenter or a bricklayer, a man who worked in the sun and fresh air, attested to by his deep tan and the sun bleached blonde, in his light brown hair.

When Arch had answered the phone late that afternoon and taken the booking, he had heard the excitement in Mr Alexander's voice. Perhaps he had a new young man to spend his time with, a midweek visit was certainly not usual. Arch supposed he would find out soon enough, as he rose from the lounge and straightened his clothes.

***

Main Street glittered damply in the lamplight, as Arch waited beside his cab for his late fare. The rain had stopped before Arch had come out, but puddles and a slick wet look covered the town. Across the road, the pub had just called last drinks and he could see people stumbling out of the shiny glass doors, looking around at the dripping world in confusion: had it rained? Gathered not far from the Pub, the local Push, drunk themselves, watched the pub patrons as they stumbled home. Laughing like a pack of hunch backed hyenas, the Push watched men until they saw the one they wanted, an older gentleman, in the dark Arch could see he was one of the town councillors. The gentleman moved with the unsteady gate of a man who has over indulged, his rotund figure, giving the impression of a wobbly man toy. Arch watched, as the rag tag group of boys, moved to surround him. The councillor was pushed and jostled, a usual preamble to a robbery or beating, but the Push had mistimed their attack, as the Pub door swung open and disgorged its patrons onto the footpath. The Push, looked up at the noise and fled, leaving the Councillor to be picked up by some of the men who now swayed and lurched along the street, back to their homes, boarding houses and hotels.

"So Mister Arch, you have gone in for motors since I last saw you?"

"Indeed, I brought her up from Sydney about six weeks ago. Speaking of six weeks, I haven't seen you for a while. You seeing other cabs behind my back?"

Arch lifted the bags and placed them in the trunk of the car, while Mr Alexander and Charlie, seated themselves in the wonderfully supple leather of the cab's seats.

"Charlie here has been too busy to visit."

"And why's that?" said Arch, as he closed the trunk of the cab.

"Because Charlie here has been in Barracks for the past six weeks, he has two days leave and then Friday week it's off to old Blighty first, then France to show the Germans what for."

"My little brother is down there too, Jack Kelly."

"I know him. Red hair, loves footy, got two little kids and a pretty wife."

"That'd be him."

Arch slammed the driver's door and pulled out into the street.

Across the road the Push had returned to the pub. Arch turned the cab so that he would now drive past the pub, and take the more circuitous road around Cliff Drive, thus avoiding taking the cab down the big hills of Katoomba or Park streets in the wet. As they approached the pub, the Push could be seen gathered around the door, watching and cheering on something above their heads.

"Stop," said Mr Alexander, craning his neck to see what the Push were looking at. "What are they doing?"

"Climbing the façade, it's a common challenge with them. If a boy can get to the top he can join the Push, if not well."

"I bet you he will get to the top, and we ride free."

"I'll take that bet, if he falls you pay double."

"Deal."

For a few minutes the climbing boy seemed to make good progress, as the Push below cheered him on, reaching the first floor with remarkable ease. Leaning over his steering wheel, Arch watched as the boy faltered and grew confused looking for some grip, to climb the tiled second story with its big central window and slick, green glassy tiles.

"They must really dislike that little bastard," muttered Arch, as he watched the boy struggle like a bug on fly paper.

"Why," asked Charlie, his voice a clear ringing bell next to his companion's sonorous rumbling.

"Because that isn't how you do it. You nip up the fire escape in the back. If they want you in, one of the boys will tell you the trick. If not, well, see for yourself."

The boy on the building recognising his predicament, neither able to ascend the glassy façade nor descend to the Push who snapped and laughed at ground level, began to panic. Even in the dark Arch could see tears beginning to stream down the boy's face, making it glitter wetly in the lamplight. Another liquid began to dribble down the boys boot, causing much hilarity among the assembled Push.

"Orright you little louts, you've had your fun. Bring him down," yelled Arch from the drivers cab, sounding his horn.

Most of the Push fled at this, rushing down the hill to Hudson's gully. One of the Push, nipped round the side of the Pub and produced a ladder, leaning it against the façade near the boy, before following his mates. Seeing the Push had fled, the boy climbed gingerly down the ladder, running off across the railway lines and into the darkness.

"That will be twice the usual, Mister Alexander, as agreed."

Chapter Six

It was late Friday night, when Jack attired in his new AIF uniform, stepped off the train at Katoomba. Several of the other passengers stopped to stare or exchange a greeting with him, as he made his way from the platform to the Main Street steps, heading towards the cab rank, where several of his brother's cabs stood, waiting for weekenders loaded with luggage to hire them.

Walking up to the nearest cab, Jack asked, "Is Arch working tonight?"

"No, he's off tonight, I think he's at his brother's house," said the cabbie, looking down at Jack's slouch hat unable to discern the face hidden in its shadows.

"Thanks Mate." Jack settled his kit bag on his shoulder, crossing the road he walked along Main Street, heading for home. As the shops receded, Jack crossed Park Street where the road changed its name, as he followed it past Blackburn's pub, past The Burlington guest house and The Balmoral, along past the homes of his neighbours, on the sweeping road that followed the railway line past his house, turned out of town and continued out west to Bathurst and beyond.

The night was cool and clear, but it no longer had the bite of winter upon it. In fact, the sting of winter had subsided with remarkable speed this year, already the Sydney air was filled with the drumming of cicadas, and even here, Jack could see evidence that they had begun to appear, their frail shells clinging to trunks of trees and fence posts. He was going to miss the cicada season this year. Christmas too, would be spent under a foreign sky, somewhere he had never been and a town he had never heard of. He would be shipping out in a week, headed to the war in France. The reality of that, made his chest tighten and his mouth grow dry. Not that he was a coward, never a coward. Just the reality of the situation made him pause sometimes, and wonder whether he had made the right choice. It seemed so when he had signed up, and when with his fellow recruits at the army barracks, only when he was alone and thoughts turned to the life he had left, did doubt have a chance to enter his mind. Besides it was too late now to back out, he had signed his name and sworn an oath; to back out now would be dishonourable.

Pausing by his gate, Jack wondered what sort of welcome he would receive. He had written to Dottie telling her he would be visiting for the weekend. But their correspondence had been patchy these past few weeks. While he had written several times a week, he had been lucky to receive more than a terse reply, usually on practical matters, from his wife. He had missed Dottie more than he had imagined he would and the children. To not have them about every day, had taken him some time to accustom himself to, he wasn't sure that he had done so yet.

Pushing open the gate, Jack entered the garden and walked up to the front door. Letting himself in, Jack heard the scrape and scrabble of people rising, as two sets of feet moved from the kitchen into the hall.

"Daddy! Daddy!"

Running into the hall ahead of the adults, Edith wrapped her arms around Jack's legs. Dottie and Arch hung back watching him from near the kitchen door.

"She's been waiting for you," said Dottie. "She watched the road until tea time."

Jack allowed his bag to slip to the floor, as he bent down and picked up his daughter. Following Dottie and Arch into the kitchen Jack sat down at the table. Edith explored his short hair and drab uniform with her tiny fingers, trying to reconcile this version of her father, with the father who had left several weeks earlier.

"Have you eaten? I saved some supper for you." Dottie fetched a plate from inside the oven, placing it on the table before Jack.

Jack looked at the butchers sausages and mash on the plate before him. The sausages had burst and were leaking grease, which sat congealing on the plate. He could see lumps of hard potato hidden within the mash, like culinary ambushes. It looked like one of the dinners his brother used to make for them as children, after the old housekeeper died.

"Thanks Dottie," said Jack, allowing Edith to sit on his lap as he ate, her fingers working at the brass buttons of his uniform. "So, how have you been?"

"We've been fine, nothing unusual," said Dottie, sitting at the far end of the table. Picking up the tea pot and discovering it empty, she rose and placed the kettle back on the heat. Rinsing out the tea pot and filling it again with fresh leaves.

"I'm sorry, Dottie."

Dottie shrugged her shoulders, but kept her back turned towards the room. Standing, Jack moved across the room to where Dottie fidgeted, his fingers hovering at her shoulder not quite daring to touch her. The easy intimacy between them had been broken, the understanding that had allowed a touch or a look to serve in place of words, was gone.

"It's time you were in bed, Miss. You can see Daddy tomorrow," said Dottie, turning abruptly and speaking to her daughter.

Surrendering Edith to Dottie, Jack watched as she left the room, ignoring his presence, as if he were no more than a piece of furniture.

Returning to his seat, Jack picked at the plate in front of him. Aware for the first time of his brother sitting on the opposite side of the table against the wall, Jack said, "She's not going to forgive me, is she Arch."

"What did you expect? You turned her world upside down, without discussing it with her. Of course she's angry." Arch leant back in his chair, his brows contracted into a frown and his mouth fixed, as if holding back all the words that he wished to say, but knew that he mustn't.

"And what about you, how are you?"

"I'm disappointed, Jack. I always thought you were better than this."

Jack turned away and looked out the window, the dark glass offering him nothing, but his own grim reflection, looking back at him. Now, sitting in his own kitchen he did not look like he belonged any more. The hair, the uniform, the man within were all alien. Just as alien as he had been, these past eight months, only now they could see what he had grown to know. He didn't work in the life that had been built up around him; he had once, but over the past few months, he had grown estranged from it and had, had to find a new way to be in the world. Turning back to Arch, he could hear his brother was still talking, his hands gesturing wildly and his usual quietly assertive voice, loud and harsh, the voice their father used when he was angry or drunk.

"I don't agree with your politics, but that's not why. It's because of the way you did it, secretly and without thinking about what it would do to us. I had to find out what you did through gossip. Do you have any idea how that felt? And Dot, you told her on your anniversary. You just kept it secret and then tell her you are leaving, do you have no respect for her? Are you listening to me?"

Unable to summon the energy to respond to his brother's arguments, Jack pushed aside his plate and rose from the table, taking Dottie's path from the room.

Searching through the house, Jack found her sitting in the dark, in the front room. Entering the room, Jack switched on the standing lamp that stood behind his arm chair. The sudden light caused Dottie to squint and cover her eyes. Jack moved the lamp out of Dottie's eye line.

"Dottie, I'm sorry," said Jack, sitting in the armchair opposite her.

Dottie looked at Jack. She had missed him these past weeks, but now was not the time to show him that. Now was not the time for weakness, or else he would spend the rest of their marriage treating her with the callous indifference that the wretched uniform he wore represented.

"What exactly are you sorry about Jack?"

"I'm sorry about how I told you. Sorry that I didn't tell you what I was planning to do before I signed up. It was a rotten thing for me to do."

Dottie looked at Jack across the tea-table. Again, he was giving her the words that he thought she wanted. Say the right words in the right order, with a suitably hangdog expression and all will be forgiven. This wasn't the man she had married.

"But not that you signed up."

Jack sighed and slumped forward in his seat, resting his elbows on his knees. How could he hope to tell her he had felt trapped in his life? That he couldn't do it anymore, this life with her and the children, this life with adult responsibilities and problems. How could he say to her that he had failed, that it had all become too much for him to cope with, that his father's death was one hurdle too many for him. Especially when it was a hurdle his brother had cleared with apparent ease, in spite of its sudden appearance in both of their lives.

"This is something that I have to do. I have to see it through. You do understand that."

"So, something in you means that you have to travel to the other side of the world and have people shoot at you and I just have to accept that," said Dottie, plucking at the hem of her apron. "I just have to accept that the children and I mean so little to you that you need to run away from us."

Jack winced at Dottie's words, turning away and pressing the backs of his fingers to his lips.

"No, it's not like that."

"Then tell me what it's like. Tell me how horribly unfulfilling your life is. About the dull dreary life, that is so intolerable that being shot at in a foreign country is preferable."

"Not preferable."

"It must be me then, you don't love me anymore and want to get as far as possible away from me." Dottie covered her face with her hands and wept.

Unable to bear the sight of his wife crying, Jack rose from his chair and knelt by Dottie's side. Holding her about her waist, he drew her down from the chair to crouch on the floor with him. Wrapping his arms about her, he held her to him and kissed her hair.

"I do love you. I do. I don't know why I have to do this, but it isn't anything you have done. It's me. I'm leaving on Friday. I don't want to leave with you thinking I don't love you."

Jack could feel Dottie's body stiffen and pull away, the words had escaped him quite unconsciously, and even as he heard himself saying them he knew that they were wrong. That once again his timing was out.

Pushing Jack away with enough force that he fell back against his chair, Dottie struggled to her feet.

"A week."

"I didn't mean to say that." Jack looked up at his wife towering over him.

"A week."

Jack picked himself up off the floor, kneeling on the carpet, he reached out to his wife.

"I know. Don't hate me, please."

"Why do you never think about me? Why is it always what you want to do?" shouted Dottie, her voice growing sharp and savage, a voice he had never heard her use before. "What do you think it will do to me if you are killed?"

"That won't happen."

Grasping Dottie about the waist, Jack looked up at his little wife.

Dottie looked down at her husband, and the innocent shock on his face, at the thought that his choices could prove fatal. This was nothing, but a grand adventure to him. Reaching down, Dottie gently stroked the side of Jack's face, watching him close his eyes and rest his head against her body.

"I swear on my mother's grave I will come home again."

"Oh, my poor stupid idiot."

Pulling Jack's arms away from her waist, Dottie moved to stand behind her chair.

Rising to his feet, Jack stood looking at the seat of Dottie's chair. "Can't things just go back to how they were? Come on Dottie, don't be like this."

"You can't just make everything right in one weekend. I'm going to bed."

***

Dottie lay awake listening to Jack's breathing, as he slept beside her. It had been so simple for him. Simple to sign up and demand that she accept his decision. Simple to come home and demand her forgiveness, in the face of being shipped off to a foreign land and a foreign war. He lived in a simple world, where his actions had no consequences and he could rise above all conflicts, demanding forgiveness and affection. How easy life must be, when one treats it with the carelessness of a child, a time when mistakes are brushed over and hurt feelings are mended with a smile or a kiss. But this wasn't one of those mistakes. She could see that Jack's cavalier attitude would be the future of her married life, if there was to be any future at all, some mistakes don't allow a second run. Though it pained Dottie to admit it, looking across at her husband, she couldn't say that his actions had not changed her feelings, had not set up ripples of disquiet on the calm pond of her affection. He had treated her with contempt, she who had run her father's household since she was fifteen, was being disregarded like a grizzling child.

Looking towards the chair where Jack had thrown his uniform, a shapeless mass in the dark room, yet there. Like a living presence. A symbol of the authority, to which Jack had submitted and to which, he in turn, expected her to submit. If only it would go away, like an image from a nightmare. A great khaki demon sent to make her bend or break. With its pervasive message of war seeping into the minds of young men across the country, across the world even, for she couldn't be the only wife who lay in bed, hating the men who had lured her husband with promises of glory and adventure. Across the country, across the world, while young Achilles sleep and dream of heroic deeds, Thetis weeps for the man she knows will not return. The longed for son or husband, who is no longer recognisable, beneath his helmet and uniform. He is a man who has had the golden summers of his youth, replaced by the mud and blood and death, of a foreign shore. He is a man who has seen the Keres up close, and who bears the indelible mark of Ares. Dottie wasn't sure she would want him back.

***

Lying in the sun, watching Edie and Alfie play, Jack at last understood what Arch had meant all those times, when he said that he had it made. Sitting on a rug in the sunshine, Alfie's red hair shone like beaten copper, throwing off sparks of light, as he watched his sister feeding the chickens. Walking beside her mother, Edie dipped her hand into the grain bucket and threw the wheat to the chooks, giggling as they gathered about her feet where she had let the grain fall. Her golden curls brushed her shoulders, as she shook her head, refusing to share the job of feeding the chooks with her mother.

Turning away, Jack could feel tears prick the backs of his eyes, his chest felt tight and his mouth empty and dry. He could have cried out at the feelings which rose within him. How had he not seen it earlier, this life that he now had to leave. This life, which he had not seen only a few weeks ago, was suddenly dearer to him than any adventure.

Squeezing his eyes tight against the tears, Jack picked himself up off the ground and moved to the wood pile by the back door. A month's supply of wood had been delivered the day before, and the logs lay in a disordered heap, where the men had unloaded them.

Picking up the axe, Jack tested the blade with his thumb. Seeing that the blade was dull, he took the whet stone from the window ledge and sat down on the back veranda, to sharpen the axe. The stone scraped against the blade revealing shining new metal. The rhythm of the stone against the blade and the flashes of silver sparking in the sun, felt hypnotic, just as cleaning and assembling a rifle had become in barracks. It was a task which focused the mind and drowned out emotion.

Taking the axe across to the chopping block, Jack set the closest log on the block to be split. Lifting the axe, Jack felt the heavy weight rush through the air, as his hands slipped smoothly along the handle and the log split cleanly in two. Again, he raised the axe, quartering the halves of the log and tossing them aside, as he reached for a second log.

By the third log, Jack had established a steady rhythm, the axe rising and falling, his powerful shoulders working beneath his shirt. Before long, the shirt was drenched in sweat, but Jack made no concession to his labouring body, occasionally shaking his head to clear his eyes, or wiping his forearm across his face as he reached for a new log.

As the hours of the morning wore on, a pitcher of water and a glass appeared on the veranda. Jack abandoned his shirt, his broad back flexing and working in the spring sunshine.

Emerging from the kitchen and standing by the back door, Dottie picked up the now empty pitcher and glass, as she watched Jack working his way through the wood pile. The naked shoulders rising and falling, as the sun burnt the pattern of his braces onto his fair skin. At last, Jack stuck the axe into the chopping block and began to gather up the split wood packing it neatly beneath the veranda.

Picking up his shirt, Jack walked across the garden to the back door, laying a hand on Dottie's shoulder, as he walked passed her into the house. Sitting down at the kitchen table Jack pulled his shirt on. Dottie, following him inside, set a plate of golden crumbed schnitzel and caramelized onions on the table before him.

***

"Will you come down to see my ship off in Sydney?" Jack, shifted his weight from one foot to the other, looking down at his boots.

"I don't know, Jack. I'm pretty busy at the moment," said Arch, his gaze fixed along the railway track, watching for the train to Sydney.

"Please. Dottie is so angry with me and with the kid's, it would be too hard for her anyway. I've messed it up with her, doing this."

"She will calm down Jack. You can't expect her to pretend it didn't hurt her. She's a good woman your Dot." Arch reached into his breast pocket and took out a flat wrapped package. "She wanted me to give you this."

Taking the package Jack opened it, his fingers tearing the paper, so that it fell in ribbons to the ground. Inside was a leather covered journal. Flicking the pages, out slipped an envelope, it was unsealed. Inside Jack saw was not a letter as he had imagined, but a photograph. There in the studio of Harry Philips sat Dottie, Edith and little Alfie. It was a simple picture, no waterfalls or cliffs cut in as backgrounds, just three people sitting against a dark curtain. Their grave faces looking out at him. Jack slid the photograph back into the envelope and tucked the book into his breast pocket.

"Tell her thanks," said Jack, as he looked away down the track for the train, his voice tight and smothered.

"I'll keep an eye on them, Jack. I'll make sure they don't go without anything."

"I know you will."

"Make sure you come back in one piece Jack. People are counting on you back here."

Hearing the train approach the station, though not yet visible around the curve of the line, Jack turned and embraced his brother. Holding him in an embrace that crushed the breath out of him, and yet was still not close enough, hoping in a single gesture to say all that he could not find the words to convey.

"Be sure to write me Arch, I'll let you know where to send letters," said Jack, releasing his brother.

"Of course I will."

The train drew up to the platform and came to a halt, flooding the air with smoke. Jack shouldered his bag, as the window closest to them flew open, revealing a compartment filled with young men, similarly clad in khaki, joking and laughing. Entering the carriage, Jack dropped his bag by his feet and leant out the door, grasping his brother's hand for one last time. The guard whistled and the engine whined.

"See you Arch."

Releasing Jack's hand Arch pushed the carriage door closed. Stepping back from the train, he watched as the train drew out of the station, vanishing around the bend.

"See you Jack."

The Women's Vigil

As the young men of Greece flocked to Aulis, the women they were to leave behind them, began their long vigil. The mothers, sisters, wives and daughters of Greece, watched as Agamemnon's siren call to war, emptied their towns and villages. For some, the wait for the news they all feared, would end too soon. The words of travellers and the wounded confirming their greatest fears; that their hero had fallen on the shores of Troy. For others the wait would be longer in coming, yet like so many others, it would come. While for some, the fearsome news would not strike, word that their men had fallen would not come. Rather they had fought valiantly, and their captains had heaped them with praise and honours. But for now, they waited, as the fleet idled away its time in Aulis, waiting for a favourable wind to carry them east to fame and glory.

Chapter Seven

It felt like an ambush, even though looking at her mother, Dottie knew that was not what she had intended. Seated opposite her at the kitchen table, Charlotte poured tea for herself and her daughter. Rather than think about the statement her mother had just made, Dottie focused her thoughts, on the stream of dark liquid and the fine bone china teapot. The soft white roses, so full they could barely raise their heads on their thin necks, against the deep green glaze of the teapot, looked about ready to fall. It had been given to her mother, by a cousin in Munich, as a wedding present. When she was small, Dottie had marvelled at the thought of the delicate china, travelling all those thousands of miles over the sea, to arrive one day, months after the wedding all in one piece.

"Mum, I know you are thinking of me, but I don't want to move back here, and I don't want Cousin Kathryn staying with me until Jack comes home."

Charlotte placed the teapot back on the trivet. She poured milk from a matching jug, her carefully manicured hands performing the ritual of tea, with the expert movements of the consummate hostess.

"Why not? Cousin Kathryn offered to come and help you," said Charlotte, smoothing the tablecloth against the edge of the table.

"The last time Cousin Kathryn came to help, was when you were sick with pneumonia five years ago. She was supposed to help me look after you and run the house."

"Yes, she was very helpful. She brought me all my meals, and helped you with the cooking. Your father said she was a wonderful help."

Charlotte sipped her tea, looking about her freshly painted kitchen.

"Do you like this colour? The painter says it will resist the wood smoke better than white. I think it's a little dark. I should get some new curtains made, to brighten things up."

"Mum, Dad only said that because he didn't want to hurt your feelings. Cousin Kathryn sat on the sofa from breakfast to bedtime, knitting stockings and smoking those horrible smelly cheroots. She only got up when she saw me taking a tray into you. I don't want that woman in my house."

Dottie looked at the new paintwork. The pale tan was certainly different from the previous clean white walls. Combined with the wood work it did make the room darker, especially in the morning, though she could imagine that with the afternoon sun it would look better.

"But Love, people will talk if you are all alone in that house."

"Some cream curtains would brighten the room, nice lace ones. You could get Mrs Murray to run them up for you. She did all the curtains for my house. She's very cheap, but her work is excellent quality, and she's fast. If you give her the fabric, she can run them up by the afternoon."

"Dottie, people already talk about you," said Charlotte, determined not to be put off.

"I'm surprised you would listen to that."

Charlotte looked quickly down at her tea cup. Her face flushed, as her daughter frowned and clenched her jaw. Ashamed to have even brought the subject up, Charlotte looked across the table and out the window. In the garden tiny honey eaters, darted about the red salvia, impossible hovering creatures. More like butterflies than birds, they dipped their long curved beaks, into the open maws of the flowers seeking nectar.

"I shouldn't have mentioned it." Charlotte rose and took the kettle from the hob to freshen the pot.

Dottie sighed, as she looked down at her tea cup. Glancing across at her mother, she could see that she had spoken too harshly. Her mother didn't mean any harm, but the topic she had struck on was still too raw, for Dottie to manage an appropriate reaction. To think of Jack these days, provoked a reaction from her, for which, she perpetually apologising or excusing herself.

"Mum, Jack didn't run off. He's not away on business or a trip. He enlisted and will be fighting God knows where. I don't think the old rules apply to this situation. The good opinion of a few, self-appointed moral guardians, don't matter to me when I am thinking about whether or not Jack will come home again."

Charlotte standing by the stove, slowly twisted her wedding ring around her finger. Looking out the window, she saw a commotion among the leaves as the lazy red tom cat leapt, with unaccustomed exertion, snatching one of the hovering birds from the air.

"Oh, you bad cat!" shouted Charlotte through the glass. Insensible to his mistress' disapproval, the cat walked around the corner of the house, his prize clasped firmly in his jaws.

"Let him have it, Mum."

"But it's the third one he's had this week. There won't be any left."

"Haven't you been feeding him enough?"

"He is supposed to catch mice in the stables, not birds in the garden."

"Maybe there are no mice left."

Charlotte moved back to sit at the kitchen table, her hands now smoothing the table cloth against the edge of the table, in a movement both unconscious and compulsive.

"Have you heard anything from Jack?"

"No, just what's in the papers. I don't know where he is going, and I don't know what is going to happen to him. I'm terrified."

Dottie buried her face in her hands, the thought of Jack alone in a foreign land had been bad enough, but to think of him actually in the war. Her Jack being shot at, by men who meant to kill, was too much to contemplate.

Charlotte frowned, drawing her dark eyebrows together in an expression that she had passed on to her daughter, a look of instant disapproval and distain. "It was a rotten thing for him to do to you."

"It was an unthinking thing to do. He hadn't been himself since his father died. I wish he had talked to Arch or me before deciding such a thing. Trouble is, the last time I saw him, I could see that he didn't want to go. That he had changed his mind."

"Isn't that all the more reason to make sure that you give no material to the gossips? You don't want Jack coming home to a bunch of lies and stories."

"There are going to be lots of women, alone in lots of houses, before the war is over. Plenty of people for the gossips to focus on, once they grow tired of talking about me."

***

The Billiard hall was hot and choked with the smell of tobacco, but Arch had been on his own too long lately. He didn't like to visit Dottie, without her having organised a companion to sit in while he visited, so the Billiard hall or the pub were his best bets. Though recently lured again into his old wild ways, he had been keeping his distance from Sally Jenkins and the 'School', since Jack's departure. Dottie had enough worries, without him drawing attention to himself with some scandal.

Walking across to the bar, Arch bought himself a schooner, scanning the room for anyone he knew. In the far corner, stood two of his drivers setting up for a game. Picking up his glass, Arch made his way through the green baize ocean, of tables and players.

"Mister Arch, would you like to join us?" said Dan, offering the cue in his hand to his boss. The first thing anyone noticed about Dan were his hands, forearms as massive as a leg of lamb seemed incongruously capped, by small square hands. Observing them, one would assume that the owner would find them as crudely clumsy, as they appeared to have been made. As if God, when forming Dan, had lost interest part way through and has assembled him using left over limbs from a selection of other men. For on closer inspection, it was not only Dan's hands which seemed to belong to another man. His legs seemed somehow too short and his torso, which had in his youth given the illusion of height, had over the years thickened and compacted, making the whole man seem almost as wide, as he was tall. Seeing such a crudely assembled man, most people were willing to dismiss him as a fool or an idiot, capable of nothing more than the brute work of driving a hansom about town. Such an assessment of Dan, would be a gross underestimation, for what Dan lacked in physical refinement, he more than made up for in skill and cunning. It had been said, that Dan had never paid for a beer in his life. While this was not strictly true, he would boast that he hadn't paid for many, and that his wife, was the only cabbie's wife, to wear a genuine mink coat to Mass in winter. Being so ungainly, it was easy for him to convince the loud, flash young men from Sydney and beyond, to play against him.

"Thanks, but I'm happy to watch for a bit and drink my beer." Arch leant against the wall, watching as short ungainly Dan transformed before him, growing lithe and slim, as he played his fellow cabbie.

"I bet the news this morning was a big relief," said Dan, glancing over his shoulder at Arch.

"Yes, if my brother is going to do damned fool things, I'd like to hope he didn't get killed before, he had a chance to fight."

"It'd be a dreadful way to go, drowning, I mean." Dan leant over the green baize and sank a ball.

Playing opposite Dan was Smithy, a man who's most distinguishing feature were his eyebrows. Which rather than framing his eyes in a curve like wings, as most eyebrows are in the habit of doing, sat at an acute angle, reaching for each other across the bridge of his nose, giving him a look of permanent apology.

"We ran her aground, The Emden, didn't we?" Unable to read more than a few words, Smithy had gleaned the story from the talk of passengers and other cabbies, throughout the day.

"That's what the papers say, off the Cocos Islands, where ever they are."

Smithy's gaze, darted from his elder companion to the boss, watching for the slightest sign of displeasure, to cross the boss' face. When he was a child, Smithy would fear the drunken rages of his own father, living life with the tensed up nerves of a mouse in a cattery. Terrified of the noise and violence, yet powerless to do anything about it, beyond shrink and hide, in the hope that he not become a target. It was an instinct that even now, as a young man, his father long gone, he could not resist. The first sign of conflict, or even displeasure, would send Smithy fleeing into himself, shrinking inside his tall gangly frame, as he sought to make himself the smallest possible target. Mister Arch had been in a dark mood since his brother had left for the war, so much so, that it had become an unspoken rule, to not mention the war in his presence.

"It all feels such a long way away, don't it," said Dan, leaning on his cue, and looking at Arch.

Silently Smithy cursed Dan for breaking the rule, and talking war with Mister Arch, himself too for unthinkingly asking a question, carried away by his own distraction and the easy flow of the conversation. The boss stood quietly enough, his eyebrows drawn together in either thought or annoyance, Smithy feared the latter, but was not sure if his fear was clouding his observation. Mister Arch looked sad rather than angry, and Smithy thought how worried and frightened he might be in that position. It was bad enough, worrying about whether there would be enough money each week, to cover all the bills. It wasn't that his wages were low, but the doctor's bills and the pharmacy ate up so much of his pay, since his mum got sick.

Presently Arch stirred and sighed, pushing himself off the wall and running his hand through his thick auburn hair, pulling it back from his forehead.

"Yeah, and at the same time really close." Swallowing his last mouthful of beer and placing the glass on the table, Arch reached for a spare cue. "So which one of you mugs is gonna lose to me?"

***

Ivy Wade, had the face of an Italian Madonna, and the willowy figure of a Pre-Raphaelite maiden. As a child, Dottie had remembered her, as having slow deliberate movements, as if actually imitating the most saintly of nuns, rather than mocking them, as the other girls did. Nearly ten years on, Ivy's movements had not sped up. Sitting in Bert Kaufmann's tea house, watching Ivy pour tea in her careful deliberate way, as if this one action taxed all her intellectual resources, Dottie wondered if she was making the right decision.

"So," Dottie picked up her cup, peering into the pale milky tea within. "How has the world been treating you Ivy?"

Ivy listened, tilting her head to the side slightly, as she stirred her tea. Her big brown eyes, betraying little of what was happening behind them. My goodness, she is like a great dairy cow, thought Dottie, placing her undrinkable cup of tea down on the table.

"I know you have plans to join… which lot was it again?"

"The Sisters of Saint Joseph," said Ivy, raising the pallid liquid to her lips, sipping delicately.

"That's the one. My mother said you were having a bit of trouble with the dowry."

"Yes, Mother and Father can't possibly afford the dowry, so I have been doing sewing to try and earn it, but it is slow going." Ivy sighed and looked past Dottie, her face suddenly registering a deeply felt emotion. "I have to believe that it is God's way of testing me and strengthening my commitment to my calling."

Dottie looked around the room, at the many fine ladies taking tea that afternoon. Feathers, flowers and straw nodded up and down, as conversation poured out of open mouths, almost as quickly as tea and cake poured in. What would her friends make of her taking, Ivy The Saint Wade, as a companion. Still, it would curb the sharp tongues of the local gossips, women who could make a scandal out of the most innocent of encounters.

"So if you could find a job where you could earn money, while still doing your sewing, that would help you to save quicker. Wouldn't it?" said Dottie, turning back to the Sistine Madonna.

"I am very particular about the type of work I choose, I would not wish to fall in with bad influences."

"I understand completely, it is very hard in this town. I've been thinking about that myself, with Jack away, it has been brought to my attention, that I might be in need of a companion, to stay with me until he returns. Would that interest you at all?" Dottie took a sip of her disgustingly weak tea, watching her companion's reaction.

"It might, what would you be offering in wages?"

"Three shillings a week, with Sundays off." Dottie watched the agonisingly slow, mental calculations Ivy was doing. "You would also get room and board. It's a small room built onto the back, we don't use it ourselves, but it has a good bed and is next to the kitchen so it is very warm. You wouldn't have to do much, just a few household jobs and sit in the room when my brother-in-law visits. You can sew and ignore us completely."

"You have electric lights in your house don't you?" said Ivy, considering the additional work possible, if she could be freed from the oil lamp she sewed by at home.

"Yes we do." Dottie topped up her teacup, from the now much stronger, pot on the table.

"Can I see the room this afternoon?" said Ivy, surprising herself, with the boldness of her question.

"Naturally, you can come home with me after we finish our tea."

"I will have to discuss it with my parents, before I give you a firm answer, but yes it is a position that would interest me greatly," said Ivy, bowing her head, blushing at the starched white tablecloth.

"Good, I knew you would be just the girl to ask," said Dottie, bestowing a toothy smile upon Ivy.

Chapter Eight

The summer tourist season was in full swing, as Dottie attempted to push her pram down Katoomba Street, past slow moving groups of sightseers. Clumps of men and woman, smartly dressed, and inappropriately shod for the damp and muddy streets, dawdled along. Oblivious to the woman, who fumed behind them, before darting past when a gap opened up. Four weeks in Mudgee, with her parents for Christmas, had allowed Dottie to forget the hell, of trying to walk streets, filled with Sydney-siders escaping the heat of the city. It had been pleasant to stroll the sunburnt yellow hills, surrounding her grandfather's vineyard, with her cousins. The hard dry heat, of the western tablelands, so different from the humidity of home. As was the custom with her mother's family, Christmas saw the house, usually sparsely populated by her grandparents, and her uncles Ferd and Reggie, who worked in the newly acquired motor car dealership, filled with as many of Dottie's aunts, uncles and cousins as the homestead and cottages on the farm could house. Four weeks of catching up with family. Four weeks, of open arms gathering up her children, allowing her time, to rest and converse with other people her own age. It had almost been enough to allow her to forget about Jack, who rather than wintering in England, as originally planned for the Australian forces, had been camped in Egypt. The last letter Dottie had received, before her holiday, was sent from Sydney. A letter assuring her of his love, wrapped around a photograph of him, smiling cheekily at her, from under his hat. She had framed the picture and had taken it with her, placing it on her night stand, so that it should be the first and last thing, she saw each day.

With Jack away, and feeling powerless to help him, upon

returning home, Dottie had joined one of the soldiers support groups which had begun springing up across the country. Groups which had sprung up as organically as mushrooms, as wives and mothers, sisters and aunts found themselves determined to show their support for their men folk, in their own way. The group Dottie joined, met once a week at the home of their patroness, in one of the big houses down by Echo Point.

It was one of those misty days, where the drizzle soaks slowly into your clothes and humidity settles against your skin, making you feel clammy and uncomfortable. Still, she had confirmed that she would attend the meeting, knowing that women who have houses along the cliffs, were not the sort of people, one could snub. Packing her children into the pram, Dottie set out to walk down Katoomba Street. Arriving hot and dampened, her hat offering no protection to her hair, which sparkled with droplets, Dottie knocked on the door. The children, who had thoroughly enjoyed the ride down the hills in their pram, sat happily in amongst the toys, with which Dottie had packed them.

The meeting took place in a large drawing room, at the back of the house with a view of the valley, through the French doors. Ushered into the room, Dottie was surprised to see not young wives and sisters like herself, but the typical committee matrons, who assembled behind the mayor, at civic functions. Looking around the room, crammed with shelves and side tables, on which balanced, porcelain figurines and glass vases, Dottie wondered just how much of a mess her children might make, and how many of the clearly expensive object d'art, they could break, before the hour was finished. Already she felt uncomfortable, envisioning the ceramic dancer losing her arms, as she toppled off her pedestal, the crystal vase shattering into millions of diamonds, as it hit the floor, and the expenses bill that would surely, follow her home. This mansion was nothing like, the rambling country homestead of her grandparents in Mudgee, widely considered to be one of the finest establishments, in the district. A house, which had seen nine children grown to maturity, now frequently invaded by dozens of grandchildren, and even great grandchildren.

Seated around a table, the women were busy stuffing envelopes. One woman sat at a desk copying a letter, handing the copies to the women at the table. Two other women sat, each with a list before her, addressing envelopes. A third, was putting stamps on the completed envelopes, while the remaining women divided the envelopes between them, stuffing them with either, a letter or a white feather.

Dottie watched this industry with some fascination, taking the children from the pram and setting them on the rug, with a few toys.

"Ah, Mrs Kelly, so good of you to make it," said the patroness, a stout woman of sixty, with a large amount of false hair piled on her head and a moustache, furring her upper lip. "We are at this moment starting a mailing campaign."

Dottie moved to the table, picking up a letter, which accused the recipient of being a German sympathizer

"I thought this was a soldiers' support group," said Dottie, proffering the letter.

"Yes, it is," replied the furry lip. "Would you like to address envelopes, or stuff them?"

Dottie dropped the letter on the floor. Challenging the woman to bend down and pick it up.

"How does this support soldiers?"

The furry lip, pressed itself against its lower partner, clearly unused to having its authority challenged. A stream of air was released from the nostrils. The lips unclasped, and as composed as it was possible for one who is never challenged, can manage, said, "We support soldiers, by encouraging layabout homebodies to do the right thing and enlist for King and Country. And through rooting out, those who would serve to bring down the country from within. Enemy aliens are an invisible danger."

Dottie picking up her children, placed them back in the pram. "I'm so glad to find that out. Thank you, but I think my husband can do without your sort of support."

The furry lip, watching Dottie wheel the pram back out of the room, would have protested Dottie's rudeness, had she not slammed the door behind her, with such force it made the windows rattle and the crystal vase fall from its pedestal. Smashing into diamonds against the marble hearth.

"I should have known not to allow an Irish woman to join. Impudent lot the Irish," said the patroness, returning to the table. Moments later, the sound of the front door being slammed shut, made the room jump.

***

"I wouldn't let it get to me, if I were you Dot," said Arch, strapping the pram to the back of his cab. "Old Lady Whatsit is a right cow and a mean one at that. Don't let her upset you."

Dottie sat in the back of the cab, with her children on her lap, blinking wetly, trying to keep the tears she had just succeeded in stopping, from again running down her face.

Dottie hadn't long left the soldier's support group, when she had burst into sudden, hot, angry tears. Dottie walked around the cliff road, towards Echo Point, where Arch had promised to meet her, after the meeting had finished. Pushing the pram past a view, that was world famous, which today, in contrary mountain fashion was invisible beneath the thick mist, which clung to her hair and clothes, the horrible absurdity of her actions just a few minutes before rose up like a tide. That she had acted so uncivilised, so like a wild thing and not a proper lady, the way her mother or Ivy could manage, the kind of woman who sits quietly and does as she is told, filled her with rage. No, not her, she had to complain, had to protest and embarrass herself in front of all those fine ladies. Ladies who behaved as they did in novels and stories. Women who moved quietly, so as not to disturb important male work, not great wild cats like her, who shrieked at their husbands, and broke parts of their dinner service in their rage. Was that why her husband had left her, had gone off to war and sent home scant news. It had been weeks since she had received a letter.

Sitting beneath one of the shelters, watching the damp drip from trees, Dottie shivered and looked at her watch, there was still another half hour before the time Arch had arranged to collect her.

On her fifteenth birthday, her father had given her a copy of My Brilliant Career, inscribing it with the words, "To my dear Sybylla, Love Dad." She hadn't understood his joke, until she read the first few chapters. How long could she expect Arch to put up with her temperamental behaviour? He had always been such a good brother to Jack, it could only pain him, to see his brother married to such a passionate and disagreeable wife. The trouble was, she didn't know how to be other, than she was.

"I thought they'd be knitting and organising raffles and cooking, that sort of thing. All they were doing, was writing mean letters to people and sending them white feathers. I left in a huff, it was so embarrassing."

"Dot, what does it matter what a bunch of toffy nosed Proddies think of you? You are not the type of person to join groups." Arch climbed into the cab, slamming the door. "You are a born leader. You should start your own group, to do what you think would be of help."

"I wouldn't know what to do," said Dottie, raising her voice over the sound of the engine.

"Sure you do, you just told me. You know exactly what kind of group you want to start. Even if it is just you and your mum and Ivy to start with, do it. If you want to know how to start write to Aunt Bette, she'll help you."

Dottie listened to Arch's sensible words in silence, leaning back in the firm comfortable seat of the cab. Watching the houses flash by, considering what Arch had said.

"What's it like living with Ivy?"

"Different," said Dottie.

"Well that's a diplomatic answer, is it that bad?"

"She's odd, it's like living with a nun. She's up at five every morning to say her prayers, and then mass at eight. She lights the stove when she gets up, so that is at least useful. Her room is covered with pictures of saints and crosses. She disapproves of gossip, so there is very little to talk with her about."

"But she's a pretty inoffensive creature isn't she. I mean, she is like a mouse when I've seen her."

"A mouse with an opinion on everything."

Just this morning it had been a comment, as Dottie had been making herself up to leave for the meeting, about how face creams, powder and rouge were unnecessary extravagances, and that they were indicative, of the moral decline of the age. For Dottie, who had been up twice with Alfie during the night, powder and rouge seemed the only option for appearing in polite society, without looking ghastly, and having people inquire about her health.

Controversial toilette arrangements, were not all that Ivy objected to, Molly Jenkins, the laundry girl, was apparently not the correct type of poor, and had not served to show sufficient gratitude for her position. Moreover, Molly's mother, had been seen leaving the ladies lounge of Blackburn's pub, very late and very drunk on numerous occasions. Ivy suspected, that Molly's wages, were what kept her mother in drink.

Even small matters, seemed to irritate Ivy, and call down commentary from on high. Dottie's library was far too full of fiction, books with dangerous ideas and sensual language, which could easily lead the unwary, from the path of righteousness. Moreover, it was not good for a lady to spend her evenings reading, when she could take up a more productive occupation, like sewing or knitting. Dottie rarely knitted, and her sewing skill's extended to buttons and emergency repairs, was besides tired after a full day of housekeeping and childcare, finding the idea of more work once her children were asleep, impossible. Besides, looking down at the cover of her book, Dottie had wondered what harm, Sherlock Holmes could possibly pose to her moral state.

"But you're the boss Dot. I've been the boss for a long time, and the one thing you can't do is let them dominate you. You do that and you're sunk. You can be as polite and friendly as you like, but at the end of the day it is your house and you pay her, not the other way around. Remind her of that, next time she offers you one of her opinions."

"But she's so…" Dottie waived her hands before her, in an exasperated attempt to summarise the quiet, disapprovingly, correct demeanour of her paid companion.

"I know what you're saying and that is how they get you, irritate the hell out of you, without ever once stepping beyond the bounds of polite behaviour. That's what makes it hard. But you just gave old Lady Whatsit a right telling off, so don't let the creeping Ivy put you off, or she will be running your household."

Pulling up outside Dottie's house, Arch stepped out of the driver's seat and walked around to the back, to unload the pram.

"Will you come round for dinner tonight after work," said Dottie, helping Edith out of the cab, following her with Alfie asleep in her arms.

"When did I ever pass up a free meal?" said Arch, lifting the pram down and carrying it up the steps to the veranda.

"Good, because I bought a leg of lamb and I don't want Ivy giving me another lecture on poverty and waste."

"Dot, remember, you're the boss," said Arch, walking with his long loose gait, down the path, past Dottie.

Dottie, absentmindedly plucked a full pink bloom, from one of the two fragrant rose bushes, on either side of the veranda steps. Watching, as Arch pulled the garden gate closed and climbed back into his shining black cab. Glittering with wet in the brightening midday light, it pulled out from the curb and turned on the muddy road, returning to town and the afternoon rush.

Reaching down, taking her daughter's hand, Dottie said, "Come on Edie, let's go in and have some lunch."

Chapter Ten

Twice a week, Charlotte Joyce would go into town, to run errands and catch up with the local gossip. Charlotte Joyce adored gossip, and what she didn't know, was not worth knowing. It amused those nearest to her, as much as it shocked those who had become newly acquainted, to discover just how much salacious gossip, filled her otherwise cultured head. As a child, Dottie used to imagine the books and musical notes doing battle, in her mother's head, with stories of accidents, suicides and sexual scandals. These days, Dottie sat and listened in shock and awe, as her mother sat in her front room twice a week, regaling her with stories. Making it near impossible, for her to meet the faces of people in the street, the next day.

After a month in Mudgee, Dottie wondered just how much gossip her mother could possibly acquire. Though, it had taken her less than a week to catch up on six whole months' worth of Mudgee gossip. A mere four weeks away from town, with her mother's contacts, could probably be caught up in a single morning.

Today, Charlotte Joyce sat at the dining room table, a room Dottie rarely used, but which being on the westerly side of the house, was the last to heat up in the morning. The full morning sun of February, making her front room prohibitively hot, until well into the evening. Charlotte wore a fine, light dress of white cotton. Now that she was seated in her daughter's home, the collar of which, was opened down to her décolletage. Her masses of fine dark hair, piled fashionably on her head, had begun to escape the hairpins, tendrils plastering themselves to her face and neck.

Taking a small bottle from her bag, Charlotte dampened her

handkerchief and dabbed her neck and bosom with eau de cologne, slipping both back into her bag as Ivy entered with the tea tray. Charlotte watched, as Ivy carefully laid out three cups and proceeded to pour tea.

"What are you doing girl?" Ivy looked up startled, the spout of the tea pot hovering over the second cup. "That tea has had no time to draw properly. Put it down and let it draw. I have no intention of drinking tea that tastes like hot water."

Silently, Ivy placed the teapot back on the tray, retreating to the far end of the table, with her cup of milky hot water and her needlework.

The silence was broken, as Dottie entered and crossing the room, threw open the window. Brushing the hair, that had escaped the combs that held it, out of her face, she gingerly took hold of the opening of her dress, fanning herself with it, as she looked at the cloudless sky.

"Doesn't look like rain any time soon."

"No, there'll be fires if it keeps on like this too much longer."

Moving to take her seat at the head of the table, beneath the open window, Dottie leant down and kissed her mother's cheek, becoming enveloped in a cloud of scent.

"You look nice Mum. Oh, good you made tea. The children are down for a sleep now, so we can have some time to ourselves."

Glancing at Ivy, sitting hunched over her tea, at the far end of the table, wearing the face not of a Sistine Madonna, but of a Roman martyr, Dottie turned to see her mother sitting in triumph, the Caesar of the teapot.

"It is beastly hot out today."

"I know, I went out early for the chickens and could tell it was going to be a scorcher, so I decided we would stay in today, hence my horrible old housedress."

Charlotte picked up the teapot and began to pour tea.

"Did you hear about Mr Reilly's accident? A terrible smash up, back up near the Burlington." Charlotte's dark eyes flashed, as she began to warm to her favourite topic, the victory of the teapot already forgotten, despite Ivy's long face at the end of the table.

"I heard a little, Arch told me that there had been a big smash with a motorcyclist, but not much more. I think he was still in Parramatta when it happened."

"Well, it appears that the young man on the motorcycle, was entirely at fault. I heard it all from Mrs Hoffmann, who saw the whole thing. The young man was travelling out of town, and tried to overtake the car in front of him, of course he was travelling far too fast, one of those young fellows who speed through without a single thought to this being a town and not the open road. He slammed straight into Mr Reilly, who was coming in the opposite direction. Mrs Hoffmann said the sound of the impact had to be heard to be believed. The motorcycle was flung clear back along the street, and such a twisted wreck it was. Looking at it, you would not believe it was a motorcycle. The whole left side of the car was crumpled up, and the windscreen smashed all over the occupants of the car, like snow."

"That's dreadful."

"You haven't heard the worst of it. Mr Quested was riding on the outside of the car, he was thrown into the street and badly shaken, but largely unhurt. The motorcyclist, however, was smashed to pieces, his left leg was broken in three places, and Mrs Hoffmann said you could see the bone protruding from his thigh. His arm was broken and his head was black with bruises. Conscious the whole time. Mrs Hoffmann said he made such a din, the like of which she had never heard come from a man before, like a dying animal. The poor lad died on the way to hospital. He came from out Cowra way apparently."

"Tragic, such a waste of life."

Sitting at the far end of the table, Ivy listened to Charlotte's gossip with a mixture of intense curiosity, and abhorrence that she could be partaking in such a low activity. Part of her knew that she should not be sitting and listening to gossip, that it was a wicked habit to fall into, not at all the behaviour expected of a Josephite nun. While yet another part of her, felt excited and seduced by the pleasure of sitting with two ladies, who could afford to spend their time talking and laughing, rather than working, endlessly working. It was as if she had been invited to spend time with Dottie and her friends at school, where due to her quick wit and friendly nature her employer ruled above all the other eleven year olds, managing to hold on to that position until she left school a year later. Though Ivy would never say, the day that her class was told Dottie would not be returning for the New Year, was one of the worst in her life. And so here she sat, desperately conflicted, as Charlotte began yet another story.

"You know Joseph Pannell, the man who runs the kiosk down at Leura falls?"

Dottie searched her memory for a face to attach to the name. "Large man, drooping moustache, big gold watch, red face."

"Yes that's the chap. Well, he's dead."

"Really, was he sick?"

Charlotte lifted her tea cup to her lips, and sipped the liquid within with all the delicacy of a honeyeater, sipping on a flower. Pausing to give her words the dramatic emphasis they demanded, while maintaining the cool disinterestedness of her tone, she said, "No, he shot himself."

Charlotte glanced at her daughter's wide eyed surprise, with great satisfaction, it is not often in one's life, that one can deliver such an earthshattering piece of information, and to pull it off so beautifully. After such a moment, the rest of the story felt superfluous, but convention demanded that she continue with her story. A convention upheld, as Dottie asked the obvious and utterly unnecessary question: Why?

"Well, I heard this straight from Mrs Pannell's sister Elsie. Let me start by saying the man was a brute. An absolutely foul man, despite what all the men about town will tell you. His poor little wife and kiddies, there were whole days when one or other of them, could not leave the house. And Mrs Pannelle, is always a little heavy handed with the powder, if you catch my drift. I couldn't stand him myself, though your father invited him to dinner several times. Uncultured oaf. I told Bessie to spit in his food."

"Mum, you didn't."

"I did, and I watched her do it. Servants are only too willing to spit in people's food." Charlotte looked across the table at her daughter, the obvious exaggeration of her words, failing to convince. "No I didn't, but I wish I had. Anyway, it was Sunday morning and they were packing up the kiosk for the day, when he began raging about a tray of scones he had knocked off the table onto the floor, which was supposed to serve them for lunch. The children, used to their father's violence, were herded outside as Pannell shouted at his wife for putting the scones in the wrong place, though she had done nothing of the kind. He was always blaming her for his own mistakes, and things of that nature."

At this moment, a small voice from the far end of the table, broke across the river of words coming from Charlotte Joyce.

"I don't think we should be discussing the dead in this manner. It seems terribly disrespectful."

Charlotte, broken mid-flow in her story, cast Ivy a sideways glance through narrowed eyes, before casually turning to her daughter with a look which said: and how my dear will you handle this?

Dottie looked at Ivy, and then back to her mother, as the realisation that she was expected to deal with her companion herself, and could not rely on her mother's biting tongue, to chasten the oh so polite rudeness, of Ivy's comment, dawned upon her.

"Ivy, if you don't like our conversation you don't have to join us, you are free to do your work in another part of the house. I don't need you to sit in with me when it is my mother visiting."

Ivy looked at Dottie, with the eyes of one cast out of paradise, finding only the impassive firmness, of a set determination that she leave their company. Lowering her gaze and blinking back tears, that had begun to form in her big soft bovine eyes, Ivy's shoulders slumped, as gathering her sewing to her as if it were a baby in swaddling clothes, she slipped from the room.

"Well isn't she a dramatic little miss. As I was saying, Elsie and Mrs Pannell noticed that Mr Pannell was holding a gun. She believed that he meant to kill all of them, wife, sister, children and himself. Just the sort of selfish act you would expect from a man like that. They both tried to take the gun from him, it really was a miracle that neither of them were shot, he pushed them aside, then shot himself through the head."

Charlotte took up her teacup and drank deeply this time, of the cooling liquid within, her greatest story telling triumph marred by the tantrums of a silly girl.

Dottie, seeing her mother visibly deflated, by the interruption to what had to be the story of the season, attempted to redirect her attention and smooth her ruffled feathers.

"Will you and Dad be going to the swimming carnival next Wednesday, down at the Baths?"

"Your father will be out in Lithgow next week. He has been so busy setting up the brewery, but once it is up and running he should have more time. I was thinking of going with my Whist group, would you like to come with us?"

"Hmm, watch athletic young men in bathing costumes competing for an afternoon, yes I think I shall. It's free isn't it?"

"Yes, though we were all going to chip in for a picnic hamper, I'll put in for you too. I'll order a car and have it pick us up. Have you heard from Jack?"

"Yes, a whole pile of letters came for me just yesterday. The poor thing was sea sick the whole way to Colombo. They kept him in the sick bay he was so poorly. He didn't have much news, just about life on the ship, and a long train trip out into the desert in Egypt. He says the camp is beneath the pyramids and that you can feel the history seeping into you, along with the dust. He said its cold and could I send him more socks and gloves, as they get ruined by their training in no time."

Charlotte half listening to her daughter's words, rose from her seat and moved to stand before the dresser, looking but not looking, at the new dinner service arranged on the display. Opening the glass door, she looked finally at the dinner plates, with their gold embossing on red backgrounds, running in inch wide bands around the edges of each plate and serving dish.

"What a lovely new dinner service." Charlotte lifted down a plate and turned it over to look at the maker's mark. "It's Schlottenhof. How on earth did you find Schlottenhof, they stopped importing it when war broke out."

"Jack bought it in Sydney, before he left. For all his faults, he does have good taste. The shop keeper said that he ought to smash it, but that it had cost him a packet and he couldn't afford to lose the money. Jack offered to pay him cost for it, so that he and his mates could smash it back in barracks. He had it shipped up before he left, but I didn't have time to unpack it until now."

Placing the plate back on its display stand, Charlotte closed the glass doors, feeling the click of the catch through the wood beneath her hands.

From her seat, Dottie could see her mother's body stiffen, as she turned her head to look at her over her shoulder. Dottie could see the tension in her mother's jaw, so that when she finally spoke, her voice sounded tight and ragged.

"Ignorant barbarians, imagine smashing something so beautiful. You may as well deface the king's portrait because his father was German and his mother half German. I wonder if they'll intern the King as an enemy alien."

Rising from her seat, Dottie crossed the room, and laid her hand on her mother's shoulder. "What's wrong Mum?"

Charlotte closed her eyes against the tears, she could feel building behind them, breathing deeply. The whale bone of her corset creaked against the pressure. Turning her face to look at Dottie, her thick dark lashes trembling with moisture, her brow knotted and her mouth tightened against the sighs, she tried to repress.

"My cousin wrote in her last letter, that she won't be writing to me anymore and I shouldn't either, for as long as the war continues. Nearly thirty years of correspondence, broken by stupid men and their stupid fighting."

Lions Meet Wolves at Troy

In the court of King Priam, word had arrived that a Greek war fleet, was headed to Troy. Knowing that war was soon to arrive on his doorstep, Priam sent his son Hector, to visit his fellow kings and tell them that war had arrived at Troy. So, just as Agamemnon had drawn together the armies of Greece under his banner, did Hector, shepherding the scattered peoples of the east under one banner, his banner. The Grey Wolf, who leads his pack out of the forest and onto the plains in search of food, led his people to war.

At sea, the Greek forces trusting to Agamemnon's word that Troy would be as easily overthrown, as it had been in the days of Heracles, joked and sang of the mighty deeds that they would accomplish on their landing. It was to be an easy victory, against a backward and disorganised people, a people who could not stand up to the might of Greece. They were in no danger of defeat; victory was in their grasp, if only they had the courage to take it.

As the Greek fleet arrived at Troy, they found not golden beaches as their leaders had promised, but ridges covered in low scrub. The rocky beaches against which the surf broke with its customary fury offered no protection to a landing, while the ridges and scrub, gave the defending Trojans a complete advantage.

"Take heart men," said Agamemnon, when he saw the bay. "Let the Trojans have the advantage of the land, for they will never survive the onslaught that we will provide. They will be running back to their wives skirts, the moment they see us coming. We will be home in time to reap the spring sowing."

The men, seeing no alternative, chose to believe Agamemnon's words. As they hauled their boats up onto the beach, not a single Trojan warrior was seen by the Greek invader, yet they made their presence felt. By sunset as the last boat was hauled ashore, the beach ran red with blood. A welcome to country the Greeks would never forget.

Chapter Eleven

William Brown, Billy to his mates, the youngest of five brothers, sat listening as his father read out to the family, the news of the landing at Anzac Cove. After the first couple of paragraphs, Billy allowed his attention to wander, focusing instead of the clink of spoons against his mother's breakfast set, as he and his family ate their porridge. The clink and scrape of spoon on bowl, began to take on the tones of a strange music, each bowl changing its pitch, as the porridge level sank inexorably, tipped into the bottomless pits of four hungry miners. Stirring his porridge with listless energy, he listened to the admiring tone in his father's voice, as he picked his way awkwardly through the newspaper article. Billy sighed audibly, looking down at his bowl.

"It's alright, Love. Joe, stop reading that, you're upsetting William."

"No Mum, I'm fine," said Billy, resting a hand on his mother's.

Ever since the day he had tried to follow his brothers down the pit, and had to be hauled out hysterical, terrified by the idea that the whole weight of the earth would come tumbling down upon his head, his mother had thought of him as delicate. His front row position in the local under 16's rugby team and his ability to butcher a whole cow notwithstanding.

"Go on Dad, when does it say we'll finish clobbering the Turks?"

The voice belonged to Billy's eldest brother David. Billy looked gratefully at David, but could see David had not so much as glanced in his direction. Billy returned his attention to his breakfast, eating as quickly as possible, so that he could leave for work. None of Billy's four brothers, had ever shown him great sympathy for his claustrophobia, teasing him in revenge for the embarrassment and loss of face the episode had cost them. However, their father's reaction to his wife's intimations that his youngest son was delicate had become not only predictable, but tiresome to his elder sons. Prompting David, in the past few months, to try redirecting his attention. A strategy with varying success. On this occasion, Joseph Brown scowled at Billy from beneath dark eyebrows, but continued to read in his slow laborious voice. Billy knew he should talk to his mother, but misguided though her sympathies were, she was his only supporter, helping him to get the apprenticeship with her cousin Henry. Conversation being, as always a minimal exercise in the household, had not erupted once the paper was read. Instead, the act of eating was resumed with greater force, as the clock chimed the quarter, reminding the men that it would soon be time to leave for work. His father's voice, had not long ceased before Billy pushed his empty bowl away, and rose from the table, pushing his chair in.

"I'll see you tonight, bye."

Heads, still busily eating, nodded from the table, as Billy turned and pulled the kitchen door closed behind him. Standing in the backroom, he pulled on his coat and slid his black cap carefully, over his pomaded blonde hair. Looking into the cracked mirror, he examined the painfully red pimples, which had recently erupted over his face. A fair downy beard had started to appear on his face at the same time, but the acne had made it impossible to shave in the bathroom mirror, as his father and elder brothers did every morning. Life really wasn't fair, not content with humiliating him with claustrophobia, he now had to put up with wearing the face of a monster.

Turning away from the mirror, Billy stepped down the back steps, walking across the yard to the shed. Fetching his bicycle,

Billy walked into the laneway behind his house. Turning down the lane, he walked past clotheslines and toilets. Looking towards town, he could see the smoke from the steel works, billowing from the big stack. A dirty stain, against the flawless blue, autumn sky.

"Hi Billy," the cracked and excited voice of George, greeted Billy, as he approached the yard. "Did ya' hear about the landing?"

"Yeah, Dad read it out to us at breakfast. Exciting isn't it." Billy climbed onto his bicycle, and began peddling slowly along the flat laneway.

"Too right. Dad said that no one will match those blokes, the men who join up from now on will be good and doing their duty, but these blokes are bloody heroes, and nothing can match that."

George, was the only son, in a family of six sisters. Six sisters, whose presence in the house, had made George the centre of his social world. As his friends hung about and littered his house, much to his mother's annoyance. Unlike Billy, George was following in his father's footsteps, now in the third year of his apprenticeship, as a fitter and turner at the new Small Arms factory.

"I got that book for you," said George, stopping his bicycle, as he reached into his overalls and pulled out a coverless book, threads coming from the naked binding. "It's got some really blue bits."

Billy doubled back and took the offered book, flicking through it, his eyes lighting on words and passages, that would require further investigation tonight, in the lavatory, with the candle he had hidden for such purposes.

"I paid Henry three shillings for that, so don't let anything happen to it." Billy pushed the book into the bag attached to his handlebars.

"Are you going to the dance on Saturday?" Billy slipped back into the steady rhythm of riding, alongside George on the wide flat street that ran nearly the length of the town.

"Yeah, you?"

"I am if your sister Gracie is going."

"I'll ask her tonight if you want," said George, as they turned into Main Street, past the courthouse.

"Orright, let me know tomorrow." Billy slowed his bicycle, as they approached his cousin's butcher's shop.

"See ya Billy," yelled George, as he sped past his friend, peddling with great ferocity down the street, standing on his peddles gliding out of view.

***

Avoiding talk of the landing proved impossible for Arch. All day long passengers and passers-by talked of war. Attempts to direct them onto the subject of the mountains, or holiday plans, proved to be useless. War was the topic of the day, war fell from their mouths, like shrapnel and their eyes blazed with the excitement of battle. Yes, now that Australia had joined the war, the Germans would be on the run. King and Country would be served by bold and brave young men of the AIF, who fought in Gallipoli. Though few could say, with great certainty where Gallipoli was, or why it was so important. What mattered was that Australia was fighting there, and fighting gloriously, if the papers were to be believed. No country had produced finer, braver men, than those who had seen their first taste of battle only a few days ago. True, there had been casualties, but that would not deter those who knew their duty.

By lunch time, Arch was sick of the conversation offered to him. Rather than take his cab down to Echo Point, to wait for the afternoon traffic of tired bushwalkers, who no longer felt possessed of the energy to make the trek back up Lurline Street,

Arch drove further afield, parking off the road heading out along Narrow Neck. Parking his cab on the rough bush grass, which grew beside the road, Arch walked along the sandstone ledge and sat down. Here, sitting on the sandstone ledges overlooking the Jamison valley, he unwrapped the half a fruit cake Dottie had given him that morning. Breaking off a piece, he ate slowly, focusing all his attention on rolling the cake around his mouth, and the sensation of it sliding down his throat. Although such concentration on eating made him gag, he was desperate for something to blot out, the desolating thought that any day now, word could come that his brother was dead.

This morning, reading the paper with Dottie, he had seen her face turn white and her whole body tremble. She had looked both, touchingly devoted and painfully beautiful. So much so, that he had been forced to remind himself that she was his brother's wife; that the beauty her fear and concern created, was for Jack and Jack alone. Arch pushed the thought from his mind, it had been such a painful morning, and he could not, after such a shock, order his thoughts and feelings into any cohesive whole. Better to let them sink, as he let all others sink, into a safe undefined mass. None of them were safe, he knew from long experience that anger and grief, guilt and jealousy could cut as deeply as any knife. What had over the years surprised him, again and again, was that pity, kindness, and especially love could lead to troubles far deeper than those which stung, but sank back down into the depths. Though he would not admit it, Arch knew it was all a distraction, his mind throwing up lust and guilt, to cover the fear he could neither suppress nor conquer, but which sat like a toad on his chest breathing its poison into every moment.

At last, Arch returned to his cab, driving round Cliff Drive to Echo Point, in time for the afternoon rush.

Chapter Twelve

The vicar's wife, Mrs Bridge had organised the dance in the church hall some weeks earlier, with a mind to raising money to help the war effort in Britain. The landing at Gallipoli, earlier that week, had caused the ladies auxiliary, of whom she was the chair, to recommend a change of focus. Stating quite reasonably that, many of the young people expected to attend, should be encouraged to actively support the Australian forces in Turkey. Mrs Bridge, who having only five years previously come out to Australia, with her husband to take up the Lithgow parish, had trouble adjusting herself to seeing the noisy ill-disciplined men, who appeared every so often in town wearing AIF uniforms, as being worthy of her support.

To her, home would forever be a small village in Suffolk where she had spent her childhood, from whence her husband, wild for adventure in the colonies, had driven her. For as long as she lived, she would not forgive her husband, for dragging her out of her life, and depositing her in this industrial hell. Had she any longing to live amongst factory workers and miners, she would have moved to Yorkshire. Certinally this stiflingly hot place, with its coarse women and rough men, who had not a name of consequence between them, and yet styled themselves ladies and gentlemen such as you would find back home, left her baffled. True, she had earned their admiration for her fine manners and the efficiency with which she conducted her household. Her accent, with its polished vowels and condescending air, sent them into ecstasies, but though they sought to imitate and recreate the life of an English village, amongst the sun, flies and soot of this strange land, she was left feeling perpetually alien. Not that her husband had fared much better, in trying to instil any moral rectitude on his flock of miners, steel workers, factory workers, railway men and their wives and children. Most of whom only attended the church for forms sake, or for the privilege of christenings, marriages or funerals. Else why, would they so consistently ignore his sermons on the evils of alcohol, which flooded the town from nearly a dozen hotels? Not that the educated classes were much better, they on the whole laughed at the temperance movement, which her husband had started. While she had had more luck with miners' wives, in spreading the word and encouraging families to sign the pledge. The contempt of many in public office, even the neighbouring Catholic priest, who regarded the movement as wowserish and impossible to maintain, had greatly discouraged the Reverend Bridge. Mrs Bridge could see very well, that despite the claims of Britishness made by those who surrounded her, that these Australians were more like children playing at a game, the rules of which had been long lost, forcing the players to reassemble it from their recollections, creating such a distortion of the original, that the mother game could no longer be guessed, through casual observation.

So when the her fellow auxiliary members, threatened to withdraw their support of her war charity, should the funds raised not go to support the Australian forces, including many local boys who had been among the first to sign up and were even now sitting in trenches in Turkey, she was forced to relent.

***

Paying his shilling at the door, dropping off his coat and hat, Billy walked into the church hall. The hall was very bright and warm, after the dark autumn evening. On the stage a small band played dance music, as couples whirled about the dancefloor. Opposite the stage, at the back of the hall, a refreshment stand had been set up, with fruit punch, soft drinks, cakes and sandwiches just like a children's party.

Taking a position against the wall, with a good view of the door, Billy scanned the dancing couples, looking for George. All week he had been applying tea tree oil and hot compresses to his face, in an effort to tame his dreadful skin. Getting ready this evening, he saw that his efforts had paid off, at least partially, while his skin still looked red and uneven, the white pimple heads had cleared up and he had been able to shave for the first time in a month. Watching the dancers moving about the floor, like pairs of goldfish in a crowded tank, some moving with great skill and flare, while others wobbled and blundered their way through the dance, he wondered what it would be like to dance with Gracie. George had promised to bring her tonight, but he could not see either of them amongst the dancers. Perhaps they had not arrived yet. The clock above the band showed seven, they couldn't be here yet, Mrs Purcell never served dinner before six thirty, and it was a fifteen minute walk from George's house to the church hall.

Relaxing, as the panicky feeling in his chest subsided, Billy wandered across to the refreshment table and bought a bottle of soft drink. His older brothers had teased him about going to the dance, as all good dances serve beer. Mrs Bridge's dance would be 'dry', thus not worth going. Though they had all taken the pledge, to please their mother, his brothers preferred to go to the bigger more raucous 'wet' dances, with their friends, held in a barn out in the Vale of Clwydd. Camping out overnight, so that their mother would never suspect, what they had been doing.

Returning to his position against the door, Billy drank and watched the dancers, a strange mix of young and exuberant dancers, none of whom could be said to be over twenty one, and older couples, parents and grandparents of the youngsters, whose presence forced a more decorous behaviour, on the young ones than was natural for them. Under the cover of dancing he could see boys, who had pressed themselves against their partners so tightly, that a cigarette paper could not be forced between them. As these couples whirled past the chaperones, they received a tap on the shoulder and sprang apart in a strangely mechanical way, only to draw together again, as the dance progressed. Billy thought of how divine it would be, to dance like that with Gracie.

Swallowing the last dregs of his soft drink, Billy was considering whether or not to buy another, when George and Gracie entered the hall. For a moment, Billy was too awestruck to move. He watched, as Gracie took off her overcoat, revealing a pale pink dress beneath. The dress had once belonged to one of her older sisters, but as this was her first dance, she had spent the week embellishing it with small, glittery, pink glass beads, the effect of which was, that she appeared to glow and shimmer like a celestial goddess, beneath the electric lights. Her hair, usually pulled tight in a plait down her back, had been curled and pinned up, so that she looked like one of the ladies in the chemist shop window, the ones in the pears soap advertisements. Her full wide sensual mouth, a copy of her brothers, which on him made his face resemble overripe fruit that had burst its skin, smiled with delight at what she saw. She hung on her big brother's arm, as he led her across the hall, to where Billy waited.

"Gracie, you look beautiful," said Billy, knowing that his whole face had turned red.

Gracie giggled, clearly pleased with the effect she was having on him.

"Gracie, I'm going to talk to Kate, over there," George, gestured to a girl who was waiting for him on the opposite side of the hall. "You two can stand here giggling all you like, come and find me when you are ready to leave, okay."

Billy watched George disappear, into the swirling crowd with a feeling of almost panic. Gracie, her face almost as pink as her dress, looked at her feet and was no help at all. She was waiting for him, if he wanted to dance pressed up against this beautiful girl, and he wanted that more than anything in the world, he would have to make the first move.

"Would you like to dance?"

Gracie giggled, nodding her head, but made no move towards the dance floor. Billy, seeing that he would have to take charge of the situation, offered his arm to Gracie in the exaggerated manner, he imagined that gentlemen did, at the big civic balls given by the mayor. Resting her hand on his arm, as lightly as if it were a dove, Gracie allowed herself to be led onto the dance floor. Assuming the stance that had been drilled into her by her dance teacher, when she danced with other girls in their schoolroom.

Billy and Gracie danced stiffly, though solidly for three quarters of an hour, occasionally meeting George and Kate, who hailed them as they passed. Billy could smell the sweet soap Gracie had used to wash that afternoon, and though she danced too stiffly to press her close, as some couples did, he was content to feel her fluttering dove hand at his shoulder, and to have his palm clamped warmly, at her waist. She looked up at him with bright, blue eyes, made all the bluer by the pink flush of her cheeks, caused at first by her shyness, though now by the exertion of dancing.

As the clock struck eight, Billy and Gracie left the dance floor, retiring to chairs placed by the refreshment table. Leaving Gracie to catch her breath, Billy wandered over to the table, to buy fruit punch and cake. Returning with the food and drink, Billy and Gracie sat in companionable silence, eating and drinking, exchanging shy glances and smiles as they did so. Billy was only thinking what a success the dance was, when he noticed a strange eager look cross Gracie's face, as she looked suddenly past him towards the door. Billy turned to see that many of the dancers too, had stopped and were looking at the latest arrival. Turning, to see what had so captured the attention of the crowd, he saw, Thomas Baker enter the hall. Tommy Baker, with his acne scars, thinning hair and a moustache that looked more like a dirty smear on his upper lip, clad in full light horse uniform.

"It's just Tommy Baker," said Billy, turning back to Gracie.

"Is it? I hardly recognised him. He looks so different, more impressive in that uniform."

Billy turned again, to look at what had drawn for the first time, such an admiring tone from his dance partner. By now, Tommy had garnered the interest of many of the girls dancing, flocking about him, as he entered the hall, leaving bewildered boys standing alone. Amongst the confused boys stood George, abandoned by Kate, who now stood amongst the clamouring girls, all seeking to dance with Tommy Baker. Billy gave George a baffled look, which was returned, as an equally puzzled shrug. Slowly, the girls dawdled back to their partners and the dancing resumed.

Billy and Gracie, finished their refreshments and returned to the dancing, though Gracie no longer looked up at him in the same way, instead she looked past him, over his shoulder, following Tommy Baker of all people as he danced with girl after girl, in quick succession. Soon, he felt George tap him on the shoulder. Turning to look, he saw George's brow was drawn together, into a painful knot above the bridge of his nose, his sensual mouth was drawn tight and pale, and through his shoulder, he could feel his friend trembling with supressed emotion.

"Gracie, we're going home."

"But the dance isn't finished," said Gracie, her voice whining with annoyance.

"I don't care, we're going." George grabbed Gracie's wrist, dragging her off the dance floor. Gracie trailed after he brother, like a sulky toddler, stumbling several times on her dress, as he rushed her out of the hall.

Bewildered by his friend's sudden departure, Billy, looked across at the dancers surrounding him and saw Kate, dancing with Tommy Baker.

The Enemy Within

As the weeks and months dragged on, stories and rumour, began to flood into the cities and towns of Greece. Stories of mutilation and violence against the wounded and dying, caused a scandal wherever they were heard. Young men were incensed, enlisting, whenever a call to arms was announced. Veterans and camp followers, returning from service repeated the stories, encouraged by the responses their stories received, to lay ever more atrocities at the feet of the Trojan soldiers. Entrenching further, the view that all Trojans were violent animals, intent on domination, conquest and rape of all of Greece.

Chapter Thirteen

No one was quite sure who they were, or where they had come from, but all would say, that they were the beginnings of the troubles in town. They had set up outside the railway station, the morning was dry and cold, the way that May mornings often are in the mountains, but they were not mountains people. Professional troublemakers, was the general opinion of most who saw them, they attracted a bad element around them, people it was best to keep as far from the tourists as possible. Bad for the town.

They called themselves, the Anti-German league and talked of establishing a branch in Katoomba. Their aim, was to hound all Germans out of positions of authority, and advocated the interning of all they termed, enemy aliens.

Their opening salvo, was to nail a German flag to the boardwalk, at the entrance to the railway station on Main Street, inviting passers-by to wipe their feet on the flag and to purchase for shilling, a picture of the Kaiser to tear up. Though nobody bothered to mention where the money would go, and when pressed, the young men at the booth appeared uncertain and evasive. Nor did it help matters, that those attending the booth, corralled the exiting train passengers through their flag wiping exercise, causing terrible congestion in both directions on and off the railway. The fact that the noise and general violence of the operation, attracted the notice of the local Push, who jeered and hustled anyone who attempted to use the second exit to the station, only made the matter worse.

By the end of the day, as the young men packed up their stack of drawings and their grubby flag, those who had watched proceedings from their shop windows and the seats of cabs, were relieved. Agreeing to prevent a repeat performance, which had so harmed their businesses, were it attempted again. None realising yet, that this was just the opening salvo, the catalyst for worse to come. The booth operators had left, but like any plague carrier, they had started an infection, that would pass from person to person, group to group, until a full blown epidemic would breakout.

One of the early victims of the epidemic, was Bert Kaufmann, the owner and proprietor of the Katoomba tea house. A large and airy establishment, conveniently situated across from the train station, where tired, thirsty tourists poured forth all day long, and the homeward bound stopped in to fortify themselves before the long trip back to Sydney. Bert's tea house was famous in town for its cakes, which Mrs Kaufmann rose at four in the morning, to bake for the day ahead.

It was a couple of weeks after the flag incident, and Bert had watched the Push gather outside his shop all afternoon. They stood by the curb, or with their backs to the windows, jostling any person who attempted to enter. There were almost a dozen of them by the time Bert wished to close up, and he had no idea, how many were lurking round the back. This was the third day, that the local Push had targeted his shop, on the corner between Main Street and Katoomba Street. Usually, the local Push would fight amongst themselves, brawling in the street, or lounging at the entrances of pubs, smoking and hurling insults, as they protected their patch from rivals. Occasionally, they turned their attention towards honest citizens, who by some act or common misfortune, had earned their displeasure, or to relieve the tedium of their days, harassing a drunk down the street, or jostling a woman carrying her shopping; petty nuisances, until now.

Inspired by the anti-German league, who had so mysteriously appeared in town and set up a local branch. The aims of which were vague, yet strangely threatening if such ephemeral demands, such as the removal of Germans from public office, implied that a threat from that quarter both, existed and needed immediate and drastic action. The Push took it upon themselves, to ensure the protection of the state, by harassing anyone with a vaguely Germanic name, and disrupting their business.

Their simplistic reading of ethnic origin, had brought them unstuck on occasion, most notably, when they had attempted to harass Mrs Hoffmann. Formerly Miss Murray, the publican of the Harp and Fiddle's sister, a woman who could be described, as neither defenceless, nor delicate. A woman, with six children at home, and arms like rolling pins. It was quite a sight, to see three young Push members running away, bleeding lips, blackened eyes and for the instigator, who had thrust his face under the brim of Mrs Hoffmann's hat, a broken nose. Bert wished he had some of her bravery, as he watched the Push, jostle his customers, or force them to step out into the street to pass along the curb. Bad for business it was.

And now it was his turn. Not that Bert Kaufmann, had ever thought of himself as German, beyond a name and a distant heritage, any more than he saw himself as Irish or a convict, for there were plenty of both in his background. But, it seemed a name, in these times, was enough to condemn even the most loyal and hardworking citizen. At least, it was in the eyes of the Push.

Bert took one last look out the windows, at the Push gathered on the street. Across the street, the cabs waited for passengers. It wasn't possible to delay leaving any longer. Pulling on his hat and coat, Bert closed the blinds, switched off the light and left his shop stepping out into the street.

"Look, 'ere comes the Hun," said the leader of the Push, a tall thin boy of no more than seventeen. Moving close to Bert, he stood, blocking his path across the street. "You're not wanted here Hun."

Bert stopped, as other Push members, began to crowd around him. He knew that they would not touch him, always waiting for their victim to break, and lash out first. A boy to his right, no more than fifteen, drew on his cigarette and blew his smoke into Bert's face. Laughing, as Bert coughed, showing a mouth full of brown and rotting teeth.

"I'm not looking for trouble. I only want to go home," said Bert, attempting to move forward.

"I only vant to go home," echoed the Push leader, laughing at his own joke.

"I'm not German. I was born in Bathurst," said Bert, his arms sweeping the air, gesturing towards the western districts, as if they could confirm his identity. Accidently brushing the chest, of one of the Push, as he spoke, Bert knew he was in trouble.

"You, hit me."

"An accident, no offence meant," stammered Bert, looking along the street for any source of help.

"You hit me," said the offended boy, shoving Bert in the chest.

Bert knew he would have to make a break for it, and try for help. Perhaps if he could make it to the cab rank, he would be all right, he could catch a cab home and escape. Reckless with fear, Bert pushed his way through the wall of bodies. Feeling fists rain down on him, he struggled forward, until a foot placed in his path caused him to fall, sprawling on the road, as the Push moved in. Crowding around the prone man, the Push began kicking, their shouts echoing across the darkening streets, as passers-by attempted to avoid attracting their attention.

"Leave him alone, you little mongrels," came a shout from across the road.

The audacity of anyone interrupting their fun, startled the Push into stillness.

"We're just havin' a bit of fun. He's just a dirty Hun, nothin' to worry about Mister," shouted the Push leader.

"I said, leave him alone," repeated the voice, from the darkness.

"You're just a Hun lover, you'll get yours," said the Push leader, turning towards the voice.

At that moment, the sound of a police whistle rounded the corner, and the Push scattered like rabbits before the fox. Disappearing down Gang-Gang Street, into Hudson's gully and its warren of dark hiding places, where the police would not enter.

The next morning, Bert Kaufmann walked up the steps of the courthouse, never to be seen again, as Bert O'Donnell, a name he had previously scorned for its convict heritage, emerged. Bert would later comment, that it was a sad day when it was better to be related to a convict, than to a free settler. By that afternoon, the sign writers were standing outside the Bert's tea house, scrapping the Kaufmann of the windows and hoardings, as the finest teahouse in town, slowly lost its prestige. The cakes, for which it was famous, with their exotic foreign names fell off the menu, followed closely by its fashionable clientele, retreating to the secure cosmopolitanism of the Chateau Napier. By the end of the war, it would be just another tea house, in a tourist town full of such establishments, which served cheap tea and dry scones.

Chapter Fourteen

The Reverend Bridge, had met with little luck, in his attempts to dry up the city of Lithgow. A failure, over which, he would be found brooding, as he lugged his golf bag across the course, with the Bishop in Bathurst. Or on lonely walks, up to Hassans Walls, where gazing down on the Hartley valley, he liked to imagine himself one of the ancient gods, perched on their great Mount Olympus. The failure of the temperance movement in his parish, had for a long time felt like a failure in himself, he was accustomed to gaining what he wished, through stubborn effort. Although the bishop had warned him, that his temperance drive was a fool's errand, in a town such as Lithgow, he had not prevented it and had even encouraged it, knowing that more than a few families would benefit from a sober breadwinner. Five years on, and the temperance that he had preached every Sunday, from the pulpit, had not only failed to dry out his congregation, it had diminished it.

Sitting on his own private Olympus, with the Eucalypts, those damned wanton dancers, swaying in the wind that tore about the rocky platform. The stubborn stunted grevilleas, clinging onto bare rock, indifferent to the winds that ripped at their spiny leaves, the Reverend Bridge knew he was a failure. It was knowledge, that sent him back to theological collage, where the masters were unmoved by his plodding, traditional interpretation of the scriptures, while heaping praise on those stars, who knew how to transform the word of God, and use it, to cover themselves in glory. The men who, even then it was clear, were heading to take up bishoprics and archbishoprics before they had reached anywhere near forty, while he, dull plodder that he was, would remain a parish curate for all his days. He had hoped, that his fortunes would fare better in this new land, which cried out for men of the cloth, and promised more rapid advancement for those who came. Reverend Bridge knew if he failed to stem the tide of his congregation, slowly drifting away to the Presbyterians, the Baptists and God forbid even the Catholics, whose priest, everyone knew was far too fond of the bottle to be seemly, he would be stuck in this grimy pit of a town forever. To never again see the inside of a fine house, nor wear the bishops purple ring before he died. Marcus Augustus Bridge, would not be curate of Lithgow till the end of his days, he would not let his wife become broken and tired, from living in this squalid place, let alone bring up children here. She needed the ocean, she was pining for it; at the very least she needed water, what a cursed dry land this seemed. Perhaps a parish by the sea would suit her, in Sydney or one of the nicer suburbs of Melbourne, as he had heard good things about the people of Melbourne, they seemed much more their sort, than these backwater hicks. The trick would be to find a theme, which would enflame the passions of the congregation, bringing them back tenfold.

Sitting in the pew on Sunday, his mother and father at the aisle end, while his brothers squeezed in beside them, leaving him sitting by the wall as usual, his view obstructed by a large pillar, Billy listened to the Reverend's sermon. Billy usually didn't listen much to what the Reverend said, as it was usually a long lecture on the demon drink, a theme that he never tired of, even at Christmas. This week, however, the familiar text failed to appear. In its place, came words of much more interest, words which resonated with those he read in the papers, and which occupied the conversation of people who he served in the shop, or met in the street. The Reverend was talking about, the war. Billy found himself sitting up straighter in the pew, his imagination fired by the images of Saint George and the struggle with evil, evil which now had a human face, that of the German race and their destructive arrogance, which threatened to enslave the free peoples of Europe. A greed for power and dominance, which if left unchecked, would extend to the very ends of the world, rendering this sovereign nation, this loyal handmaiden of Britain, merely spoils of war, and a colony of the Hun.

"This book," said the Reverend Bridge, holding up a cheap cardboard bound book, for his congregation to see. "Viscount Bryce's report to The British Parliament on German Outrages, which has been generously made available to the reading public, for only sixpence, illustrates the barbarity of the enemy which we face. Now, I know that this report is hard reading, but I urge you not to look away, not to hold your heads beneath the sand, for this fate may befall even yourselves, should we fail in holding off the advance of the Hun in France."

Billy craned his neck to see what the Reverend was holding up, it was the book he had seen for sale in the paper shop, all week. Looking across at his brothers, he could see them squirm and nudge each other, murmuring about the book he had disregarded, as some sort of agricultural manual. Billy knew he would have to get himself a copy of this book, if his brothers were willing to tax their semi-literate brains to read its contents, then it must be worth the read. Reaching into his pocket, he could feel a small sixpence, amongst the change he had brought for the collection. He must remember to save that, rather than grasp his change, as he usually did, and toss it lightly into the basket. This sixpence had other uses.

"Billy, where you going in such a rush?" George quickened his steps, until he came up alongside his friend.

"Paper shop." Billy quickened his pace, his sixpence clutched in his palm.

"Slow down, Mate."

"I can't slow down, I've gotta get that book."

George knew, from his long friendship, that once Billy had stuck to an idea it could blossom into a full grown obsession, were the desire not met immediately. He had long suspected, that his friend's oddly obsessive personality, was not something to be encouraged, but today he did not feel equal to the task of distracting him, and so hurried along the street by his side, until they arrived at the paper shop. Standing outside in the sun, George felt himself overwhelmed by a wave of loneliness. It was a feeling that had been washing over him for weeks, making him feel as if he had been drenched, by a bucket of cold, dirty, grey water. His sisters had been mocking him for being so quiet, his mother had chaffed him about moping about the house, and had sent him out to split firewood each afternoon. But neither, his mother's insistence that he make himself useful, nor his sister's mockery, had managed to lighten his mood.

"It's over," said George, as Billy emerged from the paper shop, the book held triumphantly in his hands.

"What's over?" Turning, for the first time that morning, to look at his friend.

"Me and Kate." George thrust his hands into his pockets, and began wandering slowly down the road, towards the wasteland behind their street.

The wasteland, was a town block that had been cleared years before by a property developer, who lost heavily in the 1890's depression. Over the years, the block began to slowly revert to its wild state, as the grass grew in thick tussocks, and saplings grew unhindered, in place of the stand of mature eucalypts, which once covered the whole valley. Today the rough bush grass had been reduced to stubble, as surrounding neighbours, concerned with the possibility of children lighting a fire, had set about keeping it mown and manageable. Though the absence of grass, only served to encourage children in their play, as snakes were now more easily seen. For George and Billy, this was their childhood play area, now the place where they went, when they wished for privacy, from their all too full houses.

"What do you mean, over?" Billy jogged a little to catch up. "Just because she danced with Tommy Baker?"

"Yes…No. A bit." George flung himself down on the dry grass, and lay with his arms wrapped about his head, shielding his face from the sun.

Billy looked at the prickly grass, then at his Sunday suit. Wrapping his overcoat carefully about his suit, Billy sat down as delicately on the grass, as would one of George's sisters.

"I was angry after the dance, but Tommy was out of town the next day so that didn't matter too much. I decided to wait a bit before I talked to her, you know to show her that I didn't like what she'd done."

"Yeah, course you had to let her know it wasn't on."

"She didn't think that, she got all cross with me for ignoring her all week. We got into a huge fight, with her shrieking and me shouting at her. It was ugly."

Billy looked across at George, he could tell by the sound of his voice, that there were tears beneath the arms flung across his face. His own pleasure seemed immodest, beside his friend's pain, and pain it must be, for the last time he had seen his friend cry, was when they were ten years old, and George had broken his arm, climbing one of the big trees in the school yard.

"Yesterday, I saw her and she said if I joined up, she might consider taking me back."

"So are you gonna?"

"I don't know. I mean, I don't look twenty one."

"Yeah, but you'd be over there having the adventure, not stuck here reading about it in the paper." Billy's voice grew quick with excitement and his eyes blazed, at the thought of being a part of the stories, which filled the papers everyday now.

"I can't think. She might still come round. I mean we've been walking out together for two whole months, before now. That can't mean nothing, to her." Uncovering his face, George rolled over onto his side and looked at Billy. "Read us some of yer book. Give me something else to think about."

Chapter Fifteen

Every Tuesday morning for the past three months, Dottie would host what Arch, in his letters to Jack, called her knittin' and bitchin' group. Having considered Arch's advice to start her own group, in the face of her failure with the official soldier's support group held at Kardinia Park, Dottie now presided over a group of up to ten ladies. Ladies who sat in her front room, drinking tea and knitting socks and other apparel, that once a month, they sent to Jack, to share amongst the men in his unit.

Today, there were only seven of the group present, amongst them, were Dottie's mother, her aunt Martha, her cousin Mary, who although only four, was quite competent at knitting socks, until she got to the bendy bit, or dropped a stich and had to hand her work across to her mother, to finish for her. Ivy, still smarting from the rebuke Dottie had handed her back in February, had been persuades to put aside her sewing in favour of knitting needles, for an hour a week. Though, she was more often seen fetching tea and other items, for the ladies gathered around her.

Sitting by the fire, her hands swathed in fingerless gloves, for her rheumatism, sat Beth McIntire, who always brought socks, which she had made at home during the week, when her hands were not acting up. Like Dottie, Beth was one of the few ladies of the group to have family at the front, and it had been agreed that this next box would be sent to her grandson, Alf, who had just signed up, inspired by the news of the landing.

Finally, there was Flora and Aurora Arnold, twin sisters who had been at school with Dottie, forming part of her exclusive group, and who now lived together in a smart little cottage, on Lovell Street. From whence, they could be seen walking of an afternoon, to their work at the Empire Picture Palace, where their identical faces and uniforms, caused much confusion and delight amongst the patrons. Today, they sat side by side, in shades of pink, showing off identical pink sapphire engagement rings, which had suddenly appeared on their fingers, since the last meeting.

"They're twins too," said Aurora, holding out her hand for the ladies to admire. "James and John Hastings. They have adjacent sheep stations, down in Brindabella."

"They were looking for other twins, or at the very least close sisters to marry, because only they would understand what it was like," said Flora, enjoying the way her ring caught the light, as she knitted and sent it shooting about the room.

"They came to the picture palace and we played our little trick on them…"

"They thought it so funny, when we showed that we were two also…"

"They took us to dinner every night for a week…"

"At the Carrington…"

"They went back to Brindabella last night…"

"We're going to have a double wedding in October…"

"And then we'll settle in to be farmer's wives. With lots of children between us," said Aurora, her face as pink and bright, as the dawn after which she was named, her cobalt blue eyes glittering, like late setting stars.

"Speaking of babies, when is yours due Martha?"

"About six weeks. Though he could be like Mary and come early." Martha, stroked the great dome of her belly, beneath layers of cotton and wool. "He keeps me up at night, always moving when I want to sleep and now he sleeps."

"How do you know the baby is a boy?" asked Ivy, her face usually so bland and empty, suddenly alive with curiosity. Looking at her, Dottie could see that she was actually pretty, when not consumed by her almost permanent sulking.

"They feel different, don't they Dottie."

"Yes, they do. Have you chosen a name yet?"

"We decided to go with Anthony Alfred. Alfred and I decided that given the current climate, we should choose a name that was neither English nor German."

Seated by the fire, Beth McIntire had listened to the other ladies gossip, with little interest. She had been in a subdued mood since she arrived that morning, mumbling a greeting, and then taking up a chair close to the fire. The other ladies, assuming that her hands were troubling her today, offered her tea and left her to sit until she began to feel better.

Dressed in heavy tweed against the cold, which she seemed to feel more than most, Beth McIntire had always struck them as strange, though not so much so, that she could not be admitted into polite society. Dottie had seen Mrs McIntire when her hands pained her before, she would be quiet, but would engage with the room in a polite way, apologising for her inability to help with the knitting. Today saw none of that, seated by the fire she appeared both frightened and angry, not listening to the stories being told, but ruminating on some private hurt. Listening to Aunt Martha's discussion of names seemed to peek the old woman's interest, as she broke suddenly into the conversation, in a voice that commanded attention.

"I was a girl only when the Czar ordered a pogrom of the Jews in my home of Odessa. I lost all my family. I came here because there were no Czars, but lots of gold. On the ship from Trieste, I gave myself a pretty name, like the other girls. On the goldfields there were so many people, from so many places. I got work easily, because I could talk to miners from many places. I found a husband even easier, and we chased gold all over the country. It was hard in camps with little children, but good too. We chased gold, until my Angus died. Then I came here, like the mining camps, always so many voices. I felt safe, people called me

Mrs McIntire, and not dirty Jew. Today a boy spat at me in the street, and called me dirty German!" said Beth, her accent still heavy after over fifty years of speaking English. "I am Australian, my grandson is Anzac, why they do this to me?"

Staring into the silenced room, Beth searched the ladies for answers.

"Because you sound different," said Charlotte, breaking the silence at last. "Because they believe what the papers tell them and they wouldn't know a German accent if they heard it."

"Isn't there something we can do about this?" Dottie looked from her mother to her aunt and back again, watching as they shook their heads.

"There is nothing to be done, if we complain they will be worse. You saw what happened to old Wooler, the show secretary. There are calls in the papers every week to have Germans taken out of positions of power. Not that the Blue Mountains Agricultural Show secretary is a position of power."

"And what about that awful story, that there was a celebratory dinner for the sinking of the Lusitania? Lies of course, but they stuck. Goldsmiths won't sell Alfred timber anymore. There are other shops that refuse us service. At least you and Charlotte have safe names," said Martha. "Dad says that out in Mudgee, people are being hounded out of their houses, and that they are starting to lock up all the German born men."

Dottie looked back down at the knitting in her hands, observing as her mother redirected the conversation, lightening the room. She wondered at her mother's aptitude as a hostess, she had seen the conversation taking a turn for the worst, but had been unable to redirect it. Her mother, in contrast, had like any great hostess, grasped the reigns of the runaway conversation, steering it calmly back to the centre line, smoothing ruffled emotions, settling the topic back into the safely banal. Beth McIntire's words had woken something within Dottie, which she now felt she had not the strength to conquer. Rather, it had been the tone of her words, the pride in her voice when she named her grandson an Anzac. In all this time, these long months since Jack had left, she had not once felt proud of him and what he was doing in Turkey. She had worried about him, prayed for him, missed him, and daily for one reason or another had called him a stupid, stupid man for leaving her alone with their children, but never had she found the pride, which was blazoned across the papers every day. She found it hard to reconcile the statements about keeping Australia safe from German invasion, with her husband sitting in the dirt, on a thin stretch of beach in Turkey. Jack's letters did nothing to clarify the matter for her, he spoke only of his personal safety, of unexpected flashes of beauty, a gorse bush in flower, or dust motes on the air, the quality of the sunset over the ocean, things that told her nothing of his life, yet said everything. The war he described had no killing or death, no destruction nor discomfort, in his words it was boys playing games. While she was sure his words were not entirely honest, it did comfort her to imagine him, an impervious Achilles bestriding the battlefield amongst lesser men, noticing the wild flowers, as he went. His letters, told the gratitude of the men, with whom he shared the socks and cooking that arrived. They told her that he loved her and missed her, that he would be back with her again, as soon as he could manage it.

In return, Dottie sent letters that spoke of the ordinary flow of life, as she lived it. She told of the passing seasons, describing in as great a detail as she could manage, the changes in the garden. She wrote of their children, and the great strides that they made, in their development. Alfie was nearly walking, and had cut four teeth, while Edie came up with more and more new words, chattering about the house all day, singing her little songs. She wrote about local events, sometimes sending clippings from the paper, of things that she knew he would enjoy, like the football results. The harassment, that her friends and family were increasingly being subject to, she never mentioned, such things could only cause worry, and she needed Jack to focus on returning home.

It was of his returning home, that Dottie wrote the most, talking about what their lives would be like and speculating on his possible return date. From his dusty hot trench in Western Turkey, Jack would read her hopes and dreams laid out before him in her strange spidery script. She had never got the hang of copperplate, and like her mother had found her hands wrote a much more angular and jerky alphabet, no matter how many times the nuns had wacked her across the hands for it. Reading her letters he could see himself following the life she imagined for him, a life that he had postponed and avoided by signing up. In Egypt, before Dottie had even mentioned his future, he had resolved to finish his articles and set out on his own, once he returned home. Now Dottie's letters, showed him a career, that saw him sitting in judgement as magistrate in the local court, ambitions he had never considered, but which at least offered a relief from his current position. Something he also found, in writing his letters home, filling them with the most benign and beautiful things he could find, to relieve his mind from the grim reality of his life there.

Sitting and listening to the ladies chatter, Dottie pulled out of her pocket the latest letter from Jack. It had been delivered, as her group were arriving and she had not yet read it.

Dearest Dottie,

I hope that this finds you well, I am in fine spirits and fine heath, so you needn't worry about me. I have just had leave in Cairo, and feel very much refreshed for my week away. I saw dolphins from the ship, great sleek creatures they were, one could almost say that they were playing, as they swam alongside the ship, racing us across the sea. And the sea Dottie, it is like a jewel it is so blue and bright. I wish I could scoop it up, and scatter it in twinkling gems at your feet. At night, I look at the stars and try to think of what you are doing. Are you making dinner, or hanging washing, are you getting up? Are you thinking of me?

Here in this ancient place, I think of all those lovers I learnt about, in my Latin and Greek classes. Some separated by fate, others by the gods. Lovers separated by the jealousy of others, or by death, or war. And I think how lucky I am to have you, waiting for me to return to, as Odysseus had Penelope. The red haired wanderer, who despite it all did return. As I will return, to you and our children. Think of this time, as our great trial, all lovers go through some trial in these stories, so that in the end their happiness is all the sweeter. At night, I look at the stars, and think how sweet it will be once I am back with you.

All my love

Jack.

Blinking back tears, Dottie folded the letter and slipped it back into her pocket. It had been a mistake to read it amongst company. Such intimate words, always made her feel as if Jack were wooing her all over again, using words and tricks that were guaranteed to work, now that he was not a stumbling youth, but a man who had known her intimately, for many years. It seemed so strange, that their faltering marriage should be strengthened by the very thing, which threatened to break it open in the first place.

Taking several deep breaths and a mouthful of tea, Dottie steadied herself and turned her attention towards the conversation, continuing around her.

Chapter Sixteen

Walking from the Butcher's shop, where he worked, to the Pie shop for lunch, Billy knew that he would once again, have to run the gauntlet of laughing jeering faces, as he walked past the recruitment office. They had collected there after reports, in the paper, of the August offensive in Turkey and the battle the papers called, Lone Pine. The dance last May, had failed to help him get any closer to Gracie, and Billy longed for some girl to pay him attention. It had been divine to hold Gracie close, to feel her warmth and the rise and fall of her breasts against his. If George hadn't been so angry, he might have had a chance to kiss her, then she would have walked out with him, or at least attended another dance. Truth be told though, it was not Gracie especially that he wanted, at this point any girl would do. Any girl, to pay him attention and give him back that, warm and lovely feeling, as she pressed against him, would be fine by him. Which was why, despite knowing that he could avoid the recruiting office, by crossing the street, and much as he hated being jostled by the girls, who stood calling out at men, as they passed and handing out white feathers, part of him liked it.

The part of him, that nightly dreamed of laughing girls pouring feathers on his head, their mouths red and wet, the feathers obscuring their bodies showing here a bare arm, there a thigh or a calf. A tangle of shapely limbs, flickering in and out of the ocean of feathers, they dumped on him. He woke from these dreams, into the bedroom he shared with his youngest brothers, Allister and James, hot and panting, hoping that they were still asleep, and did not see him.

So every day, since the girls had arrived, Billy walked the gauntlet, collecting white feathers as he passed, feathers that were thrust into his sweating hand by eager grasping fingers. Feathers, that he took home of an evening, and placed in an old shoe box, that he kept in the back of his bedside table.

Leaving the pie shop, Billy returned by the opposite side of the road, knowing that Cousin Henry would not be pleased, if he dropped their lunch on the footpath.

Sitting in the back room of Cousin Henry's shop, a room that was barely warmer than the biting August day outside, Billy ate in silence, despite his cousin's attempts to draw him out in conversation. Cousin Henry, was talking about a letter in the paper that told of the German's cunning in battle, using German Australians, who fought treacherously against their own countrymen, to lure Australian troops out into the open. The letter writer claimed, that killing was a strange sensation, but one that quickly grew natural.

"So you see, when it comes to it, killin' them, is no different to the slaughter men in the abattoir," said Henry, his brown moustache peppered with pie crust. "I'd go m'self, but I've got to think of m' littlies and besides they wouldn't take me with m' bad leg."

Billy looked at his cousin and his twisted leg, a legacy of the polio he had suffered as a child, and the reason he had remained above ground in the shop, in a town whose prosperity came from below.

"If I were a young bloke like you I'd be over there in a flash. It is the great adventure of our time, be a shame to miss out."

Billy nodded, filling his mouth with pie, so that no reply could be expected of him. After Kate's ultimatum to George, he had tried to join up, upping his age and looking the recruiting officer in the eye, daring him to challenge it. The recruiting officer, a man with a quota to fill, wrote down George's lie of twenty one, despite it being obvious that it would take over half a decade for him to reach such an age. George had proudly shown

Kate the recruitment papers, expecting the impossible, that a girl of fifteen, could keep her word and reward his bravery with fidelity. But Kate had no interest in him anymore, with a toss of her golden curls, she coolly informed him, that she was walking out with Howard Babbage, who was eighteen, and drove about town in his parent's old barouche. George had informed his mother of his actions, and she had marched him down to the recruiting office, utterly humiliating him by demanding they tear up his papers, showing them his lie, on his birth certificate. George swore that it was the worst sort of luck that he had been stymied like that, but Billy had seen the relief in his friend's eyes, as he spoke of his escape and found himself doubtful about what had truly happened. Billy was right to be sceptical, as George hadn't shared the whole story, omitting the part about how after Kate's refusal to take him back, terrified of what he had actually done, he had buried his face in his mother's skirts and sobbed out the whole sorry tale, begging her to help him.

Swallowing his mouthful, Billy looked at Cousin Henry. "I'm not afraid of a bit of blood."

"No?"

"No, not a bit. The Hun are animals after all, not men. I'm not afraid of killing animals."

Henry, wiped the crumbs off his moustache. Billy's enthusiasm for the subject of war had surprised him, and now he felt that he had better hose down his young cousin's enthusiasm, lest it get him into trouble. "You're too young anyway. It probably won't last until you are old enough to join up."

"I'll be sixteen in October."

"Sixteen is nothing, there are boys still at school at your age."

"It's old enough. I can shoot as well as any of my brothers, and I'm the biggest in the under 21's footy team."

"I'm not saying that you couldn't do it, just that you need to have more life before deciding such things. Besides your mum wouldn't let you sign up, look what happened to your friend George."

"George was a coward, I'm not a coward."

"No, then why don't you go down the pit like your brothers?"

Billy scowled at Henry, turning away he walked out of the cold close room, into the yard. Standing by the back door, Billy took out his clay pipe, forcing the tobacco into the bowl with such force that the bowl cracked. Lighting the pipe, he drew on it, letting the smoke settle his nerves. What cheek of Cousin Henry, to bring up his fear of the pit. He wasn't a coward like George, he would do what none of those around him dared. As soon as he was sixteen, he would sign up and show everyone how brave he was. The girls outside the recruiting office, would smile and stroke him, George would be shamed for pulling out the way he did, and no one would ever call out to him 'Silly Billy scared of the pits' again. It was only nine weeks until his birthday, only nine more weeks of waiting, before he showed everyone that he was brave. Far braver than his brothers, or their father, or George. He would follow those heroes of Gallipoli. While failing to be in the forefront with those lions, he could at least add his name to that list.

The Loyalty of Wives

In the court of Agamemnon, Clytemnestra quickly divested herself of the old bard, who had been instructed by her husband, to watch over her. The blind old man, was easily led into the forests, during a hunting party and there left, to wander, as night stole in and the beast of the forest came out to hunt. With her chaperone absent, Clytemnestra was free, to indulge those passions, that a good husband knows to keep in check.

Aegisthus, brother of the former king, taking advantage of his cousin Agamemnon's long absence at war, began to make a play for his kingdom. For Aegisthus lived, banished, in an impoverished kingdom, far from the reins of power. Deciding that the quickest way, to the throne of Mycenae, was the path Agamemnon himself had taken, Aegisthus worked his way into the bed, of his onetime sister-in-law, Clytemnestra. For her part, having released herself from the bounds of wifely decorum, Clytemnestra welcomed her new lover with open arms.

Chapter Seventeen

"If it's dry, do you think you'll have time to prune my apple trees this weekend?"

Arch looked up from the paper, he held above his face, as he lay sprawled on the lounge, a position that he had taken up regularly, after dinner with Dottie and the children, now that Ivy was in attendance.

"I can't do this weekend, but I'll have time during the week, while work is slow."

Dottie nodded and returned to her knitting, not socks tonight, but a blue jumper for Edith, which she hoped to get finished, before the European winter's demand for socks and gloves and scarves, began again.

"Have you heard from Jack?"

"Only the usual about flowers and sunsets. What does he write to you about?"

Arch thought for a moment, trying to recall the last letter Jack wrote, but like those he wrote to Dottie, they were all filled with a strange jumble of images and sensation, none of which could tell the reader much about his present situation. Letters which all began assuring the reader how well he was, continuing on with recounts of funny stories and promises for the future. Nothing to suggest the fighting, or the discomfort of his present situation, nothing that might give clues about how he felt or what he had done. His writing was so vague at times, it made Arch wonder at his state of mind, not that he wished to read about killing and death, much less have Dottie forced to read such things, still it concerned him. To believe Jack's letters, he had spent the past nearly four months, lazing in the sun, watching the birds and flowers. Meanwhile, the papers shrieked of nothing, but casualties and stalemate in Turkey, of one failed offensive after another.

"The same. I wonder how he is."

"Living in some strange dream world, like he did before he left. When the children ask him what he did in the war, he'll tell them he looked at flowers and talked to people and lay in the sun. And they'll think he is lying, and ask me what he really did, and I won't have anything to contradict them with."

"Why would you want to?" Arch looked at Dottie, his auburn eyebrows knotted into a frown. If Jack wished to make his war experience nothing, but an extended picnic, then there must be reasons for such a wish. Just as he had managed to forget the five years, he lived at home with Arch and their father. Turning Arch into a villain, who had separated him from his saintly suffering father. Arch knew that Jack, had spent his time at school, with Aunt Betty, quietly rewriting his family, until it resembled something from one of his story books. An image that he could live with. An image, which had been dashed upon his return, and the realisation that their father, was not the father he saw when he visited with Aunt Betty, but a resentful, angry and frequently drunk old man. If Jack had again resorted to fantasy, to cope with what he saw, Arch knew that he should be worried.

"Because…" Dottie's words trailed off, as she struggled to finish her sentence, the firm, but tranquil expression on Arch's face, making her doubt the arguments she had heard advanced by others. Suddenly, it felt foolish to argue that Jack behave as others did. Jack had never acted, as others expected him to, at least not entirely. To expect him to do so now, when no one yet knew what the accepted behaviour of men in his situation was, seemed suddenly altogether foolish.

"Ivy, be a lamb and make us a pot of tea," said Dottie, remembering that their conversation could be over heard, by the small grey mouse in the corner of the room, bent over her sewing. Ivy's presence in the house, might be necessary to prevent scandal, but she did stifle the free flow of conversation, and despite her protestations that she abhorred gossip, Dottie had never felt secure in speaking freely before her.

Dottie and Arch watched, as the grey clad figure rose from her corner and crossed the room, closing the door behind her.

"Do you think Jack is alright?"

"In all honesty Dot, I don't know. He has always been one for a bit of fantasy. Perhaps you need it over there?"

Dottie looked at Arch, her eyes searching his face for the knowledge that she needed, sure that if any one should know, it would be him. Listening to Ivy bustle about the kitchen, Dottie turned away, screwing up her courage to ask the question, she desperately needed answering, while knowing that there was no answer.

"Do you think he kills people?"

"Why would you ask that?" said Arch, sitting up and leaning towards Dottie. His voice feigning shock, as Dottie put into words, what he had also been thinking.

"Because I think he could, but I think it might break him," said Dottie, leaning close to Arch, her voice dropped to a whisper. "He told me once, when we were still courting, about your mum. That he felt it was his fault that she died. I have always known that Jack, has been trying to give himself the family he never had. Not pretending that my parents were his, but creating the type of home he had never known. The trouble is he has no idea how such a home is supposed to function. His idea of marriage, comes from books and Christmas cards. I love Jack, but I know I can't rely on him the way he would like me to."

Looking up at Arch, Dottie expected to see his firm somewhat forbidding features looking down on her, with disapproval at having spoken to him thus. Instead, she was surprised to see, that usually closed and mature face, suddenly open, vulnerable and younger even than Jack. There was relief, in those big rose brown eyes of his, and his whole frame seemed to grow soft and slack, as if relieved of a heavy burden. When he at last spoke, it was in a voice that Dottie had never heard him use before, a voice full of softness and vulnerability, the voice of the lonely little boy.

"He's trying to be what he thinks everyone expects of him. I never even tried to do that, I'd seen too much to believe Jack's daydreams. Dad was always too hard on him, and Jack tried to do his best to please, but it was never enough. Dad expected the impossible. I wish Jack hadn't seen Dad that last time. Mum died because she was sick, and Dad was too stubborn to get her help. It had nothing to do with Jack, but Dad was so angry, that he made it our fault."

Arch paused, looking deeply into Dottie's face, searching her dark eyes and the lines in her forehead, which showed when she was concentrating. Having reassured himself, his words were being listened too and understood, Arch pressed on.

"If Jack wants to create a fantasy to live in, rather than tell us what is really happening, then it must be bad over there. I don't think he's killed people, but I think he's seen a lot of death. When he gets back we'll have to be gentle with him."

In the hall, the sound of footsteps, halted the words beginning to form on Dottie's lips. Rising from his seat, Arch opened the door, as Ivy entered with the tea tray. Placing the tray on the tea-table, Ivy returned to her sewing, as Dottie moved forward in her seat, using the mask of hostess, to settle the tumult she could feel within her. Arch too availed himself of his new position, to stand with his back to the room, before the fire, composing himself to speak lightly again, as the past sank slowly back into the depths where it usually dwelt and his body resumed its former stiffness. He heard himself asked to pass tea to Ivy, and felt his body respond, as the big German clock with the carved surround on the mantel chimed the quarter. Taking his own tea, Arch returned to his seat on the lounge.

"What time is this late fare of yours coming?"

"The ten o'clock train, I've got enough time to finish m' tea, then I'll be off."

"It's quite late, are they a regular?"

"Yes, Mr Alexander, the producer from Sydney. Always comes of an evening, always orders the big cab, always wants me to drive him, and best of all always pays whatever I ask," said Arch, relaxing back into his mask of casual indifference and bonhomie. The image of the 'good bloke', that over the years he had pasted about himself, like the tough carapace of a crab, something that would prove a substantial barrier to any curious probing. A tough exterior, which hid from the world that his true nature, was as soft and yielding, as any invertebrate. Stripped of his mask, he knew he would collapse before an indifferent world, and be picked apart. But the mask was so cold, and his armour felt at times like a prison, denying him the chance to touch another and be touched in return. As a coral, in the shallow water far to the north, spreads its tentacles awhile in the sun, and retreats back into its stone reef, at the slightest threat. So too, did his defensive mechanisms kick in, ever alert to changes in the atmosphere about him, frequently spooked, by even shadows.

Half an hour later, Arch sat in his cab, waiting for the Sydney train to arrive with his fare. Talking to Dottie had bewildered him, amiable as he had found Dottie in the past, he had never expected to find in her the sensitivity, or understanding, that she had displayed that evening. Had never expected, to be impressed by her grasp of Jack's past, or what that might mean for her, or him for that matter. All these years, he had thought her a mere doll, an ornament for his brother's pleasure, a fixture in his brother's game of happy families. Now he saw, that the doll knew it was all a game. That she smiled and sparkled, because it pleased her husband, not because she could not see, the cracks and repairs, and broken beyond repair, parts of Jack's character. And now, here she was bracing herself, against the return of a man, who could only return home more broken, than he had been when he left. Not that they had any idea what, that would look like, so far while many men had left, none had made their way back to Katoomba again. The papers carried stories of wounded men, returned home, who wished they could return, but their wounds were slight, and had not disfigured them, as they stood proudly in their uniforms and spoke to the reporters. Their words printed to encourage recruitment, not assuage the fears of families; such words were distressingly absent.

Hearing the train approach the station, Arch pulled himself from his dreaming, setting his mask straight, as he stepped out of the cab, to wait for his fare. The air was cold, but dry, a hard frost would shroud the town by morning, making it glitter like a jewel in the dawn light. Unlike at other times of the year, the streets were deserted, light and noise came from within pubs and restaurants, but patrons rushed for cabs or rooms as they left, unwilling to linger in the frigid air. Even the Push boys, were safely home in bed, or beside the fires, or kitchen stoves, in their family homes. The only sensible place to be, on a winter's night.

Turning his coat collar up, against the chill, Arch watched, as his breath competed with the steam of the locomotive. Folding his arms, as he waited, he pressed his hands against his ribs, trying to keep them from becoming numb, in his thin leather driving gloves.

Presently, the few passengers began to emerge, up the steps and looked about for a cab, or walked quickly down the street, towards boarding houses and hotels. Trailing the crowd, lost in his own thoughts, came the heavy black clad figure, of Mister Alexander. He carried no luggage, and wore an expression which spoke of profound distress. Waiting until the last of his fellow passengers had left, watching as Arch waved away several requests to hire him, Mister Alexander approached the cab.

"Travelling light are we, Mister A?" Arch noticed the lack of bags. Looking up at his fare, Arch found himself for the first time in his life, dropping his cabbie's patter. "You look like you need a drink. The Pub's still open for another hour."

With a barely perceivable nod of his head, Mister Alexander followed Arch across the street, to the bright and noisy opening, in the dark shop fronts. Following Arch, with a passivity, that had become a dominant feature of his life for weeks now, the elegant theatre producer, found himself seated in the snug, away from the noise and smoke of the main bar, while Arch went for the drinks. From where he sat, the sounds of the main bar, washed over him, as an indistinct clamour. The whole place, was thick, with the sounds and smells of men, in a way that he had never experienced before. The maleness of his club, was one of hushed solemnity and fierce rivalry, it was not a place to relax, as much a place to be seen and to work. Here, the aim was quite the opposite, here the men sounded relaxed and jovial, amongst the glare of the lights and the dark wood panelling. Charlie had never taken him to a place like this, they had met on the beach at Coogee, Charlie parting the waves with the great power and elegance of a dolphin. He had been enthralled, snared immediately, by the younger man's lithe athleticism, so much so, that when Charlie demanded more of him than he had previously offered any of his other boys, he gave it. For the first time in his adult life, he had loved one of the men, he had only ever seen as outlets for his urges. He had loved Charlie and now Charlie was gone.

"Sorry about the state of these, got them for free 'cause they're half head," said Arch, placing two glasses on the table. The foam slopped over the side, pooling on the tabletop.

"I think they're at the end of the keg. This is larger, you take that." Arch slid one of the two glasses across the table, as he took his seat opposite, still unsure of the impulse that had led him, to invite his fare for a drink.

Picking up his beer, Mister Alexander raised it to his lips, and poured the whole glass of amber liquid down his throat. Placing the glass back on the table, he found a second before him, and used it to chase the first.

"How'd you find out?"

"His family had put a notice, for his memorial service, in the paper."

"I'm sorry, Mate."

"He still sends me letters. They're from weeks ago. I don't know if I can bear it when they catch up. When I hold in my hand the last letter he ever wrote to me."

So you're here to make sure that day never comes, thought Arch, taking Mister Alexander's words to their logical conclusion.

"He wouldn't want that you know. If you meant as much to him, as he means to you, he wouldn't want that."

"What would you know? What would you care?"

"Not a great deal, except I don't want the police round mine tomorrow morning, asking why I dropped you in the middle of nowhere, in the middle of the night."

Mister Alexander looked at Arch, how obvious was his design, that this rough cabbie could see, what he had managed to deceive all his friends and colleagues about. He, who concealed half his life, had been so careful to appear his usual self, tidying up his accounts, and leaving no loose ends in his affairs. On his desk, in the office, sat his freshly drawn up Will and the keys to all his properties. Every bill had been paid, down to the last penny, and every contract signed for the next season. He was ready to walk out of his life, with as little fuss, as possible.

"Living up here, it gets pretty easy to spot the jumpers. I'll take any fare, except them, they can find their own way down the mountain."

"You are very absolute about that."

"Too right I am. I hate it. I hate how it spreads the pain about. You think no one will notice you going, but there is always someone. Someone else to have to bear the grief, even if you don't know who that is. Even if you think you are alone in the world, there is always someone."

The vehemence of Arch's words, impressed themselves upon his companion. So used was he, to the coolly dispassionate words of those in his circle, men who reasoned out every move, with an icy self-interested logic, that this burning fervour, this conviction, seemed almost obscene. It was as if here, in this public place, a man had stripped himself naked, and stood before him saying, this is me. So like Charlie. Faced with such a revelation, he knew he had one of two choices, he could continue as he had begun, burying his heart, beneath layers of tweed and respectability, like the proper gentleman, he had learnt to become. Or, he could continue what Charlie had begun, with his fierce devotion, and exhume that which had been buried, to feel again no matter how painful.

"You are a good boy, but you cannot understand my situation."

"You loved him and he left you. It's not that hard to see. I love my brother, and every morning I wake and wonder, if today will be the day I lose him. I don't know what I will do if that day comes, but I would never do that."

"You think about that?"

"Yes. I hate that I do, but I do think about him dying. I know his wife does too." Arch stared at the table, and the pooled foam now run to liquid, unsure of why he was sharing such things, unsure of why he cared about the life of this man. Somehow though, it seemed important, as if this would offer some weight, thrown into the balance that would keep his brother safe, for a few more days.

"I encouraged him to join up. His family didn't want him to, but he did and I encouraged him. And now he's dead. I feel responsible."

Mister Alexander paused, he could again see Charlie before him, advancing his case for why he should sign up. Again, he could hear the anger in his words at his parents, who argued that there was no need, unless Australia were directly attacked. Charlie had fallen out with them, and sought refuge with him, spinning tales of heroism and glory, so that he too, could see how it was more than right that Charlie join up, it was his duty. Objectively, he knew that there had been no stopping Charlie, he was his own man, and it was that quality that had been so beguiling about him. If he had of objected, Charlie would have fallen out with him too, so passionately did he believe, in the rightness of his actions. He had acquiesced, out of love for Charlie, and months of letters, from half a world away, were his reward.

"I miss him terribly, but no one knows what he meant to me, or that he even existed."

"How about I take you to a nice hotel, somewhere quiet."

Mister Alexander shook his head. "No need, I'm going to go back to Sydney. Thank you."

Rising from his seat, Mister Alexander pulled on his coat and hat. Reaching inside his jacket, for his wallet, he took out a wad of notes, pressing them into Arch's hand. Arch looked up at the theatre impresario, with a look of confusion. There must have been a hundred pound in his hand, though he knew better than to count it.

"Your fare, Mister Arch. Perhaps I will see you again one day."

Arch would have protested, that it was unnecessary and besides far more than twenty fares, but all he saw around the partition of the snug, was the retreating back of Mister Alexander, as he was swallowed up by the crowd in the bar.

Chapter Eighteen

It was late spring, and the warm weather had arrived at Lithgow, the dry heat that rolls off the western plains, and sits in the Lithgow valley for the duration of summer, had arrived. In every tree, cicadas throbbed, giving the heat its customary soundtrack, a monotonous droning that made the listener drowsier than the heat. Men and women, stripped of their winter layers, gloried in the sunshine. On the sports field, cricket, with its white and gleaming players, replaced the mud spattered warriors of rugby league. Skeletal trees, first foaming with flowers, now covered their nakedness in fine green leaves, and the roses began to bud.

In town the ladies of the soldiers support groups, knitted with hot hands, stopping frequently to gossip and drink tea, loathed to touch the wool again, but knowing they must, for those brave boys sake. The girls outside the recruiting office, glowed in the heat, as they handed out their feathers, each looking more like a wilting lily, as the day continued, as they stood unflinchingly, under the mercilessly hot sun, remembering their self-appointed duty.

Across town, at the Small Arms factory, George laboured in the double heat of the day and the machinery. The humiliation of his failed signup attempt, had finally worn off, though he could see that it had nevertheless, caused a ruction in his friendship with Billy. It was clear to him, that Billy knew or suspected, more than his official telling of the story, and that his friend did not approve. That was the problem with Billy, he was so damned absolute. A man couldn't change his mind, in Billy's presence, right was right and wrong was wrong, and no shades of grey could be admitted into his logic. So, if signing up was the right thing to do, then to be thwarted in that, even as legitimately as his mother had thwarted him, made George wrong. As a result of the critical judgement, George now found himself subjected to in Billy's presence, he had begun avoiding his friend of over ten years. Not that he hadn't had compensations, for the loss of his friend. While his gesture, of duty and loyalty, had done little to impress Kate. As news spread about town, he found that Helena, the daughter of doctor Tennant and a girl, far out of his social standing, began to seek him out after church and that he, in turn, was beginning the tentative process, of walking out with her.

For his part, Billy devoured every newspaper report he could find on the war, especially those that spoke of the Anzacs. Usually, so secretive about his obsessions, Billy hid his growing obsession with the war, from no one, and yet somehow no one objected. It seemed, that the whole world, was giving tacit consent to his plans. Even so, Billy knew that he would need to plan his intents carefully, lest he find himself caught out in the same way as George, humiliated by his parents, forced to remain in town, with everyone knowing what had happened. The fact that George seemed to have no shame, at his failure to sign up, and continued as if nothing had happened, made him wonder about his friend.

Over the months, Billy had rehearsed his moment in the recruiting office, hundreds of times, practicing in the mirror, how he would stand and hold his face so that he looked like his loose-limbed confidant brothers. What words he would use, to avoid the cracks and shrieks, that followed ill-judged words or high emotion, as his broken voice, tried to find the right level, alternating between a low rumble and sharp aggravating squeaks. He experimented with his hair, combing it this way and that, until it framed his face, in a way that accentuated his jaw and diminished his baby cheeks. He grew out his beard, partly to hide his acne, but to add that aura of age and maturity, that his cleanly shaven face lacked. In the end, all his careful preparation, seemed startlingly unnecessary. Walking into the recruitment office, the man behind the desk, a man with silvering hair and a bored expression, greeted him at once ushering him to a seat. The cooing of the girls outside, as he walked into the office had been bewildering enough, but to have a man as old as one's father, treat him as an equal, was almost enough to make Billy forget all his careful preparation.

For the recruiting officer, Billy appeared to be exactly what he had been hoping to find all week, a man who would not be rejected by the doctor, because he had lungs full of coal dust. He was charged to find fit young volunteers, and where do the Army in their wisdom send him, a mining town, full of men who work in protected industries, or whose health is broken before the age of twenty five, as they toil away in the dark. He had lost several promising lads, to inflexible parents who would not sign consent forms, and the incessant chatter and giggling, from the girls camped outside in the street were driving him mad. Clearly the army was punishing him for something, though he couldn't think what, except perhaps that he had dared to get old, and was no longer fit for active service. Not that he felt old most of the time, but then he would look into the faces of the girls who stood about outside, watching their admiration for the uniform, fight with the pity that the man within was on the wrong side of forty. He knew that his lady killer charms, so effective when he was a waspwaisted young officer, no longer worked, leaving him to feel every one of his forty-eight years. Now sitting opposite him, was Billy, eager to join, feeding him the most obvious lies. The lad was so nervous, that he forgot what year he had been born in, and had to be reminded by the kind Major, with his rounded vowels and glossy salt and pepper hair. He looked like a good lad, one of many brothers he had confessed, in his excitement. The officer wondered how many of those brothers, he would see enter his office before this war was won, for jaded though he was, there was no question in his mind that Britain would win this war, Britain and her allies would emerge bloodied and bruised to be sure, but victorious.

Years later, when he thought back to this time, and the sea of faces, he had sent to barracks and then beyond to the battlefields of Turkey, France and Belgium, he would struggle to remember a single face, to think of a single fate among those eager boys and desperate men. In the early days, his job had been easy, as the unemployed and the desperate drought plagued farmers, flocked to his doors, eager for the money his offer promised, money that their wives and parents could use to keep their struggling households running. In the early days, his bonuses came thick and fast, today he was lucky to see a bonus every few months. When at last the victory, of which he had been so sure of, came it felt hollow, as he thought of all the men, who hadn't returned. He had done his duty for King and country, but somehow, that reasoning felt flawed and he could not fully stifle the guilt that gnawed at him, as he looked at the memorials, which began to grow like mushrooms in every town, a testament to his work and the work of so many others like him.

Billy left the office elated, in his pocket he held his instructions to report to barracks in Sydney, Friday week. Outside, the girls fluttered about him, their hands touching and caressing his head and shoulders, as if he were some pagan idol and they his anointed priestesses. Billy at first revelled in their attention, lingering longer than was strictly seemly, as girls who had never shown interest in him before, jostled each other to get close to him. Though as their attentions continued, he found the girls and their desire for him, or rather the uniform that they already imagined him wearing, panic inducing, as he broke free and hurried back to work.

As Billy felt the letter he had written on the lunch room table, slip from his fingers into the mail box opposite the railway station on Thursday afternoon, he knew it was too late to turn back. It had been an agonising week, his urge to boast and crow about what he had done, rubbing his bravery into the faces of his brothers, mother and father, was one he could scarcely supress, as it fought with the need for silence and secrecy, to assure his success. Not even George, could be considered reliable these days, all he did was talk of Helena. Strangely, though Gracie was among the girls at the recruiting office, George gave no intimation that his visit was public knowledge. He had made no attempt to stop them talking, but as he would reflect glumly of an evening, perhaps, despite the fuss they made of him, he was not noteworthy enough to become public gossip. William Brown has signed up for the army, was not sufficiently exciting gossip for those girls, with their pale skin and red mouths.

At church on Sunday, Reverend Bridge preached a sermon about the importance of duty, to Billy, every word felt like he was giving his encouragement and approval. How he had felt like jumping up from his pew, shouting that he had done his duty, challenging them to follow in his wake, like the lads on the recruitment posters. He was going to be a hero of the Dardanelles, while they sat safe at home, protected from German invasion, by lions like himself.

Sitting and fidgeting in church, was nowhere near as tormenting, as sitting and trying to conceal his actions, in the face of his brothers and their teasing. All week long, they ribbed and chaffed him, about one thing, or another. All four, had organised dates for the weekend, and this fact alone, was enough to start their teasing, mocking Billy for his dateless existence. It had grown so bad, that by Wednesday night, in the bedroom they shared, at the back of the house, Allister had offered, across the black gulf which separated their beds, to find Billy a date for the weekend.

"No one would pick on you, if you didn't take it all so seriously, Billy," came Allister's quiet voice, through the darkness.

Billy listened in silence, staring up at the ceiling, so as not to see his brother, in the bed beside his.

"Billy, Mum and Dad are worried about you, I heard them talking the other night when I went out to the lav. They think you might be one of, them."

"What them?"

"You know, a shirt lifter."

"They think I'm a fairy!" Billy was stunned, his words hurtling out of him far louder that he had intended.

"Well, think about it. You spend all your time cutting pictures of soldiers out of the paper. I know you have them in a box in your bedside table. You never talk about girls, despite our best effort to help you find one. You don't go down the mines, so in Dad's eyes that already makes you suspect. What are they supposed to think?"

"You should mind your own business." Billy turned his back to the room, staring at the wall beside his bed. He felt suddenly so alone, and was unable to stop the tears, which began to flow, quickly creating a damp patch on his pillow. Tomorrow, he would be out of here. Tomorrow, he would be able to start a new life. Tomorrow, he would be a hero, and everyone would envy and admire him. Tomorrow, he would no longer be William 'Silly Billy scared of the pits' Brown. Tomorrow, he would show them.

***

Crossing the road from the post office, Billy hurried to the ticket office, buying himself a one way ticket to Sydney. In his pocket, he had his week's wages, and he hoped it would be enough to buy him a room for the night, so that he could report to barracks in the morning. Sitting waiting for the train, Billy felt an unaccustomed lightness, as if at last he was travelling on the right path, a path which he did not have to fight against, impossible pressures and ignorant people. He had at last found his calling, he would be a soldier, a magnificent soldier who covered himself with glory and honour. And when he returned in triumph, a conquering Caesar, all of those people who had thought so little of him, would lionise him, as he deserved to be. Small children would rush after him, begging for stories, girls would cross the street to talk to him, and his brothers would shrink from him, jostling each other to be of most service.

In a cloud of steam and smoke, the Sydney train came to a halt by the deserted platform. Opening the nearest carriage door, Billy stepped onto the train, sitting down, as his old life, along with the railway station, slowly slipped away.

Chapter Nineteen

"Have you heard from your brother lately?" asked the voice from behind, as Arch sat on the back patio, gazing into the increasing gloom across the manicured lawn. The sun had already sunk beyond the mountains, and the drone of the cicadas, had given way to the quiet chirping of crickets, and the lower, more calming, croaking of frogs.

Arch looked up at the ginger haired woman, standing by his side, a glass in her hand. Taking the glass, Arch waited for his aunt to take her seat beside him, in the large wickerwork chair.

"Yes, he's back in Egypt for the winter. He was already in Egypt when they evacuated, he'd got the flu and by the time he was better, there was no front to go back to."

Elizabeth looked thoughtful, as she sipped her drink, the crystal tumbler growing damp in her hand.

"So army life suits him then?"

Arch shrugged.

"Well, something had to suit him, eventually. Perhaps he can make a career out of it?"

"Does he write to you?"

"Occasionally, he tells me what he is up to, describes the world around him. They never say much, really. I write back and tell him how the peace movement is going, he often asks about that, and about things happening here. I send him newspaper clippings and pamphlets from our group."

"I think it's hard to say if army life suits him. Dot and I get the same types of letters, they remind me of the ones he used to send home as a child." Arch took a mouthful from his glass, feeling the years old liquid slip down his throat. "She told me to thank you for the material on the peace movement."

"There are whispers about conscription about. We've been liaising with British colleagues, to work out how we will fight it, if it comes up. Do you think Dorothy would be interested in taking part?"

"I'll ask her, but I'd say she would."

"How is Dorothy?"

"She's holding up. It's hard for her, two littlies and no husband at home. Her parents help, and I help with some of her bills. I feel really sorry for her."

Listening to Arch speak, Elizabeth noticed the tone, rather than the substance of her nephew's words. Turning a curious look upon him, she searched his features for the emotion that matched, the softness and tenderness in his voice, causing him to frown and turn away, focusing on the darkening garden.

"When I was a girl, and lived in Surry Hills, we had nothing. Dad had been killed years before, when your mum was still a toddler, and my mum, your grannie used to take in washing. I remember her hands, they were as red, as crab claws, after being boiled in a pot. It was really hard, we never knew if there would be enough food, or if Mum would spend the food money on drink. She did that sometimes, when she got down about Dad. She would sit in the ladies lounge, drinking port and lemonade, until she had to be escorted home by the publican, at closing time.

"Your mum and me, we were sent out to work, as soon as it was legal. We'd been working long before then at home, doing the mending and helping Mum with the laundry, but now we could earn actual wages. We both worked in big, sea-front houses. Walking together of a morning, we would arrive at our respective houses, I would go down to the laundry in my house, but Edith was being trained to be a parlour maid. She wasn't old enough to live-in yet, but it was a much flashier job than mine. Edith was charming and pretty, like your brother, people loved her, they couldn't help themselves.

"In the big houses, it is the custom to give the staff a present at Christmas, usually something small, to keep their renewed loyalty for the year ahead, without raising their wages."

"You talk like a trade unionist, Aunty."

"Why, thank you. Anyway, Mrs Stratton, Edith's employer, rather than giving her, the same gift she gave to the rest of her staff, gave her a little porcelain bird. It was a robin with a red breast, and Edith loved it. When she came home that evening, she showed us her little china bird, while all I had was a fragrant soap. She put the bird on her windowsill, and used to tell it things when she was upset. It was the most beautiful thing she had ever had, and I wanted it."

Elizabeth looked across at Arch, he had dropped his head looking away from her, listening, but not wishing to appear to be.

"I wanted her bird, I thought it unfair that she should have got something like that, while I had nothing. I chose not to remember, that she equally had nothing, that her life was as hard, if not harder in some ways, than my own. I didn't know what the lives of the house maids were, until much later, all I could think of was that their job was dry, and they didn't ruin their hands in hot water and lye. I didn't know about Gentlemen or their sons in those days. All I knew was that I wanted her bird. So I stole it.

"The problem with stealing it was, that I had to hide it. I could never enjoy it openly, because then I would have to give it back. Edith was devastated by the loss of her bird. She cried for a week, and we tore the house apart looking for it, eventually Mum took the blame for its loss, claiming to have sold it for rent money. Edith wasn't happy with that, but she accepted it, there was no arguing with Mum. I felt so guilty about what I had done to Edith, but I knew after Mum had taken the blame, I couldn't return it. So one evening, I walked down to the harbour, and threw the little bird into the sea."

Elizabeth raised her glass to her lips and took a large sip.

Behind her the lights of the dining room came on, and the maid began to lay the table.

"I know you think, Jack has led a charmed life, and that your childhood was much harder, but it doesn't help to think like that. Jack used to come and see me when he was training last year. He was so worried that he had ruined his marriage, he was like a little boy again, crying on his auntie's knee. We talked about a lot of things, about your mother and the fact that you have a memory of her, while he doesn't. How, though he wants it desperately, the family he always wanted is much harder than it seems. About how envious he was of you and your father."

"But Jack only saw the outside of that, he had no idea what living with Dad was like." Arch, turned defensively towards his aunt's words, ready to fight for his own perspective, against a lecture. Turning to look, he saw in his aunt's face not the stern and critical woman, who told him off when he had done something wrong, seeing instead the inward thoughtful gaze of persuasion and self-recrimination. Did she too feel as if she had failed Jack, had failed to see what he needed before it was too late, and he had set his feet on such a dangerous path.

"I know you think, because Jack had a good school and a nice house to grow up in, that he was better off than you. For weeks, after you had gone back to live with your dad, Jack used to cry for you. He didn't know who I was. To him, I was the old lady who took him away, from his brother and father. He used to be so excited when he knew you were visiting. He used to tell all his friends, and all the staff, that his big brother Arch was coming. When he met Dorothy, he brought her down for a visit. I could see at once, he had found his precious china bird."

"I don't want to take Dot away from Jack."

"You may not want to, but mind that you don't."

Rising from her seat, Elizabeth turned and entered the French doors, leaving Arch alone on the veranda.

Chapter Twenty

It was Ivy's odd way of announcing a visitor that had disturbed her. She had burst into the kitchen, with more speed and force than were characteristic of her, announcing, "Mrs Kelly, there is a man with red hair come to see you."

Dottie, who had been doing the washing up, wondering what she was going to make for dinner that night, felt a trembling begin to creep all over her body. A man with red hair; that could only mean Jack. Jack back home at last, and not a word given or even hinted at, that he was returning. Drying her hands on a towel, Dottie took off her apron, running a smoothing hand over the fly-aways in her hair. Was over a year's worth of waiting, to end like this, with a sudden knock at the door, wondered Dottie. She stood for a moment, trying to catch her thoughts, scattered like the chooks in the yard. Steadying herself against the table, she took a few deep breaths, composing herself so that she could make it, the few yards from the kitchen to the front room. Finally feeling confident, that she could traverse the slight space, in a few quick strides, Dottie set off, barely feeling the floor beneath her feet, as she ran to the door and pushed it open. Standing in the centre of the room, was a man with his back to the door, admiring the stone cats on the mantelpiece.

"Ohhh." The sound flung itself out of her with more force than she had realised, and yet she could not stop it. Voicing her disappointment, as the man turned and looked at Dottie, with genuine concern.

"Dottie, are you alright?"

Dottie felt her breath begin to catch in her throat, choking her. As the man appeared by her side, guiding her to the nearest armchair. She felt her head gently pushed down, to between her knees, and the man's voice encouraging her to breathe with him. His big warm hand, pressing down between her shoulder blades.

"I'm alright now Uncle Ferd," said Dottie, sitting up straight, watching as the man crossed the room, and filled a glass from the bottle on the sideboard.

"Drink this. Are you sure you're alright?"

Dottie sipped from the glass, looking up into the concerned brown eyes of her uncle.

"When Ivy said there was a red haired man waiting for me, I thought she meant Jack."

Ferdinand moved back towards the sideboard. His hands thrust in his jacket pockets, as he shuffled his feet on the floor, chewing his bottom lip, looking down at Dottie. "That was my fault, I told her to say that. I wanted to give you a surprise. I completely forgot about Jack."

Dottie took another sip from her glass, her mind steadying itself again, concentrating on the firm horsehair head rest behind her head and the smooth silk satin, of the arm rests beneath her hand. The strong brown liquor in her glass, made her think of Jack. It was Jack's last birthday present, she was drinking. Twenty year old scotch, given by her father, for Jack's twenty first. He had accepted it in the spirit it had been intended, but when he brought it home and placed it on the sideboard, Dottie could see he had no intention of drinking it. Wine with dinner, on special occasions, was as much as Jack ever drank. Looking at the torn foil, Dottie wondered if she ought to replace the bottle, though where she was to find a bottle of twenty year old scotch, she didn't know. As she regained her balance, on the fine line she walked between hope and worry each day, Dottie felt she had better reassure her uncle, who stood just out of view by the sideboard.

"I forget about him too sometimes. Not that he exists, but during the day, when I'm busy with the children and all the work

I have to do around here. I think of something and say to myself, I must tell Jack when he gets home from work tonight. And then I remember that he's over there."

Ferdinand took his hands out of his pockets, rubbing the palms of his hands together in a brisk motion. Moving closer to the chair again, he took Dottie's glass and swallowed down the remaining amber liquor, himself. "I'll let him know how much you miss him, should I see him over there."

"You joined up again?"

"Had to really," said Ferdinand, sitting down on the arm of her chair. "They are harassing Dad worse than ever, and there was no way any of us wanted Reggie to join up, he'd end up in the infantry like your husband. I join up, I end up in a nice safe motor pool behind the lines with my old unit."

"You make it sound like fun." Dottie frowned up at her uncle, noticing the set of his jaw, and the dark cast of his honey brown eyes. "Have you told Mum what you've done?"

"Yes, Lottie and your dad are putting me up for the night, before I catch the train down tomorrow. Your dad said he'd store m' car for me, so I can drive it back when I come home."

"You know Dad will drive that thing around town while you're gone."

"Yeah, it's better for the motor if it is driven regularly." Ferdinand stood, picking up his driving coat from the sofa. "I'm here to collect you for my farewell dinner. So gather the kids and we'll be off."

***

Dinner at Dottie's parents, was typical of any gathering when the Spies family collected in one place, with talk, wine, and food. This evening however, was marked by a febrile atmosphere, and the jollity seemed brittle and forced. Seated around the dining table, six adults, three men and three women, their usual free flow of family conversation, reduced to a staccato of polite phrases and complements, about food or dress, as the words which everyone feared to utter, were chewed and swallowed back down, with food that no one tasted.

As the evening wore on, more wine than usual was drunk, and spilled onto Charlotte Joyce's pristine white table cloth, like so much blood. It became clear that an inarticulate conversation, had been being carried out, between brother and sisters. A sigh, a glance, the set of a jaw or the pursing of lips, had rendered words redundant as elder and younger sister, alternately cajoled and scolded, their brother for his actions.

"I hear your husband is doing well," came the blundering voice of Dottie's uncle Alfred. A man with little subtly and no tact. He was oblivious to the angry glance that Harold Joyce threw him, and the beleaguered glance of her uncle Ferd, silently begging the table, not to give his sisters an excuse to harangue him.

"As far as I know he is doing well. They made him a Sergeant, so that makes it two promotions in under a year. He's in France now and I don't know if I should be more or less worried about him now, than when he was in Turkey."

Picking up her glass, Dottie stopped the flow of conversation by filling her mouth with wine, following that, with a fork full of roast beef. Understanding at last, her husband's fondness for the silence that eating allows, when feelings are raw and companions careless.

Around her, Dottie could hear the conversation becoming strained to breaking point, as the buried argument, rose closer to the surface. The tone though, as yet not the character of the conversation had grown sharper, as words were edged with sarcasm and laced with anger. She could hear the serious, almost comical tone, her uncle Alfred employed, when defending himself from an act of his own stupidity. Her aunt Martha, provoked, as much by the tone, as the words themselves, narrowed her eyes and listened in that way she did when angry. Recording all a person's words, so that they could be fired back to them at a later time, in evidence to support her argument.

Dottie, would have liked to have called a truce to the arguing, but found she had not the will to do so. Her blundering uncle's words had touched a dam, which had been threatening to spill all evening. Excusing herself from the table, Dottie retreated to the quiet of the sitting room across the hall. Sitting in the dark, Dottie felt fat, warm tears, chase each other down her cheeks, dropping onto the lace front of her dress. She had had enough, of giving polite and loyal statements about her husband. Had enough, of casual questions, that brought the worry and the pain to the surface, without a moment's notice, and with no regard to how she would struggle to supress them, so as not to cry in the middle of the bakery, or the butchers shop. So many people were relying on her to be strong, and she had been, though at times like this, she wondered how much longer her strength would hold out.

"Here. I made a tactical retreat, and left the Germans to it."

Dottie noticed the folded white square, of a pocket handkerchief, thrust into her field of vision. Taking the offered object, Dottie wiped her eyes, as her father sat down heavily on the sofa, beside her chair.

"They're all at it now, like a pack of chooks. I think your aunt Martha is ready to kill Alfred. Your mother is going at Ferd like a banshee, but I prefer that to her silent treatment. If she says everything to him now, I won't have to listen to it all tonight in bed."

Dottie looked at the dark, comfortable form of her father, sitting beside her. Rising from her seat, Dottie moved to sit beside Harold on the sofa. Leaning against his big solid body, inhaling the smell of good tweed and cigar smoke that enveloped her. She felt Harold wrap his arm about her, holding her close.

Dottie watched, as the darkness briefly parted in the flare of her father's lighter, before pushing back, forcing the light to coalesce about the glowing tip of his cigar.

"Mum will be angry with you smoking inside."

Harold Joyce drew on his cigar thoughtfully, knowing that his defiance of his wife's rules, a secret signal of long standing, would lead to punishment later that night, and distraction from the events of the evening. "That's better than angry about her brother."

"Dad, do you think he'll come back?"

"Jack? Yeah, 'course he will. He might be a bit of a dreamer, but he loves you and your kids, he'll come back, even if he has to walk the whole way."

Dottie wished she could share in her father's confidence. No doubt it was easier to be confidant, when worry didn't steal your sleep, and the silence in the night, was broken only by the fighting of possums, in the neighbouring trees. How much longer could the question, how is your husband? Be answered in the affirmative, that he lived and breathed still, upon the earth, even if it was a world away. People who had not seen Dottie for some time, commented on how thin she had become. While her friends noted, but were too tactful to mention, how much the worry for her husband had left her looking frayed. Dottie herself felt, that every action required all her attention. Tasks which she had once taken in her stride, now stumped her, as household items lay where they had been placed, sometimes for days on end. Had her mother not come to her rescue in the summer, her kitchen would still be filled with ripening and rotting apples, from the trees in the yard, waiting to be preserved. Her mind, once as focused and calm, as a deep slow flowing river. Was now a scattered mess of fragmented thoughts, which itched and buzzed, refusing to settle on a single thought, like a hive of angry wasps.

"What if he doesn't come home Dad?"

"Don't think like that, it's not a good place to go."

"But…"

"No, you can't start to mourn someone who is still alive."

Dottie looked down at the crumple handkerchief, and blew her nose, wiping the last of the wet from her eyes.

"Can you run me home?"

"Yeah, I'll run you home, and be back before Ferd even notices his car is gone."

Chapter Twenty one

Sitting in his cab waiting for fares, Arch watched the shining green face of the pub disgorge its contents onto the street, like so much vomit. Groups of men, too quickly drunk, in the hour or less permitted them after work by the new laws, stumbled along the street, swaying and shouting. Small scuffles broke out, as the men split off and began to make their ways home, either singly or in groups. While others leaned against the shining green tiles, and vomited. They looked like so many animals. About to stagger home to wives and children, sitting peaceably around their evening meal. Men who usually ate sober, and drank after dinner, the pub being their meeting place and a social outlet, had begun drinking their whole night's fill in one short hour. Emptying their pockets, before their wives could see any money. Not that he was one to romanticise drinking, but at least the old times seemed more civilised. He had been able to make sure he and his brother were safely in bed, before their father came home after eleven. What child would be in bed, safe from the spectacle, of a drunken father at six o'clock? And yet they argued that this would help the wives and kiddies. In church halls and civic centres across the country, the Temperance movement were celebrating a victory. Passing laws that would have been a violation of a man's rights before the war, but which in these nervy, dangerous days of war, so many new constraints were both, offered up and accepted.

Across the street on the corner of Katoomba and Main, just down from the tea shop, where all the ladies used to take tea and cake, but which since the change of name last May, they declared impossible to frequent. Arch looked at the burnt out ruin of the three shops that until a couple of months back had stood there.

No one could quite agree, on who had lit the fire at the back of Ashcroft's. There were those who argued that the culprit had been a disgruntled punter from The School up stairs. Others claimed it was the Germans, though they could not explain why the Germans would want to burn down the Two-up School. Even if someone writing under a German name had sent a letter to The Echo threatening to blow it up. Others suspected the Temperance wowsers, who seemed determined to make sure that there was no fun for men, left in town. Perhaps that was the aim, strip the world of all comfort and fun and pleasures. Reduce life to the monotony of animals, working and sleeping with no chance for humanity to creep in between the necessities, men made docile and obedient through boredom, and more willing to sign up. Though grinding people down only works for so long, before they break out and rebel. All one had to do was look at what had happened in Ireland, only a few months back. The Easter Rising had been big enough for even Jack, on leave in London to mention it in his letter home. Still, it made Arch wonder what would be coming next.

But he already knew what was coming next, the papers all screamed about the need for conscription. As the focus of the war turned from Turkey to France, the enormity of the fight, that had already been going on for nearly two years, had become apparent. He had not been following the course of the war in France, only talk of Gallipoli where his brother served, had been of interest. Now, turning to read about the war in France, even from this far off vantage point, Arch could see that no quick end was in sight. The tension of that, and the worry and fear for those aboard, seemed to be slowly, but surely, breaking people apart. He could see it on the faces of those he knew, their bodies carried on, their mouths spoke intelligently, they functioned as regular people, but still some part of their minds were perennially absent. Following some beloved form across the ocean, into a sea of mud, pain, and fear. It felt like a physical trembling through all his limbs, a trembling that he could neither control, nor ignore. Yet the trembling was better than the alternative. The sudden collapse that came once the tension was released, with the coming of one of those fearful telegrams. Already one had come for Mrs Richardson, informing her, that her George had perished during the landing at Gallipoli. She had been so overbalanced by her loss, she had to go away, for a rest by the seaside, for several months. Returning not long before Christmas, visibly diminished in both body and spirit, the matronly hen in her customary tweed, reduced to a sparrow, hesitant and nervy, a piteous creature in anyone's eyes.

Yes, it would be conscription next, he had already amassed a large collection of white feathers, from anonymous sources. People who felt they had the right to comment, on his private business, the intolerable cheek of it. Sending things anonymously was a cowardly act, if any one wished to call him a coward, they should do it to his face, give him the chance to deck them for their effrontery. For he was not a coward, but he struggled to see how a war in France was any of his concern. They said to think of England, but England had just shot his father's people, struggling for their freedom. Thinking of England only made him angry, he owed them nothing. As for here, and the pseudo-English who wished to press him into war and muddy death, well he knew where they could go.

The talk of conscription had so concerned him that Arch had written of it to Jack, asking for his opinion. It had been a surprise to receive his reply, only a few days ago. Jack, in an abrupt departure from his usual chatter about scenery or funny stories, had launched forth in a passionate rebuttal, of the idea that he should be forced to fight alongside men who had no wish to be there. He talked of the state of the English forces, which had increasingly been composed of conscripts. How they knew nothing of how important a common sense of purpose and mateship, kept not only oneself alive, but also those around you. It was hard enough to deal with young recruits, whose heads were filled with idealised notions of the war, and images of heroes, to have men who actively resented being there, would be intolerable. He was so incensed at the idea of conscription, that he had told Arch to have the letter published in the local paper.

Straightening up in his seat, as the first train passengers began to mount the stairs, and pour forth onto Main Street, struggling with luggage, looking out for cabs, Arch watched, as his handsome cabs began to pull out from the rank. Watching the crowd, for the fare that had phoned ahead that afternoon, and booked him for the weekend. At last he saw her, parting the crowds like a great bark, swathed in furs, with a small man, he at first took to be a porter trailing in her wake, loaded down with a quantity of luggage, more suited to a long sea voyage, than a weekend in Katoomba.

Stepping out of the cab, Arch opened the passenger door watching, as the woman and her male companion, settled into the fine leather seats. Waiting in dignified silence, as Arch strapped the luggage to the back of the cab.

"Welcome to Katoomba, your Ladyship."

Tales from the Front

The stories that made their way back to Greece; either on the tongues of bards or wounded men, both of whom were sought out equally by eager and anxious family members, were composed and polished. They spoke of heroic deeds, and glorious deaths, which could console those who had been left behind. Knowing that though their loved one had gone, his name, would live in the annals of their history. His deeds, were writ large by the gods, and the favours they bestowed, would provide them with glory everlasting. That their loved ones had died, a hero's death, unsullied and buried with due honours, reassured and comforted them in their loss. Their death had meaning, and they had not fallen victim of violent Keres, to wander on the edge of the underworld, ghosts, without honour or purpose.

Chapter Twenty two

Arch didn't need to do more than look at Dottie, to know the news that had brought him rushing to the house. He had run rather than driven, it felt somehow more urgent and allowed him with each footfall to bargain with God that the worst not be waiting. Let Jack be wounded, broken, mad even, but not dead. Jack cannot be dead.

Bursting into the house, he saw Dottie sitting in the front room, shaking with sobs. She held a scrap of paper in her hands out towards him, as he entered the room, dropping it on the carpet at her feet. Instinctively, Arch wrapped his arms about his chest, as if to hold in the great pain, he could feel building within him. Sinking to his knees, he found he could not breathe, air gulped in and stayed trapped, agonisingly in his chest, his mouth opening and closing futilely like a fish out of water. For a few terrifying moments, he felt as if he were going to die. And suddenly, that thought was not as horrible as it first seemed, if only it wouldn't hurt so much. He stared wildly at Dottie, who leant towards him in her chair watching him curiously, from wide frightened eyes. Arch felt himself pitch forward, a horrible animal roaring, filled his ears. He no longer felt the tightness in his chest, but the awful noise would not stop, it just went on and on, until he could not bear it any longer. He tried to form words, to make the noise stop, only to find that it was his voice making the noise. He no longer felt as if he were dying, but somehow that only made it worse, there would be no easy escape, he would have to lie on the floor making this grotesque animal noise, until something else came along to take its place.

As Arch collapsed on the floor, Dottie rose from her chair, moving over to where he lay. For a few moments she stood hesitating, as she debated within herself what to do. She wanted to join him, lying on the floor, screaming. The idea of letting the restraint and control, she had lived with for over two years, go and abandon herself to the wave of emotion that she could feel rising, barely below the surface was tempting, but it was an idea she could not submit to. To let go of all restraint, would mean falling from a height, from which there would be no recovery. She would instead do, as she had always done, press on with life. Seek out the firm ground, in a landscape which changed and shifted with each step, opening chasms and swamps, in the path before her, threatening to derail her. She had thought, she had become skilled at negotiating this ever changing terrain, but events like todays, which opened up the earth at her feet and forced her to back away, as the ground fell away, reminded her of how hollow her pride in her adaptability was, in the face of the mercilessness of events, that had ensnare all their lives. Kneeling down, Dottie reached out, and ran her hand down the back of Arch's head, stroking him, as if attempting to quiet a distressed animal. His hair was thick and soft, far softer than she had expected. She had never heard a man making the kind of noise, which issued from Arch, at this moment. As she stroked his hair, she allowed her hands to sweep down his back, her movements rhythmic and slow, listening to his cries quiet, and his breathing calm down.

Arch lay quietly for some time, letting the tears which finally arrived, roll down his nose and splash onto the rug, beneath his head. Dottie's hands ran down his head and back. For the first time in his life, he felt there was someone to help him bear the horrible pain, which threatened to burst out of him. Someone else, who could understand how much this hurt. For the first time, he didn't have to hold himself aloof, for the sake of those who depended upon him. He didn't have to sublimate his pain, into chores or a stoic front, to spare the feelings of others, or avoid being criticised and told off. Sitting up, he faced Dottie and looked at her, not as his brother's wife, but as a fellow sufferer, someone he could turn to, and receive comfort from. Wrapping his arms about her he pulled her to him, pressing her with all his strength to himself. Feeling her return his embrace, neither hesitating, nor breaking away.

***

Sitting on opposite ends of the couch, Dottie and Arch, drank Jack's whisky. Drinking just enough, so that the warm buzz of the alcohol, temporarily blurred the sharp edges of grief, offering if not relief, at least making the sharpness of the pain manageable.

Dottie allowed her gaze to wander about the room, it felt as if she had found herself in a stranger's home. The home of a happy woman. Somewhere, at the edge of her mind, she wondered what had become of her children, but the thought was too vague to cause much concern, flitting across her consciousness, vanishing again beneath the weight of her grief.

"I'm gonna have to call my aunt," said Arch, breaking the silence. "Oh God, what am I gonna say?"

Dottie bit her lower lip, looking at Arch, too exhausted by her own distress to offer any word of comfort. In the kitchen, she could hear someone moving about, and the babble of her children's voices. Vaguely, it occurred to her, Ivy must be looking after her children.

"Then there is a requiem mass to organise." Arch walked slowly to the sideboard and refilled his glass. Returning to his seat, he sat contemplating the amber liquid.

Dottie found herself noticing, how quiet her mind had suddenly become. The finality of the telegram's words, had quieted the wasp nest of worries that had consumed her life, since Jack had left. It felt, as if, all the gears of her mind had become clogged, with a horrid, black thickness, a density without texture, warmth or substance, yet, which had in a moment, stopped all the central workings of her mind. At the edges, she could observe stray thoughts emerge, and flit across her perception, only to be consumed by the darkness. Arch's words, entered her ears, as disjointed sounds bereft of meaning. She was vaguely aware that, as the room grew dark Arch left, the quiet thud of the front door and the creak of the veranda boards, serving as his farewell.

As Arch left, Ivy entered the front room and rebuilt the fire that had been allowed to burn out, bringing food that Dottie failed to eat, and cups of tea that trembled when she picked them up, spilling the contents onto the rug.

When the clock struck ten, Dottie, found herself raised from her seat on the sofa. Her clothes were stripped from her, leaving her in her slip and knickers, as the same guiding hands pulled back the warm soft covers, making her lie down in her bed. Like a child, responding to a parental order, she slept.

Chapter Twenty three

The morning was eerily still, as Arch walked to the train station, to meet his aunt. A stillness, matched only by the dazzling brightness of the cold clear day, reflecting off the thick blanketing whiteness of the snow, which had stopped all sound and movement. Walking ankle deep in snow, Arch listened to the squeaking of his boots, and the occasional slither and slump, of snow falling, as trees released themselves from their icy shroud. Here and there, a sudden sound would reach him, as overwhelmed by the weight of the snow, a branch gave way with a crack, reverberating around the valley like a gunshot. He listened to his breath, which poured forth in great clouds, into the frigid air, as he walked. Desperately trying to focus his mind on anything, but the endless unanswerable questions, which had kept him up all night. How had his brother died? Had he suffered? Or was it sudden and painless? The scrap of paper from the telegraph, had offered nothing solid, but the final solidity of death. He was tired of death, there had been far too much already in his life, death linked to death like dollies in a paper chain, each new one dragging up the others that had gone before, reopening griefs that stubbornly refused to heal.

Each death had made him feel older, so much older, than his now thirty years. Were the deaths quantifiable, orderable in scales of magnitude? Did this new death hurt more or less than the last, having been infected for the first time twenty years ago now, had he developed a tolerance to grief, as one could develop a tolerance for certain poisons. The whole situation seemed unreal, allowing him to think about the practicalities of tying up a life, and yet somehow believing that the owner of that life, would soon return. It had felt the same twenty years ago, when his father had told him, his mother would not be coming home again. That there had been an accident on the railway line, and she had died. It had not seemed real then either. For weeks he expected that his mother would come home, imagining that she had just gone to stay with Aunt Betty, like she did the time when the baby didn't come. He remembered being told about the baby that was supposed to come, watching his mother's belly grow big and firm like a melon, running his hands across the taut flesh, to feel the baby kick. But the baby never came, and his mother was gone for months. When she came home again, no one mentioned the baby. Arch began to think that he had dreamt the whole thing until again, some years later, his mother again began to swell up, like a balloon at a fairground. This time the talk of a baby had been quieter, more subdued. He knew that a baby was a good thing, as every visitor or friend of his mother's, asked him if he were excited to be getting a new baby brother or sister, but his mother looked frightened and he hated to see her like that. When at last the baby came, he had expected his mother to be happy like the other women, who proudly showed off their babies. Wheeling them along the rough streets, in sturdy black prams, their older children clinging to the sides with proprietorial pride. But this baby, produced no such surge of maternal joy or pride in his mother, instead his reserved, but loving mother grew silent and still. She would stay in bed long into the morning, leaving him to be bustled off to school, not with the hugs and kisses of his mother, but the rude impatience of the housekeeper Mrs O'Dwyer. Some days, he would catch her weeping, unable to stop, no matter what he said to try and cheer her up. No longer, did she dress up to go into town, or to pay calls on friends, but wore the same worn old house dresses, her hair hastily pinned up or tied back, for days on end. And then for a time, she would brighten, and be her old self again, cheerful and friendly, paying calls and keeping house, as she had done before Jack was born.

But these times would never last, and as Jack grew, the intervals between their mothers depressions, grew shorter. Until, by the time Jack was three, the intervals had ceased altogether, and the whole of their lives came to be dominated, by the fear of what their mother's mood, would bring next.

In the weeks leading up to his mother's death, Arch remembered how the whole house came to feel, as if it had become infested with his mother's mood. As if her depression, had escaped her body and spun its web, like a spider across the whole house, filling the space with threads, which connected to her and caused her pain when tugged. Slowly, the whole house had grown quiet, all the occupants loathed to say or do anything, that could tug at one of those silvery threads. And then, after months of silent inactivity, she made a choice. A choice, to walk by the train tracks and disappear from their lives, once and for all.

In contrast his father's illness, while sudden and painful to watch, was positively prosaic. The kind of death that happens every day, in homes the world over, as illness gains the upper hand and the poor mortal dies. There had been nothing dramatic, nothing shameful, about anything in Patrick Kelly's death, besides his insistence on bequeathing his misery, to his youngest son, with his spiteful words.

And now it was Jack's turn to die, and he felt numb. His death was too obscene to be believable, was he truly to believe that his brother, so alive with animal health and youth could now be dead. To believe that those muscles, which drove their owner in a mad charge, across a football field, were now inert and useless. To believe that voice which boomed with joy, or confided his softer secret feelings, in a stream of warm rich sounds, which only recently had settled into a man's voice, leaving the squeaks and cracks of teenage years behind, would never again be heard. To believe that love, had been extinguished, snuffed out by the hatred of men, leaving his own raging and bereft, unable to comprehend the loss that had been communicated, on a small strip of paper. And the worst of it was, he knew the letters would keep coming, words from a dead man, sent into a future he would not see. Words, that offered no presentiment of the death, which lay ahead.

Mounting the top of the hill, Arch was assaulted by the sounds of laughing and shouting, as children having emerged from houses played in the snow, in the gardens of the guest house, at the top of Station Street, opposite the courthouse. Hurrying past, Arch saw more children playing and shouting in The Crushers, by the railway station. Looking at his watch, as he crossed the tracks, Arch saw that he was nearly twenty minutes early, to meet his aunt's train. Entering the waiting room, Arch stood by the fire, warming his chilled legs and hands. As the warmth seeped into his body, chasing away the numbness of the cold walk, the hideousness of the situation began to dawn on him. Here he was, standing in the warm, invigorated by his walk, able to feel his heart beating in his breast, and across the world, his brother's heart had been stilled, and his body lay in some filthy wasteland.

Twenty minutes later, when Elizabeth Ebsworth entered the waiting room, she found her nephew, all six foot three of him, slumped against the wall, sobbing like a child.

Chapter Twenty four

It was the lack of a body, which distressed Dottie most of all, about her husband's death. The lack of a place to say, here lies John Michael Kelly, my husband, made her feel, as if she had been somehow cheated out of, one of the important trappings of widowhood. Moreover, she felt the need for some focal point, to remind her children of their father, who was now in heaven. For the formal words and ceremonies of a Requiem Mass, without the closure of a funeral, where the coffin stood central to the proceedings, had seemed as insubstantial, as the words on the telegram. Especially, when Jack's letters insisted on arriving, their dates making for a dreadful countdown, to an end the writer barely suspected. With this in mind, Dottie went to the local stone masons, ordering a small memorial stone for her husband, to be placed on her parents' property, to give her and their children, a place to remember Jack.

It was a fine September day, when the memorial was ready. A cool breeze played with the tips of the trees, but a bright warming sun, shone down on the party of soberly dressed men and women, gathered around the engraved stone, on the formal lawn, that surrounded her parents' house on the hill. Across the lawn, two magpies dug the lawn, looking for bugs, their glossy black and white plumage giving them a formal, sombre appearance. Perched in the tree above the party, a wattle bird cried out, in its harsh primordial voice, only to find itself chased away, by the pair of magpies, who again settled themselves on the lawn, watching the humans. They appeared to listen, as first a young woman spoke, her voice steady from rehearsal though filled with genuine emotion. Next they listened to a man, with bright tempting hair, the kind of hair they would like to line their nest with, had they not already stolen plenty from the ginger tom cat. He spoke in a voice which cracked and broke, like the voice of the wattle bird, they had so successfully seen off their patch. At last, the human party moved off, leaving behind a pile of bright yellow rocks. Curious, the two birds moved forward, investigating the new addition to their territory, before again returning to the far more important business, of hunting grubs in the lawn, to feed their chicks.

***

"So, Dorothy dear, how are you bearing up?" The words came from above, the same words that had dogged her weeks now. Polite words that needed a polite, suitably restrained reply, not the reply that she wished to give, the reply that spoke of grief, loss and loneliness. The reply that made her wish, to shout and scream how unfair it was, that she should have lost her husband, to a war that seemed to have no end.

Dottie sighed and stared at her tea cup. Looking up into the face of Elizabeth Ebsworth, she found herself unable to supress the bitter laugh that escaped her, as she realised, her reply need not be formulaic. "I'm managing, though there are so many things to deal with. Jack didn't leave a Will, and Hector Johnson can't find the deeds to the house."

Dottie's hands trembled, causing her tea to spill into the saucer, and onto the skirt of her dress. Placing the cup on the tea table, she dabbed ineffectually, at the spilt tea on her lap.

"Perhaps Jack kept them at home?"

Dottie shook her head. "No, I've been through all the papers in Jack's desk, there is nothing. I don't know where that leaves me. I'll probably have to move back home here. I don't want to though, I've grown to love my little house."

Standing and scanning the large room, which opened out

onto the veranda, via a pair of open French doors, Elizabeth searched for her nephew, among the crowd of people assembled there. Watching the people move to and fro, assembling into small groups, which burst with sound or broke away, as quickly as they formed, like ripples on a pond. When Dottie had invited her to come for the memorial ceremony, she had thought it would be merely a small affair, close family only, so was surprised when she saw so many people. More even than had attended his requiem, now crowded into the Joyces' sitting room and spilled over, onto the terrace outside. She was even more surprised, when upon speaking to guests, found that all had some connection to, or story to tell about Jack. Whether they were the young men from his football team, or little old ladies whose affairs he helped manage at work, all spoke of Jack as being a most considerate, dependable, generous and affable young man they had met. Her little boy, for that was how she thought of Jack, who had so craved affection and love had, unbeknownst to him, in his short life achieved what many men cannot achieve, in a life four times as long.

At last, spying Arch standing, listening half-heartedly to a man, with a Katoomba football club pin on his lapel, Elizabeth caught her nephew's eye and beckoned him over, with a slight movement of her head. She watched, as Arch, spoke quickly to the man and broke away, making a path through the crowd, towards where she and Dottie sat, on the opposite side of the room.

"Dot, I have to say again how grateful I am that you did this," said Arch, leaning over Dottie's chair.

"Archie, Dorothy and I have been discussing Jack's affairs, and I was wondering, if you would know where the deeds of the house are," said Elizabeth, settling herself back into her chair.

Arch smiled, confused by his aunt's interrogative tone. "I have them at the Bank, you should have told me you were looking for them, Dot."

"Archie, why do you have the deeds to Jack's house?" Elizabeth's eyes narrowed, suspecting some male trick was afoot.

Arch looked away from his aunt's penetrating gaze, her green eyes like hard jewels, as he shuffled his feet on the floor. Dottie too looked up at Arch, her face luminously pale, against her dark hair, and the black hat she wore.

"Because, technically, it is my house. Dad didn't leave Jack anything. I told him Dad left him the house. I couldn't tell him that Dad left him nothing. I was waiting for probate to expire, to sign them over to him, but he signed up and left, before I got the chance."

Arch looked at Dottie, watching the quavering look pass across her face, as she wondered what further upheaval, her life was about to undergo. Kneeling down beside her chair, his long limbs crushed into such a tiny space, that he resembled a praying mantis, crouched on the floor. His hands resting by Dottie's arm, on the arm rest, yet not daring to touch her, he continued, his voice betraying his alarm.

"I've already spoken to my solicitor, about having them signed over to you, Dot. I was waiting until the paperwork was ready, before I said anything. He says that they'll be done next week, I'll take you in to sign them when he calls me. I didn't mean to worry you. I'm sorry."

Dottie let out a shuddering sigh, leaning back in her chair, searching Arch's face for signs of deceit, finding instead only concern and regret that his action should have caused her such distress. Reaching across, she patted Arch's hands, as they lay next to her arm.

"That's alright. I'm glad that it is so easily sorted."

Arch, lifted himself up off the floor, sitting down on the edge of the tea-table, his knees folded up to his chest.

"Have you been able to sort out the rest of Jack's affairs?"

"Yes, he didn't really leave much. Just a few stocks and bonds and a bit in his savings account. It was the house that was worrying me."

"Tell me, Dorothy, how your work with the anti-conscription lobby is progressing?" said Elizabeth, changing the subject. Watching, as Dottie brightened and grew animated, her mind drawn off that which was most personal, to that which she had used as a safety line in her grief. The anti-conscription lobbying, had grown out of Dottie's soldier's support group. Her interest in knitting socks, having waned with Jack's death, she had thrown her energies, into preventing forced participation, in a war that seemed so unnecessary.

"Quite well, thank you for asking. We now meet at the church, because there are so many of us, and we don't all fit in my front room. I've been speaking at various groups, we have some of the more progressive social groups onside, and I spoke at the mechanical institute, in Lawson, only a few days ago. The men there were very impressed by our arguments. We've been leafletting and door knocking, all over the district, and we have a whole lot of ladies, ready to hand out leaflets at the polling stations, on referendum day. I think Jack's letter in the paper, saying how the men in France don't want unwilling fighters, helped."

"She's a real warrior, Aunty," said Arch, grinning up from his seat, the admiration in his voice unable to be concealed, as mere politeness.

Dottie blushed at the complement, shielding her face with her hand, but then as happened so often, she found herself thinking of Jack, and the thought of him cut through her distraction, with piercing clarity. Blinking back tears, she struggled to express the turmoil she could feel within her, to those who watched, distressed by her sudden weeping.

Reaching out, Arch lay a hand on Dottie's knee.

Pressing Arch's hand with her own, Dottie offered a tight quick smile, as she rose from her seat. Arch watched, as making her way across the room, Dottie disappeared through the door, into the depths of the house.

Chapter Twenty five

It started with blackberries. An afternoon spent like so many others, Dottie had walked across the tracks to pick blackberries, which grew in great hoops of tangled vines, on the westerly boundary fence, of Arch's horse paddock. The berries hung in clusters, like miniature bunches of grapes, and had been tempting Dottie for some time. Her mind, was filled with the idea of making jam, when she arrived at the stables, armed with a basket and a sturdy pair of scissors. The afternoon had progressed well, with blackberries falling into the basket, Dottie appreciating a quiet afternoon in the sunshine. A rare child free day, while her mother and father enjoyed their company for the night.

With the anti-conscription battle won, her mother took a greater lead in the soldier's support group. For she found it hard to go on baking and knitting, knowing that her husband was not the recipient of her handy work. The finality of Jack's death, had been liberating in some ways, she could see now. Not that she wished for her worry and terror to end, in such a way, but she was forced to admit that, despite the grief that it caused her, she at least now knew the fate of her husband. And with his death, she felt removed from the war, no longer did she feel the need to follow battles, or scan the papers for news, that might offer some clue to her husband's activities. The letters from Jack, had finally petered out just before Christmas. And though she had read every one a dozen times, she was glad that at last this communication from a dead man, who did not know he was dead, had finally ceased.

Standing in the sun, it occurred to Dottie, that for the first time in months she felt happy. The terrible ache that sprung up whenever she had thought of Jack was absent. As she recalled their courting trips to the wilds of North Katoomba. In search of blackberries and illicitly acquired apples, which they had eaten with stained fingers and many kisses. It was on a lazy afternoon like this, in the weeks before they married, that Jack had made love to her in one of the horse stalls. To this day, she could not smell freshly mown hay without becoming aroused. It was the first time she had been able to think of Jack, and not picture him lying in the mud and dirt, of a battlefield. It occurred to her, that perhaps this is how one recovers from grief. The loss is still there, but the memories change. Her thoughts of Jack did not, for once, spoil her mood, rather her mood allowed her to remember fondly the man, who had been her husband.

As the sun began to drop down, towards the lip of the valley, striking the earth at that awful blinding angle, while at the same time, offering apology in the form of golden dying light. Dottie finished filling her basket and began to move out of the blackberry patch, only to find that her skirt had become entangled in the vines. Their thorns, eager grasping hands, ready to tear any exposed skin. Dottie looked about for some sign of life. Listening to the crickets pick up their instruments and serenade the gathering evening with their throbbing call. Arch and his men would be bringing their cabs in soon, so she would just have to wait, and hope that someone noticed her.

"Dot, what have you done to yourself?" asked Arch, as he strode across the paddock.

"Picking blackberries," said Dottie, squinting against the setting sun, at Arch's silhouetted form.

"Getting caught more like," said Arch, as he looked at Dottie's tangled skirt. "Here, give me them scissors, and I'll cut you free."

Stepping into the blackberry patch, Arch took the scissors from Dottie, and began to cut the vines, clutching at her skirt.

"I got in alright, and then I couldn't get out again," laughed Dottie, the growing dark, mercifully covering the deep blush, which had risen to her cheeks.

Dottie looked down at Arch, bent over her skirt. She could see where the nap of his neck, rose from his collar. The dark red hairs, which lay against his creamy skin, looked like the pelt of a mature fox. She had to fight the urge not to stroke him. She could feel his side, rubbing against her breasts and belly, as he worked. She smelled the scent of a day's work on him, the powerful animal smell, of a working man. It had been so long since she had last been touched in any way. Too long for her to bear any longer, as she reached out and lay her hand on Arch's back, as if to steady herself. His back was warm, and the muscles beneath her hand, powerful and so very much alive. Without warning, she felt herself lifted off the ground, as cut free of the briars, Arch carried her free from the patch.

"Thank you," said Dottie, as Arch placed her on the ground, his hands lingering for a second only on her body. His face, mere inches from her own. It would take very little, to traverse those inches, and press her lips to his. It would take nothing more than a flick of the eye, or a movement of her head, to give him permission to move those few inches. Her body ached to be touched, after over two long years of abstinence. But looking now at Arch, all she felt, was how much she wished it were Jack who held her fast in his arms, and hung above her wanting to be kissed. Closing her eyes, turning her face away, Dottie smiled.

"Come round tomorrow, I'll give you a pot of jam."

Arch straightened up and stepped back again, to a respectful distance.

"Do you want me to walk you home?" Arch stepped into the briar patch, retrieving Dottie's basket.

Inspecting her skirt for damage, and plucking free the odd piece of twig, Dottie said, "It's not dark yet, I'll be fine."

"I'd better go see to the horses then," said Arch, handing the scissors back to Dottie and rubbing his hands together, for want of anything better to do with them.

"'Night Arch."

"'Night Dot."

***

Returning home, Dottie picked up the envelopes from her mail box, as she walked around the back of the house, and entered via the backdoor. Tossing the letters unnoticed onto the kitchen table, with her basket of fruit, she removed her hat and gloves. She rebuilt the fire in the stove, before placing the kettle on the heat. Gathering up the letters, Dottie took them into the front room, to read while she waited for the kettle to boil.

Seating herself beneath the lamp, Dottie tossed the first few letters aside, knowing them to be bills, which needed no urgent attention. Another, she could tell, was from one of her cousins in Bathurst, who she had been helping set up a soldier's support group. Dottie felt in no mood, to read a letter full of inane questions tonight, and tossed it unopened, with the bills for her attention tomorrow. It was the final letter, which stopped Dottie in her tracks, postmarked London, she assumed that the shaky handwriting was her uncle Ferd's. His script had always been barely legible, despite his substantial and expensive education. Opening the letter Dottie read:

December 3rd 1916

Dearest Darling Dottie,

I am so sorry to have not written to you in so long. You must be worried sick, wondering what could possibly have happened to me. I've been in hospital these past four months, having copped a good one fighting at Poziers, last August. Don't be alarmed though, I am in one piece, all limbs attached and as ugly as I ever was. I was knocked about pretty bad, with a touch of blood poisoning though, and it has taken a while to shift that. But I am all recovered now, Darling and they are sending me home in the New Year. I should be home in time for little Alfie's Birthday, in March. My baby boy, will be all grown up, when I see him again. And Edie turning four, she will be a big girl, off to school in a year. How much I have missed.

And you Darling, how I have missed you these past years. You can rest assured, that I have been a good boy while I've been away. It has always only ever been you that I wanted, coming here proved that to me, more clearly than anything else could have. I go to sleep, and think about how I will fold you in my arms when I return, and much more besides. I am counting off the days, until I leave for the ship, and then I will be counting the days of my voyage, that brings me safely back home to you, and all I love.

When you get this letter, go out into the backyard and look up at the stars, I am sending you kisses to match every one of those stars. Kisses to cover every inch of your delectable, precious body.

All my love,

Jack

P.S. I have also written to Arch and Aunt Betty, so you don't have to share this letter with anyone.

P.P.S. There seems to have been some trouble with my identity, after I was wounded, I hope they didn't tell you I was missing, or anything awful like that.

Death or Glory

Home. The dearest wish of every man, on every battle field is to return home. Men will wander for years to find it. They will slay Cyclops, or visit the realm of the dead, to find their path home. Some will go to extraordinary lengths, to avoid leaving it, in the first place. Among those who had attempted to avoid the war in Troy, were Achilles, secreted amongst the women of Scyros, and Odysseys, feigning madness to avoid his military duties.

However, once placed in the thick of battle these men learnt their true calling, death or glory, would claim them for their own, and all vain thoughts of home would vanish. To think otherwise, would be to bring shame upon oneself. In the company of men, only rugged self-sufficiency was to be respected. Weakness was dishonouring, and the shame of that disabling. So much so, that a man would rather die, than rely on another for support.

Chapter Twenty six

The last thing Jack could remember, before waking in hospital, was a blast, which threw him up into the air, like a rag doll, and let him drop into the mud. Between then and the hospital, ten weeks later, was one long stretch of wandering, lost on an ocean of illness and injury, like some vivid dream, from which he could not wake. The fleeting moments of lucidness, that had allowed him to surface, were not enough to press upon his memory. Instead, he found himself to be no more than a leaf, or a stick tossed upon a stormy sea. Debris of a once great thing, which would eventually be caught, and dragged down to the depths. And those depths were tempting. Every day he could hear their call, luring him down, confusing and blurring the idea that kept him afloat. Home, the idea that day after day, forced him to strike out like an exhausted swimmer, against the lure of the depths, seemed so far away. Some days he floated, listening to the sound that called from the deep, the soft warm sound, promising an end to all the dogged effort he had engaged in. The siren call, which said no ill could come, from sinking down to where all fighting finished. Sometimes, he felt himself heeding that call, gently sinking down into the darkness, only to see the image of home flash before him. Forcing him to strike out again, resuming his slow progress, across the wastes of water.

When at last, Jack's doctors declared him out of danger, he had endured nearly six separate surgeries, including two skin grafts, and had survived a dose of blood poisoning. The nurses, not having a name to give him, called him their miracle man. The man who survived what had killed, so many of his fellow patients. Safe now from the depths, but swathed in bandages from his right shoulder to his left knee, Jack floated in the hallucinatory world of painkillers and sleeping powders. Slowly, the drugged haze lifted, like a morning mist lifts from the mountains, showing the bright face of day. And Jack was able to reclaim himself from this strange battlefield.

Reclaiming, his temporarily mislaid name however, involved more paperwork than Jack had ever seen pass through Mr Johnson's office, in his old civilian life. In fact, he became so adept, at interpreting the army's forms that it passed in whispers through the hospital, that he was the man to speak to, if one needed a form explained or filled in. Strolls through the hospital grounds, to strengthen the remaining muscles in his leg, became his office hours. Men from different wards, mingled outside in the sunshine, freed for a little, from the suffocating smells of the wards.

Mixing with his fellow patients, Jack marvelled at the different ways, a man could be wounded. The most obvious, were those who had lost a limb or more, their pinned up pyjamas and distorted silhouettes, proclaimed for all to see, how they had been damaged. Then there were the gassed and the blinded, some of whom lived in hope of recovering, at least a little, of the sunshine they felt on their faces. And then, there were the men like him; men who could stand up in their pyjamas and need only show what had happened, if they chose. Men who carried bits of metal, in their seemingly whole bodies, bits of metal, which could at any time move and kill them. Men like him, who had lost more of themselves on the operating table, than they had in battle, for whom their subsequent illness, had weakened and damaged them in ways their doctors could only guess at. Then there were the men who had left their reason somewhere in France, lost amid the constant noise and fear of battle, though he rarely saw these. The hospital keeping them away from their fellow patients, their injuries making them a special class of wounded. Finally, Jack came across the men with head wounds, these men were among the most grizzly of the wounded. The distorted shapes, their injuries had made of their faces, were a shock when Jack first encountered them in the garden. Just as the expressions of those who had come from different wards, embarrassed and depressed the men with head wounds, as they saw for the first time, expressions which would haunt the rest of their lives.

Seeing the reaction his expression provoked, Jack sat down by the nearest man, who sat with the intact portion of his face turned towards the sun, his injured side still swathed in bandages. Like most of the men, he was young and looked at Jack with his good eye. Jack could see that he was frightened, but he would not hold that against him, truth to tell who among them was not frightened.

"So, where are you from?" asked Jack, hoping that he could bluff his way through, until he could bear to look at the injured man.

"Lithgow," said a voice that still cracked and boomed, in the way of young men.

"Lithgow, I'm from Katoomba, we could almost be neighbours."

"I think I recognise you. Did you play Rugby? The Lithgow Katoomba match in '14? I think you're the red haired bastard, who decked m' brother Daniel."

"That sounds like me. How long have you been out here?"

Jack looked at the uninjured side of the face, blonde hair stuck up at odd angles, where the bandages ended. The good eye was clear and pale blue, the undamaged skin was marred by acne, which looked painfully inflamed. He could see the boy was far younger than the age he had given his recruiting officer. He wondered how many older men had risked their own safety, out of pity for this silly boy.

"I don't know really. I was at the front about three days," said the boy.

"Three days, shit. I mean, there were a fair few blokes who copped it when we landed in Turkey, but that was more bad luck, and piss poor management. I managed eight months at the front, in Turkey, and not so much as a scratch. Don't let anyone tell you the Turks let us off easy, they fought like buggers. After that, I thought France was going to be easy. It's a bigger bloody shambles here than over there, and all the bigwigs are here." Jack noticed the impressed look, in the wounded boy's eye. "What's your name?"

"Officially it's David, but he's my older brother. I'm William Brown, my mates call me Billy," came the crackling and booming voice.

"So Billy," said Jack, seeing the boy's face brighten, at being addressed so intimately. "Are you headed home soon?"

"New Year, you?"

"Same, we're probably on the same ship. We'll end up with two bloody winters this way. A whole year waiting for summer, that's no way to live."

Billy laughed, for the first time since he had arrived in the hospital, he did not feel sorry for himself and his wretched fate.

Jack shuffled, crossing his legs and pressing himself back away from Billy, making the wicker chair he had sat in creak. The admiration that shone forth from the one clear eye, in the boy's ruined face, was something he had not encountered before. Certainly he had been looked to and admired in his uniform. Knee deep in mud, his Sergeants' stripes conveying competence and confidence, to the raw recruits he found himself in charge of. A symbol of his ability to survive. To be admired with no practical cause, merely for being and having been in the fray for a good spell, was unnerving. The boy hadn't been at the front long enough to learn there were no heroes as he imagined. Just men who hung on longer than others.

"Well, I've got a few more blokes to talk to, before they shut us all up for the night, but I'll see you around."

"What's your name?"

"I only just got it back, so don't lose it. It's Jack Kelly."

Supporting himself on his walking stick, rearranging his dressing gown. Jack turned and shuffled off along the terrace, returning to his wheel chair, asking the nurse to take him back inside to bed.

Chapter Twenty seven

Ultimately, the war had not been quite as Billy had expected, when he joined up a year ago. He had enjoyed his time at the training camp, and on the ship to England. There, the camaraderie of other idealistic young men, buoyed his spirits and allowed him to forget, what he had so hurriedly left behind at home. Wintering in England had been a great adventure, for a boy who had never travelled further afield than Bathurst. To see places he had only read about in books, made him feel as if his life had become some fantastic dream. He and the fellows in his company, who had travelled with him from Sydney. Spoke together after training in the barracks, made cosy with a fire and intimate manly company, of what great deeds they would do, once they found themselves at the front. When at last in April, the call came, Billy found himself a mere speck. Swept up in a great movement of men, supplies and horses, and the scale of where he was going, began to dawn on him.

France itself, when he finally landed, proved an even greater shock than the train or the army depo, at South Hampton. The port surged with men, travelling in both directions. As fresh new recruits disembarked, he watched exhausted, battle hardened men take their place, travelling back across The Channel for leave. Wandering the port he saw a hospital ship, being loaded with wounded men on stretches, the full extent of their injuries, concealed from prying eyes by blankets. Though Billy could tell by the distorted shapes, that some of these men had lost limbs and the realisation filled him with horror. He was here to be a hero, heroes return home whole, or die in battle covered with glory. They don't lie groaning on a stretcher, horribly diminished, a burden on their families for the rest of their lives.

The train to the front was slow, as it cut its way through fields and towns, which grew ever more degraded and battle scared. The rear position, to which they were heading, was outside a small village mostly abandoned, but for those who felt there were a few francs to be made from the army, that had advanced into their midst.

Billy and his mates, spent a week behind the lines, waiting for their turn to join the 'fun', as some of the more experienced soldiers called it. Their voices tinged with a sardonic jaded tone, which neither Billy, nor his mates understood. Behind the lines, they discovered the joys, offered by French wine and French girls. Their eagerness for new experiences, rendering them blind to the apathy and cynicism, the girls brought to the exercise. Discovering too late, that what the girls offered was not as they imagined, and that the result, was not what they expected. They didn't feel like men, unless it was manly to itch like crazy or for the truly unlucky ones, discover an increasing burning when they peed.

When their time to join the 'fun', came at last, Billy found himself walking through a ruined orchard. The splintered trees, making horrible distorted mocking shapes, some with leaf and blossom emerging from the ruined trunks. Tenaciously clinging to life, making Billy think of the wounded men he had seen at Calais. Approaching the trenches, which slowly wound their way deeper and deeper into the earth, as the front grew closer. Billy found himself forced to swallow down the fear that rose in him, as the sky grew to be little more than a strip of blue, between tall mud walls. He watched, as the men they were relieving filed past. Men of clay, their eyes the only part of them that distinguished them, from the muddy bodies in no-man's land. And yet, it was they eyes that frightened Billy, most of all, the haunted exhausted look, no man should ever wear. He felt ashamed that he could not look at them, these were the heroes he had wished to join, could he now shrink from them as from devils.

The front itself, with no offensive in the offing, offered Billy its usual casual chaos, of random shelling and sniping. Far from being engaged in any heroic acts, Billy found himself handed a trenching shovel, and sent with other men, to dig out a section of trench, which had collapsed under German shelling.

It was on Billy's third day at the front, his second of clearing the trench. As he and his companions picked up their shovels after their smoko, that a German shell hit the line they were working on. Two men were killed instantly, buried alive beneath the falling earth, a third was badly concussed. Billy, himself, lay clear of the land slip, with a mass of shell fragments in the right side of his face.

***

Days later in hospital, waiting to be evacuated back to England, his face a mass of bandages and dressings, Billy waited for his friends to come and visit him. Never in his life had he felt so lonely, or frightened or foolish. His dreams of heroism had turned to ash, and he now faced months in England, before he would be declared fit to return home. As day after day, his waiting proved fruitless, Billy grew increasingly despondent. Until at last, as another visiting hour, produced no friends to cheer him, Billy could not stop himself from weeping. Hiding his face, what was left of it at least in his pillow, as his body shook with sobs.

"Mate, are yer in pain? Do yer want me to call the nurse?" came a voice from the bed beside Billy's.

Billy looked up, seeing a man with his arm in a sling, sitting up in bed with a tin of biscuits on his lap. Billy shook his head and looked at the young man beside him.

"Do yer want one of m' biscuits? M' Sarge's wife makes 'em," said the man, offering the tin.

Billy reached across the space between the beds, and took a biscuit. He sniffed the biscuit and lay it on his bedside table.

"Aren't yer gonna eat it?"

Picking up a note book from the same place, Billy wrote: I can't eat solid things.

Looking again at Billy, the man saw that alongside the mass of bandages, his jaw was wired shut.

"Look on the bright side, we're goin' home." Noticing Billy's puzzled look, the man opened up his bed, revealing a bandaged torso and legs. "Got caught in barbed wire and was pretty cut up. I was a bit worried 'bout m' old man, but the Doc assured me he's fine. M' hand is pretty useless at the moment, though. Nerve damage. It's a good thing I'm a leftie."

Billy stared at this chirpy young man. Bewildered to find such good humour, at the prospect of returning home less than a man.

"So what do you do? I'm a teacher, in a little one teacher school out beyond Tamworth. Farm kids mostly. Got a good excuse to use m' left hand now." Billy could see vast wheat fields, reflected in the man's blue eyes, as he spoke.

Thinking of home, the man could almost feel the hot dry heat, which blew in from the west and the hard frost of winter. He could see his pupils, as they looked up at him, bored or confused by his lessons. Occasionally wrapt, as he told stories and banged out simple tunes on the piano, accompanying the children's singing. He'd miss the piano, but he had seen too much of what could happen to a man here, to see that as too great a sacrifice. Looking at Billy, with his face all mangled, the loss of the use of his hand was nothing; he'd go back to work, find himself a nice girl, get married and have a family. He had been prepared to lose more than a hand for such a future.

Falling silent, the man sighed, returning his attention to the biscuit tin on his lap. Turning to the patient in the bed on his other side, the man reached across his body, offering the tin to a man with no legs.

Billy listened a while to the two men talking, swapping stories and adventures, thoughts of home and future plans. He felt alone, not just in his silence, but also in his understanding of how things were. The stories at home in the papers, did not resemble the stories these men told, of mud and chaos, of becoming lost in the night and sleeping in a shell crater. The stories at home, were all heroic, beating the enemy and showing ones worth as a fighter. From the talk about him, few if any of the wounded men had seen the enemy, let alone fought them. Now he would be going home, and he would have nothing to tell them, for he could not say that he was injured digging out a stretch of trench. They would be expecting stories of bravery, while here amongst the wounded men all he heard were stories of bad luck, poor timing and misadventure. This was not what war was supposed to be.

Billy didn't feel any more a hero, once he arrived in the hospital, in England. Without friends or relatives to visit him, he began to feel depressed. His dark mood, was not helped by the fact that, the men who shared his ward, died with alarming regularity. It was not hard, to imagine, it would be his turn next. So lonely did he become, that he began to write home, long childish letters which omitted to mention the exact nature of his injuries. When the replies came, as he hoped they would, they were filled with excitement and prayers for his future safety and health.

The treatment for his injuries, was itself gruelling, as doctors took skin grafts from different parts of his body, to rebuild a passable right side to his face. His broken jaw had healed, and a plate had been made to replace the missing teeth, but the open raw wound, that had once been a cheek bone and an eye socket, along with a section of skull had to be covered and rebuilt; a process of months. Billy had just had the last of these surgeries, when Jack shuffling along the terrace, sat down beside him and began chatting. Finally he had met a real hero.

Chapter Twenty eight

Jack, had not been relishing the thought, of the ship home. He had travelled on ships now many times, yet every voyage, no matter how short, began the same way, him lying on his bunk, trying to keep from vomiting. Travelling home this time, Jack swore by all the Saints and Angels that this would be the last, the very last time, he stepped onto a boat. It wasn't until Alexandria, that Jack finally felt well enough to join Billy on the deck, and join in the social life of the ship. Waiting in the port of Alexandria, where members of the Light Horse were set to join them, Jack remembered his arrival in Egypt, just two years earlier. How innocent he was then and how confused. Looking now at his younger self, Jack pitied him. He pitied his lost and struggling self, and the fact that he only now felt secure in his skin, once his skin was so horribly mangled. Yet, looking at Billy sitting beside him, who still harboured ideas of heroes and glory, despite losing half his face, he knew that he had at least got something out of his experience.

Though Billy's hero worship, at times frightened him, it was too vast too hungry. He sometimes felt that it were lucky, Billy only had one eye, for were the boy to turn such hunger on him with the strength of two eyes, he should feel himself completely devoured. He certainly didn't feel himself to be, the brave fighter Billy admired. Were he brave, he would dare to look beneath his clothes, and see the work of the surgeon's knife. If he were truly brave, he would have told Dottie what had happened to him, and not allowed the vagaries of medical jargon, to shield him from identifying the doctor's talk, with his own body. He wasn't brave, he was frightened. Frightened, that if he told Dottie the extent of his injuries, she would not be waiting for him when he arrived home. Frightened, that if he allowed himself to understand what the doctors and nurses said, he would have to admit that the past five months were actually real. Frightened, that if he allowed himself to look at what was hidden by his clothes, he would not be able to overcome his own revulsion.

Had he ever been brave, or had he rather been a good sport and a team player, and been rewarded accordingly. He didn't like to think that there was anything special about him, he had been lucky that was all, to say otherwise was to condemn all those good men he had known, and who had fallen, as lesser men for having fallen. Luck was all it was, good or bad luck. Or if one wished to view things from a more classical vantage point, Fate. Each man was weighed against his foe, and one must dip towards the earth. No personal qualities could change one's fate. Was Hector a lesser warrior than Achilles? Both bestrode the battlefield of Troy, laying havoc in their wake, Hector's love of country could no more save him than Achilles anger could condemn him, since it was fate that determined their end. Jack wished he still had his Iliad, to offer to Billy. Though he doubted that his hero worshiping young friend would have managed the ancient Greek.

"Do I look really bad Jack?" asked Billy, as they sat together, beneath blankets looking out to sea.

Jack looked across at Billy, he always sat to the left of his friend, where he could be seen and heard and tried to consider him objectively. Jack saw a face marred, but no longer repulsive, as his first instinct had suggested. From this side, his face looked more or less intact. The right side of Billy's face had been badly damaged, his jaw once broken had been patched together. Metal plates had been used to replace the missing skull, the hair tufted and patchy. The right eye, and much of the socket were missing, delicate pink skin had been grafted over where the eye had been.

Giving that side a rather sunken look, due to the missing cheek bone.

The damaged portion of Billy's face was at least whole, unlike some men he had seen, wounds that would not heal cleanly leaving them with gaps and holes in the place of jaws, noses and eyes. Men whom made one question the kindness of saving them, but who never the less stood, as a testimony to the will to live regardless of the obstacles. In the scheme of things, Billy had come out fairly well. Then again, coming home at all was a feat, while the slaughter in France continued.

"Well, considering what happened to you, they did a good job putting you all back together," said Jack, flashing a smile. "If you focus on the good half, you don't look any worse that you ever looked, ya ugly mug."

Billy smiled, looking out at the white wake of the ship, drifting behind them. He sat for a while, watching the sea and the other men on deck, as they strolled and chatted, were wheeled around by nurses, or like him sat in the sun.

Looking back at Jack, Billy decided that it was time to admit his most shameful secret, the one which had tormented him since he had become aware of his wounds. He envied Jack, who would be going home to a wife and children. A hero returned from the wars. And he was just Silly Billy, who hadn't lasted more than a week at the front, returning, looking like a monster. Billy swallowed hard, feeling the parts of his face that still had feeling flush hot. He could see by the look in Jack's face that he must be blushing.

"Mate, you've gone all red. You're not about to propose are you, cause I'm a married man."

"Do you think girls will like me now? I'm worried they will be frightened of me. I went with a girl in France, before I was hurt, but back home I was never very popular before and now..."

"Billy, you fought for your country and were wounded in the

line of duty. That's a pretty good pick up line," said Jack, laying a hand on Billy's shoulder.

"But I didn't do anything. A shell fell on our trench and I woke up in hospital with half my face gone," said Billy. "I didn't fight. I didn't do anything brave or heroic."

"Mate, make it up, tell a bloody good yarn, about capturing a German trench single handed. Or tell how you saved wounded men from the field, and were hit going after one more. They will lap up stories like that. The papers back home must be full of that sort of rot. The girls in Lithgow aren't going to know any different." Jack wrapped his arm about Billy's shoulder, pulling him into a one handed embrace. "Billy, remember, we are the lucky ones, we get to go home again."

Billy grinned his broken smile looking out across the water.

Homecomings

From the moment, Clytemnestra saw the watchtowers blaze; she knew that her days of freedom were coming to a close. Agamemnon was returning in glory, after his victory over the Trojans. Years of war, which had stripped the land of men and wealth, had ended with the king's return, loaded with treasure, as promised.

For Aegisthus and Clytemnestra, the return of Agamemnon could only mean the revelation of their affair. It would reveal the treachery of both, wife and cousin, something that would cost them their lives. For both knew, that Agamemnon would not be beguiled by the exposition of his wife's breasts, as his soft brother Menelaus had been. Falling to the feet of the faithless Helen, forgiving her all her sins. And so a plan was hatched. Aegisthus and Clytemnestra would travel to meet Agamemnon's victory caravan, before it arrived at Mycenae, along the isolated road on which stood Aegisthus' palace.

Arriving at the palace of his cousin, Agamemnon, attended by his loyal men, surrounded by caravans of slaves and booty, had all the confidence of the lion of Mycenae returning home. The feast, before which he found himself seated, was of a fitting magnificence. His cousin having emptied his store houses for his benefit. Hungry for the comforts of home, after years of campaigning in foreign lands, Agamemnon and his men fell on the feast, with the ferocity of starving animals.

As the evening wore on, the strong wine took effect, and it became clear that one group of men had not taken full part in the feasting. Abstaining from the un-watered wine, alert for a sign from their master, Aegisthus. As the merriment was at its height, the signal came, and the lion of Mycenae, along with all his loyal men found himself slaughtered, like the cattle, he had so recently devoured.

Chapter Twenty nine

The arrival of the hospital ship in Sydney, was considerably different to the departure Jack remembered, back in '14. Then, streamers and crowds packed the port, waving to their brave men, sending them off, with prayers and hopes. This time the arrival was more subdued, though welcoming parties and crowds stood on the dock, the mood was not as jovial, as when Jack had left. The families dotted about in small anxious huddles, as they watched the men disembarking, searching for their own, with faces upon which fear and hope waged war. Each man who walked down the gangplank, gave hope the upper hand, while those confined to stretchers gave fear a minor victory. Alongside the families, were groups of men and women wearing rosettes and ribbons, handing out packages to the men, as they emerged from the ship. Hansoms and motor cars, were lined up, waiting to take the wounded men away from the port. While behind them, discreetly out of direct view, were a fleet of ambulances. Waiting for when the crowds thinned out, to take the traumatised and the badly wounded straight to hospital.

Gazing at the crowd, Jack wondered if it would be possible to avoid the whole circus, and slip away without anyone noticing. It couldn't be that hard to walk quietly away, from the cars and crowds, and catch a tram to Central station. Turning to Billy, Jack was about to suggest such a plan, when he caught sight of the elation that played on Billy's ruined face. All those months in hospital, he had been wishing for something like this, a hero's welcome. Jack knew he could not deny his friend so simple a joy, so despite the fact that he could feel every stranger's eyes upon him, assaulting him with their admiration, he stepped into one of the waiting cars, joining the slow procession to Central station.

Although it was March, it was still hot in Sydney, so passengers waiting for the Lithgow train to leave, milled about the platform rather than boarding the train. Wishing to avoid the crowds, Billy and Jack slipped into a compartment, drawing the blinds that looked out towards the platform. Even with this precaution, as they sat in the compartment, Jack and Billy found themselves the objects of scrutiny. Sitting by the window, so that Billy could hide the damaged portion of his face from curious passengers, they were joined by two women, who had been at the official welcoming ceremony. The women, both wore ribbons pinned to their dresses and hats. The younger woman wore a skirt, falling to a good six inches above her ankle. They looked like mother and daughter. The elder of the two women, as she sat down, after a polite nod in Billy and Jack's direction, took a book from her handbag and began reading immediately. Sinking into her own private world. The younger, of the women, seemed incapable of the absorbed self-containment, her mother displayed. She drummed her fingers on her skirt, in quick rhythmic waves, drawing attention to her lack of gloves. Jack and Billy could see the neat well shaped oval fingernails. Once she had grown bored of this, the young woman began whispering in the ear of the elder, giggling at her own cleverness.

"Deirdre hush. If the poor young bloke has a half a face, I don't think he needs you pointing it out for him," said the older woman, her words brittle in the hot close compartment.

Billy pulled his hat further down over his face and sank into his seat. Jack, watching his mate's reaction, scowled at the two women, until they left the compartment. For the first time it occurred to Jack, as it had occurred to Billy long ago, in the hospital in England, that he had become an object of pity. But far worse than pity, he had also become the object of ridicule. Silly creatures, like that young woman, treating him as if his wounds made him an exhibit in a zoo, or circus, and not a man.

Jack thought of the walking stick, rattling in the luggage rack above their heads. That would have to go as quickly as possible. To have been wounded was one thing, but to have to advertise it to the whole world, was quite another.

Shifting his seat to sit opposite his friend, Jack smiled at Billy.

"Don't let a tart like that get you down, Bill old man. You don't need the good opinion of that kind of girl. She wasn't even wearing gloves and did you see how short her skirt was?"

"They're all gonna be like that, though."

"No they won't." Jack felt the train move off with a lurch. "The good ones won't, the ones who are worth it won't care."

"Like your Dorothy?"

"Yeah, like my Dottie," said Jack.

"So, what are you planning to do with yourself once you get home?" asked Jack, as the train began its long slow climb up the mountains.

"I don't know if Mum's cousin Henry will want me back, I was half way through m' butcher's apprenticeship when I joined up. Perhaps I'll take up one of those settler farms they're offering us, out Bathurst way. I could raise chickens or sheep. I don't think they will be upset about having to look at me."

"That's a bit dramatic Billy. You just need to give people time to get used to you."

Billy looked at Jack, the intact portion of his face looked serene and accepting, as if he had already decided long ago, that his actions and their results, had separated him from other people.

"Won't you get lonely?" Jack looked out the window and down into the valley below, before it disappeared into the Lapstone tunnel, plunging the carriage into darkness.

"I shouldn't think so. I'd rather live by m'self than have people look at me all the time."

Emerging again into daylight, Billy looked at Jack with the air of a martyr. As if his decision had conferred upon him some Grace, Jack was too base to understand. Not that Billy's solemn moods ever lasted long. As once again a childish thought crossed his mind, and he turned with beaming enthusiasm upon Jack, saying, "Mum said that they are planning a reception when I get home. Are your family doing anything special for you?"

"I don't know. I'm sure Dottie will be at the station. I don't think she will have anything special organised. She only knew I was coming this morning."

"If your wife is anything like m' mum, she'll have a whole party organised by the time you get to Katoomba."

Jack sighed, looking out the window, watching the bush rush past. After all this time he was finally home. Resting his head against the window, he let the swaying of the carriage, and the flickering of the afternoon light, lull him until he dozed. Waking when the train stopped at Wentworth falls, to take on water.

***

"Well, this is me Billy" said Jack, standing, watching the town come into view around the bend. "Keep in touch."

"I will Jack." Billy grasped the offered hand, shaking it warmly. "Good bye, you've been a real Mate."

Shouldering his kit, Jack leant heavily on his cane and stepped out of the compartment. Looking at the platform slowly come into view. And with it a crowd of people, like those waiting at the dock hours earlier, waving flags and throwing streamers.

Seeing the party waiting for him, as the train approached the platform Jack blenched, for a moment he considered remaining on the train. He looked back at Billy, his shattered face composed, excited even, as he considered the welcome, which awaited him at home. Jack walked the few steps to the doors and stepped off the train, looking towards the welcoming party, standing by the station entrance. Reminding himself, that those standing waiting were his friends and family, rather than the anonymous crowds who lined the roads in Sydney, Jack forced himself to approach the group.

"Who is all this for?" said Jack, as he approached the crowd. "Is the King coming to visit?"

No sooner had he spoken, than he felt Arch grip him in a bear hug, crushing the breath out of him.

"They told us you were dead, Jack," said Arch, releasing Jack enough to look at him. "Come on, let's get you home, Dottie is waiting for you."

Walking out onto Main Street, Arch loaded Jack into his cab, which had been decorated with ribbons and a large banner, the paint still wet, bearing the words, Welcome Home Jack!

Sitting in the back of the cab for the journey home, a trip that had never warranted a cab ride before. Jack wondered how Billy would cope, with the welcome he would soon receive. Billy had seemed excited that he was to be welcomed home a hero. They had discussed it on the train, Billy explaining, that to be welcomed by friends and family, even if they would stare, was different to being welcomed by strangers. Strangers could only comment and stare, because you were not know to them, and so your feelings didn't matter. Jack couldn't agree, surely friends and family were worse, they would pity you and ask what happened to you, while the attention of strangers was easy to disregard. In the hospital, he had been useful, able to support his new mates, drawing attention away from himself. If only he could do the same thing now. How many times tonight would he be asked what had happened to him. How could he avoid answering the questions he found hard to ask of himself?

Dottie stood at the gate waiting for Jack. She had heard the train pull into the station, and rushed into the yard to greet him, when he arrived. Now she stood, hanging off the front gate, ready to swing it open and welcome her husband home. Gazing down the street towards the station, Dottie watched as Arch's cab drew near, stopping outside the house. Pulling open the gate, Dottie could feel herself trembling, as she waited for Jack, to emerge from the cab and cross the footpath, towards her. She saw a man who moved carefully, supporting himself on a stick in his left hand. His face was thin, his nose pinched and the once plump and youthful curve of his face, had become lean and angular, there were deep lines about his mouth and at the bridge of his nose, giving him the face of a man, ten years his senior. And yet those eyes, those bottle green eyes which lit up with joy, as they turned to look at her, were unmistakeable. Dottie could no longer contain her emotions, with a shriek of joy, she wrapped her arms about Jack's neck.

Wrapped in Dottie's arms, Jack felt himself begin to fall. Grasping on to her to hold himself up, he felt his feet slither on the garden path, as his legs gave way beneath him, leaving him sprawled on the ground. Quickly, before anyone noticed what had happened, Dottie and Arch, lifted Jack back to his feet, and hurried him into the house.

Jack spent the evening, seated in his armchair, in the front room. Edie and Alfie, both much larger than he had imagined they would be, climbed on his lap and inspected the man, to whom the adults gave all the attention. Edith, now a little girl of three, seemed to recognise him as the man on the mantelpiece, who Mummy called Daddy. Trying out the word on him now, she was delighted by the results, as the man smiled and called her a good girl. Alfie having no memory of his father, sat on Jack's knee, regarding him with cool green eyes, relaxing only when his granny picked him up and took him to bed.

Despite his initial misgivings, Jack soon relaxed and enjoyed the party. The relief his friends and relatives showed, at his safe return made Jack feel ashamed he had thought to slink home without telling anyone. Looking across the room at Dottie, as she mingled and laughed, Jack wondered what he had missed in the past two and a half years. Dottie laughed, her head thrown back and her fine white teeth shining in the glare of the electric light, above her head.

"She hasn't laughed like this in months… years," said Arch, standing by Jack's chair. "It's like your wedding day all over again."

"She deserves to be happy," said Jack, looking back at his wife with a sigh.

"So do you Jack."

Jack smiled up at Arch, holding out his empty glass. "Get us another beer, would you Arch."

Chapter Thirty

"That's the last of the guests," said Dottie, returning to the front room, sitting down on the arm of Jack's chair. Reaching up, Jack rubbed Dottie's back, burying his hand in her hair, pulling it free of the combs which held it in place, allowing it to fall down her back. Laying his head against Dottie's back, Jack buried his face in her hair.

"Would you like me to run you a bath?"

"I'm very tired Dottie." Jack's arms wrapped about Dottie's waist.

"We can go straight to bed."

"You can have a bath if you like."

"I think I will," said Dottie, rising from where she sat, disappearing deeper into the house towards the bathroom.

From the front room, Jack could hear the tub being filled. He could see Dottie standing in the steaming room, undressing. He followed each item of clothing, as it made its way to the floor, as if he were watching her. First the fine lacy blouse, then the pink skirt she was wearing, the one that she hadn't fit into since before Alfie had been born. Then, there were the slips. The corset would come off next, he had felt it through her blouse, and it was her pink, fancy one, with the little roses at the front and the red ribbons at the back. If she was wearing that corset, that meant she would be wearing, the pink silk drawers, camisole and pink stockings. These too would be cast off. Finally, she would reach up, searching her hair for any combs or pins, still hiding in amongst the waves. These, she would tug roughly free and place in the dish, on the edge of the sink. Jack looked down at the tortoiseshell combs, he had pulled from Dottie's hair. He heard the taps turned off. Now he knew she would be climbing into the bath, sinking down into the water, she always ran just that little bit too hot, making her skin flush pink. She would dip her head under the water at first, wetting her hair, though she would not wash it. She saved that job for every second morning in the sink. She would stretch out, and luxuriate in the hot water, passing the soap across her body, until she was slippery and shining. A lover of hot baths, Dottie would be out before the water was anything approaching warm, after which he would usually take the bath, which had by now cooled to a more human temperature. Wrapped in towels Dottie would be returning to the bedroom by now to dress for bed. If she had worn the pink corset, then she would put on her lightest, most tissue paper thin, silk night dress. The one he had bought her in Sydney, during their honeymoon. She would be waiting for him to come to bed. She had been waiting over two years for him to come to bed.

Rising from his chair, Jack made his way to the bathroom, which was still steamy from Dottie's visit. The bath looked inviting, but lying in the bath, would mean looking at his damaged body. As he did every time he dressed, Jack fixed his gaze on a spot on the wall. Focusing his attention there, he undressed and washed himself with the water from the bath. Never allowing his gaze to return to his body. Fighting the morbid curiosity to look, with a greater will not to know. He washed his hair and shaved in the foggy mirror by the sink, clearing only enough to see the task at hand. Draping towels about his naked body, Jack drained the bath and switched off the light.

Entering the bedroom, Jack could see Dottie lying on the bed, waiting for him. Keeping his back turned, Jack took a night shirt from the dresser and slipped it on, allowing the towels to fall to the floor.

"Are you going to wear that?"

"You don't mind?"

Dottie moved aside, so that Jack could climb onto the bed. "You just didn't used to, that's all."

"I didn't mess about with any of those girls, overseas."

Dottie kissed Jack. She kissed him hard, holding his head in her hands, so that he could not pull away. He smelled like soap and shaving cream. She felt Jack's hand between her legs, his fingers growing wet they moved. Forcing her to break off her kisses, as she erupted into giggles. Jack kissed her neck and shoulders, his teeth grazing against her skin. Lifting up her night dress, he took her nipples in his mouth first one and then the other, flicking them with his tongue, until she came. Now she felt him push himself into her. She looked up at him, lying between his forearms, as he thrust inside her, his face flooded with pleasure, as he slid back and forward. His lips sought hers out pressing deep kisses onto her mouth. Lifting her feet up from the bed, she wrapped her legs about his waist, linking her feet at the small of his back, feeling his thrusts gain in speed and force. Until pulling against her shoulders, his palms pressing into her collarbones, he came with a great shuddering yell.

"Are you going to let me see?"

Jack opened his eyes and raised his head from the pillow.

"You can't hide it forever."

Dottie rolled over to look at Jack. Reaching out she touched the fabric of his nightshirt. Jack flinched, at her touch. Dottie sat up leaning against the bed head.

"You don't look at it yourself, do you?"

Jack sighed and rolled onto his back. Unbuttoning his nightshirt, Jack allowed Dottie to look at the damage, which had been wrought on his body. The scar, for it was all one, looked like a giant claw had been run from right shoulder to left knee. Bright pink scar tissue ran, in a sunken valley down his body. The edges where it met undamaged flesh, were ragged and uneven. Across the right side of his chest, Dottie could see his ribs where so much muscle had been cut away, there was little to cover the bones beneath. Further down his stomach and leg, the scar, bit deep into the big muscles, which had been patched together, as much as the doctors could, but they no longer joined up. The missing tissue uneven, craterous and ugly.

"They told me you were dead. We had a Requiem mass for you."

Dottie pulled the nightshirt closed and buttoned it, as Jack curled up and laid his head in her lap.

"I'm so sorry, Dottie. I'm so sorry I went away, and ruined everything."

Jack, buried his face in Dottie's lap, and sobbed.

'No more Panels, No more Story.'

Standing by the walls of Carthage, watching as the sculptor and his assistants packed away their tools, Aeneas looked at the carvings that graced the walls. They showed the story of the war in Troy. Here Paris stole away the queen of Sparta. There Achilles sulked in his tent, while the Greeks fought at Troy. Hector now, is dragged behind the chariot, before the walls of Troy. Ending with the sack of Troy, where he saw himself, carrying his father and leading his son from the burning city.

"Why are there no more panels left?" asked Aeneas.

"The story is ended, the war is over," said the sculptor.

"But my story is not finished yet."

"It mightn't be, but the war is."

"But what happens now is a direct result of the war."

"Not my problem. No more panels, no more story. What happens to you now is private life. History isn't interested in that. It is only interested in grand narratives, heroes and myths."

"But the war goes on, in my head, every day."

"People don't want to want to hear about your headaches, or pains, or sleepless nights. Heroes die in battle, or disappear into civilian life. They want to forget. It's easier that way."

"You say my wounds are inconvenient?"

"You were wounded, you came home. That is your place in history."

"If I die of my wounds years later?"

"Men who die on the field, fit into myths easier."

"That's not fair."

"That's history," said the sculptor with a shrug, picking up his bag of tools.

Aeneas watched the sculptor walk away.

Chapter Thirty one

Dottie had taken his suit out of the trunk, and hung it up to air over the weekend, but it still smelt of mothballs. When Hector Johnson had offered him his old job back, at his welcome home party, Jack had accepted. Here was a chance to return to the life he had left. Now standing at the foot of the stairs to Hector Johnson's office, Jack realised just how far from his reach, his old life was. The stairs reared up before him, an insurmountable obstacle. The three garden steps, from the footpath to the garden path, and the four steps onto the veranda, had been difficult enough to manage. Seven steps with a flat path between them, had already almost beaten him, numerous times over the weekend. The steps leading to church, had caused him to falter, and had it not been for his brother's arm supporting him, he would have slipped down them, as they left Mass the day before. If five steps could defeat him, how was he to manage the two dozen steep stairs, to Hector Johnson's office?

Jack looked at the stairs, his leg ached already from the walk into town. He shrank inside his too big suit. He could feel sweat, prickling in his armpits, and the back of his neck. Placing his good leg on the first step, Jack hauled himself up, his injured leg joining his right. Slowly, painfully slowly, Jack climbed to the flat turning point of the staircase. Pausing to rest his aching leg, Jack looked at the next rise of stairs. Twelve more steps, and he would be at the office door. Mustering his strength, Jack hauled himself up the remaining steps to the office door. Crossing the office, Jack sank down into his chair. As he sat, catching his breath and massaging his aching leg. Jack heard Hector Johnson race up the stairs, taking two at a time, appearing at the door ready for his day at the office.

The morning proceeded with the same, monotonous torpor as if he had never left. Though Jack found that his job was not, as he had remembered it. Now that his leg ached with every step, and his arm trembled, unable to carry any great weight. The dull light tasks, he had in the past, performed unthinkingly, his youthful, animal strength, frustrated by his passive job, were over the course of the morning, becoming ever more difficult. It didn't help, that clients looked at him and his walking stick, with expressions of pity. The sighing and commiserations, that followed him as he closed the office door behind them, bit into his pride far deeper, than his inability to perform simple tasks. Just a few months earlier, he had been a twice promoted, experienced soldier, placed in charge of young recruits, the three stripes on his arm, a symbol of not just admiration, but respect. Now he was back in the job he had held since he was sixteen, and the clients looked at him, as a feeble creature. Despite the Returned Service man's badge that he wore on his lapel. He was no longer the brave young warrior who called for reinforcements from the posters. The warrior with fine strong limbs and manly self-sufficiency. It was as if he had aged fifty years, suddenly becoming an old man, who had to be helped from his chair.

***

Pouring out a bucket of water over the tiled step of the Harp and Fiddle, cleaning up after the six o'clock swill, Sid Murray watched, as Arch crossed the street and approached the pub.

"Mate, sorry to drag you over here." Sid put the bucket down on the step.

Arch, stepped gingerly over the stream of water and vomit, seeping into the sand of the foot path, to stand by Sid, on the newly sluiced steps. "What's the matter?"

"Your brother is in the snug. I don't wanna call the cops on him, but I've gotta lock up."

"No worries."

Sid led Arch, into the pub, directing his attention to the morose figure, sitting in the back of the bar.

"How long has he been here?"

"Since lunch time." Sid went back to putting up chairs. "He's pretty drunk."

Stepping deeper into the bar, becoming enveloped in the smell of spilt beer and vomit. Arch could see his brother's features in the dim light, of the few lamps that were still lit. Sitting beneath one of the lamps, its light giving his face a jaundiced look, Jack looked up, from the empty beer glass before him. His eyes were heavy and unfocused, as he rested his head, on the heel of his right hand. Close now, Arch could see that the left side of Jack's face, was bruised and swollen.

"Since when did the pubs close at six?"

"A halfway through last year, Jack. You missed a few things while you were away," said Arch, pulling out a chair and sitting opposite his brother.

"Fucking wowsers! Go to war and they won't let a man have a drink." Jack lifted his glass to his lips. Discovering it empty, he held up his glass and called across the bar. "Beer!"

"I think you've had enough already" Arch gently took the glass from Jack's hand, placing it on the table behind him. "Sid says you've been here since lunch."

"So?" Jack steadied his unfocused eyes on Arch, in a silent drunken challenge.

"Wasn't today your first day back at work?"

"I'm not going back there again." Jack allowed his gaze to wander about the bar, throwing his head back and sighing. Resting his head again on his hand, he whispered, "Fucking stairs."

"Did something happen at work?" Arch knew, trying to talk

to Jack in this state was futile, but attempting to drag him out fighting and shouting was going to be more futile, than listening to his brother's drunken ramblings.

"I can't do it. I can't even carry, a bloody tray across a room, without dropping it. They look at me. They look at me like some cripple. Like I'm some fucking nothing."

"Jack, have you been fighting."

"Yes, I've been fighting. I fought in Turkey and in France, what did they do?"

"I mean today. What happened to your face?" Arch gestured at the angry looking bruises, running down the left side of Jack's face.

"I fell. I'm not going back. I fell down the stairs, and people looked at me as if I was nothing. I'm not going back. I need another drink."

"You need to go home," said Arch. "Sid needs to close up, and he doesn't want to call the cops."

"I'm not going back to work," said Jack, as he rose from his seat, leaning on the table and his cane for support.

As Jack stepped out from behind the table, Arch could see where Jack's trousers had torn, as he fell. His knees were grazed, and his black trousers glistened with dried blood.

Taking his cane in his left hand, Jack grabbed his brother by the shoulder, drawing him close, confiding in a conspiratorial whisper, "It wasn't like they said. It's not an adventure. They try to kill you."

Chapter Thirty two

It was a quarter to eleven and Jack still hadn't got up. Dottie had thought to allow him to sleep, but after a week of Jack sleeping up to thirteen hours a day, she knew that something was wrong. Rather than feel better for his sleep, Jack would rise irritable and tired, drifting about the house in his pyjamas. The bruises on his face had almost faded now, and Hector Johnson had asked repeatedly, when Jack would be back, but Jack had so far, refused to return to work.

Standing in the doorway to their bedroom, Dottie looked into the darkened room, at her husband in the bed.

"Jack, are you getting up, Love."

Jack lay curled into a foetal position, under the blankets. Dottie could tell, from the tense stillness of his body, that he was not asleep. Entering the darkened room, she waited for Jack to pull the blankets, back from his face. When at last he did, Jack looked at her, with blank, uncomprehending eyes. Sitting on the bed, Dottie ran her hand across her husband's back.

"Jack, I'm going to get the doctor. You're not well, Love."

Jack groaned, rubbing his face with his hand, clutching the bed clothes about his neck. "I'm tired, that's all. I don't need the doctor."

"Do you want something to eat? I can make you some soup, if you don't feel up to much," said Dottie, casting round for something substantial to cling to, some practical help, to occupy her. "You forget to eat too much, I don't think you ate anything yesterday and only toast the day before."

Jack looked at Dottie. She wasn't like the jolly nurses at the hospital. She looked at him and grew frightened. Her voice trembled on the edge of tears, and her face wore a mask of worry, all furrowed brows and compressed lips. It was the face of a worried mother, who has sat up all night with a sick child. Is that what he looked like then: an ailing child. Surely, he wasn't so frightening; he was just tired. So tired.

"Make me some soup then. I'll get up when it's ready."

Jack watched Dottie leave, following her foot steps down the hall, to the kitchen. Pulling the covers back up over his head, Jack lay still in the dark. He could feel the pillow case bunched up beneath is cheek, it was soft and comforting, the fine texture of the sheets had become thin and delicate from years of washing. He felt swaddled in home, and yet it would not hold him. He could not stay here, in this safe warm place, he had longed for. Closing his eyes, he saw again the mud and blood. Again, he felt the shock, which had lifted him off his feet, depositing him on the ground, broken and bloodied. He saw men fall, and never get up again, through the sights of his rifle. He was again, sitting in a hole, all night long, shooting at men, as they moved under cover of darkness. Again, he saw the faces of dead Turks, washed from no man's land into the trenches on top of him, in the torrential autumn storms. He heard men screaming, their voices those of beasts, as they struggled to safety across the dirt. Again, racing along the beach in the dark, as bullets sparked off the stones and the roar of the big guns shook the air. Again, he was face to face with the enemy, a man like himself, hesitating and frightened, knowing that one of them, must not survive this encounter. He had willed the Turk to turn away and run, to save himself, for an instant he had implored him to run. Seeing that he would not, that this man would stand his ground, Jack had done what he had been trained to do.

And people looked on him with pity. That was the worst part. They looked on him, as if he were a stray dog, a creature to pet and fawn over. It was worse than being called a hero. It was worse, than listening to them discussing the war, as it was shown in the papers. A matter of feet taken and enemies killed, all clean and precise, as it must seem in the reports that arrived, on the commanders desks. Nothing mentioned of the sounds, the smells and the sights, of the dead and dying. Nothing about, the fear that drives you on, and makes you act without thinking. Makes you do things that you wish you hadn't. They talked, as if it were a matter of chasing the enemy away, like in a children's game, not at all a case of turning living men, into corpses. Pity, saw neither the horrible things he had done, nor the horrible way it made him feel. Staying in bed, at least spared him that.

"Jack, lunch is ready," said Dottie, standing at the door.

Jack pulled back the bed clothes and sat up. Reaching down, he searched for his slippers under the bed, pushing his feet carelessly into them. Standing, he picked up his dressing gown, from the foot of the bed, wrapping it tightly around himself. Catching sight of himself, in the dressing table mirror, it occurred to him that he could do with a bath. Nearly a week's growth of beard, covered his face, and his hair felt greasy and mattered, sticking up from his head at different angles. The purple bruises, along the side of his face had faded to a greenish yellow, the pain had gone from them days ago, but they still graced his face, reminding him of his own infirmity. Padding out to the kitchen, Jack sat down in his usual place at the head of the table, before the bowl of soup Dottie had prepared for him.

Picking up the wedge of bread by his bowl, Jack tore off chunks and dipped them into his soup, swallowing them down one after another. He was about to lift the bowl to his lips, and drink off the warm liquid, when he caught sight of Dottie watching him. Placing the bowl back on the table, he saw that he was at home in his kitchen, not sitting in a trench, eating food out of a mess tin. Bewildered, he looked back at Dottie, sitting to his right, the spoon in her hand hovering just above her soup. On the other side of the table, sat two little children, his little children, spooning soup from their bowls, as if to show him how it were done.

"Isn't Daddy a naughty boy, telling us he wasn't hungry? Alfie, Edie you better eat up or Daddy bear will eat up your lunch too," said Dottie, speaking to the children, as she reached across the tablecloth and squeezed Jack's hand, suddenly lying idle beside his bowl.

"I thought..."

"It doesn't matter Love, its only soup. It's only us, you don't have to be embarrassed." Dottie lifted the hand she held, and kissed it. Releasing it, as she continued her meal. Watching not Jack but the children, as they wiped out their bowls with their bread.

"Edie, Alfie, now that you're done, you can go and play."

Jack watched, as the two children slithered from their seats and ran from the kitchen, eager to return to their games, which had been interrupted by lunch. Picking up his spoon, Jack resumed his lunch; how could he have mistaken Dottie's cooking, for the swill he had been eating for over two years. Drinking his soup, he looked across at his wife, watching, as her face relaxed.

"Would you like me to run you a bath? I'll sit with you and talk with you if you like."

Jack placed his spoon in his empty bowl, pushing the bowl away from himself. He held his head in his hands. "I don't like to look Dottie."

Rising from her seat, Dottie crouched beside Jack, running her hand over his head and shoulders. "You don't have to look Jack, I'll look for you."

"I don't want you to see either," said Jack, turning to look at Dottie, his green eyes glittering with tears. "I don't want pity."

"I know you think this is the worst thing that can happen, you look at yourself and your scars, and see what was lost. I spent months thinking you were dead. I look at you, and see what I gained. Jack I love you, it would be a pretty poor love, if a few scars could change that."

"I was somebody Dottie, people looked up to me."

Holding Jack's face in her hands, Dottie brushed aside the tears that began making tracks, down the hard angular plains of his face.

"You are John Michael Kelly, my husband, the father of my two children. Beloved, brother and nephew. You are so loved. When you were dead, everyone we knew, everyone your father knew, everyone who had ever had any contact with you, sent messages of sympathy, or flowers, or came to your memorial services. If people pity you your wounds, it is only because they love you Jack."

"I can't go back to work. I don't want to spend the rest of my life, sitting home on a pension."

"We'll find you a new job, something that will make you feel needed again. You know, you are the only one, who doubts your value."

Jack smiled, wrapping his arms tightly about Dottie, pressing his face into her body, inhaling the smell of her freshly laundered dress and warm animal smell, of her beneath.

"I'll have that bath, if I can I keep my eyes closed."

"Whatever makes you happy."

Chapter Thirty three

It had taken all of Dottie's persuasive powers, and a lot of cajoling from Arch. But between the two of them, they had managed to get Jack washed, dressed and out of the house, on Saturday afternoon. Thus, he found himself perched on a stool, drinking a beer in the Billiards hall, watching Arch and his cab drivers, Dan and Smithy, playing.

"Mister Jack, you are quite welcome to play," said Smithy, as he pushed himself off the wall he leant against, to take his turn playing Dan.

Jack shook his head, his shaggy hair, that he had not yet bothered to have cut, since leaving hospital, fell into his eyes and he pushed it back with his free hand. Smithy could see how thin, the hand that raked back the thick ginger hair looked. He saw how a tremor gripped the other hand, making the amber liquid, in the glass it held, shimmer, like the disturbed surface of a pond.

"I bet you're glad to be home, Mister Jack," said Smithy, swallowing down the pity that rose in him. That Mister Arch had told both him and Dan, to hide when they saw Jack. Not that such an instruction was easy, poor Mister Jack looked so frail and ill. One only had to stand near him to see how the walk from his house, left him panting and drenched in sweat. He blamed the sultriness of the March afternoon, coming as he had from an English winter, but Smithy who was well acquainted with illness, could see it was more. How else, was one to explain the terrible agitated expression in his eyes, staring out of his pale face, or the sudden fits of trembling that shook him, even in the hot billiard hall.

"Best thing in the world." Jack drained his glass, placing it on the counter.

"Do you want another?"

Turning to look at the bar, Jack saw Arch approaching with a pair of schooners. Fishing in his pocket, Jack pulled out a ten shilling note, and held it out to Smithy. "Why don't you nip down the chippie, and bring us back some chips."

Grasping the money, Smithy smiled, pleased that he could offer some small service, to Mister Jack. Relieved as well, that he had not caused offence, as he struggled to contain his pity for the man, not much older than himself in years, but ages older in experience.

"I sent Smithy off for chips," said Jack, as Arch perched on a stool, handing him a fresh beer.

"He's a good bloke, Smithy."

Rather than reply, Jack plunged straight into his fresh beer, drinking down silence, in long deep swallows.

"Steady on mate, give a bloke a chance to catch up."

Placing his now half empty glass, on the counter, Jack looked at Arch.

"So, what was so important that you had to get me out, to watch you play billiards, for half an hour?"

"I thought you'd enjoy the change of scene. I've hardly seen you since you've been back, you're usually in bed before dinner."

Jack frowned, flashing Arch an irritated look. "I've not been feeling well."

"It wasn't a criticism, just an observation. I've missed you."

Arch picked up his glass, and swallowed deeply of the dark liquid. Wiping the froth from his moustache, he resolved to try again.

"Dot tells me, you want to find a new job."

Jack ran the nail of his index finger, absentmindedly, through the spilt foam on the counter. Vaguely, he wondered how long Smithy would be, with his chips. That he hadn't eaten all day, despite Dottie's best efforts to persuade him, and now the beer he had drunk, was making his head swim. At times like this, he would usually have a smoke, but after the months in hospital, he had found he had lost the taste for cigarettes. Even if he hadn't, the smell of smoke that permeated the room, was enough to drag him back to the trenches, before a push. As men smoked, what they hoped would not be, their last cigarette. Picking up his glass, Jack washed the memory away, in a mouthful of beer.

"Anyway that got me thinking. I'm moving m' offices out of m' cottage and into town. Now usually, I have Dan or Smithy sit in m' office and man the phone, but they'd both much rather be driving the cabs. So, I'd be looking for someone to run the office, answer the phone, and do the books, an easy job for a clever bloke."

Arch raised his glass to his mouth and drank, watching Jack's expression, as he considered his words.

"I'd have to have new signage, with a new office. To my way of thinking, the man who runs the office should be just as invested in the business, as I am, driving the best cab. That way, the best of the business is on show, for all to see. When Dad was alive, it was Kelly and Son Cabs, at the moment it has gone back to its original name of Kelly's Cabs, but I think it lacks something, the familial quality; the customers like that."

Jack looked at Arch, growing suddenly bored by his brother's long winded, round about, job offer. Looking away, he saw Smithy entering the hall, with a newspaper parcel, which the young cabbie quickly deposited on the counter, along with a handful of coins. Tearing open the paper, Jack began shovelling hot, crisp, fried potato into his mouth, luxuriating in the pure physical pleasure, of eating.

"I was thinking, Kelly Bros Cabs, might make a good name," said Arch, pressing on, with his interrupted train of thought. "What do you think Jack?"

Jack looked up from his meal, sucking his greasy, salty fingers, as he considered his brother's words.

"Two things. Firstly, I'll do the books and run the office, but I'm not answering the phone, get a girl in to do that. Secondly." Jack paused, searching Arch's face for the understanding of what had been obvious to Smithy. After the past week, he could see that Dottie, was beginning to understand what had become clear to him. Now that he was away from the safe cocoon of the hospital, and the unreality allowed for by the doctor's incomprehensible words. But Arch's face, with the dopy smile that had become almost a permanent fixture, said nothing more than it had said all week. That a miracle had occurred and he had no wish to question or examine it too closely, lest it be taken from him.

"Secondly?"

"Do I really have to say it? You might want someone whose health is more, reliable, than mine is at the moment."

Arch smiled, reached across the counter, pulled a chip from the steaming package, slipping it into his mouth. "I'm not opening for a couple of weeks yet, you should be back on your feet by then."

Chapter Thirty four

Lying awake had become uncomfortable. Staring into the darkness, Jack had lain thinking, his thoughts taking on no settled form. Preferring instead to ambush him, with a general anxiety about himself and his future. As the clock in the front room, struck five, Jack climbed out of bed. Donning his dressing gown and slippers, he shuffled out of the bedroom, and went to sit on the back veranda. Outside, the air was cool and fresh, though the day, like those before it, was going to be a warm one. Warm days were always horrible up on the line, when the smell of no-man's land rose up and drifted, in great gusts, into the trenches. Checking his thoughts, Jack steadied his mind, bringing it back to his present. He watched, as the growing light, touched first the top of the tallest eucalypts, their leathery leaves, standing out darkly, against the lightening sky. He could hear the chooks, down the back of the yard, begin to rouse themselves, their clucking and gabbling, reaching him across the lightening yard. He could smell wood smoke, as neighbours began lighting their stoves, putting on the kettle, for the first cup of tea. Now he could hear Dottie moving about the kitchen behind him, not noticing him, as she concentrated on lighting the fire.

Jack had no great wish to be noticed, this morning. For this was the morning, he was due to start working, in Arch's new office. In the bedroom, his suits hung newly cleaned and altered to fit his new, slighter frame, ready for his new job. How long he would last in that new job, was anyone's guess. He knew that for Arch's sake, he would try. Much as he was loathed, to sit at home on the pension the Repatriation Department had assessed him, as qualifying for. As the letter he had hidden under a pile of papers, almost as soon as it arrived, had informed him on Friday. Sitting at home on a pension, was infinitely better than the alternative. How close that alternative had come, too. Young Billy may see himself a failure, as a wounded man rather than a dead hero, resenting his survival, or at least the mode of his wounding. Jack could no more, now understand Billy's sentiments, than he could when he first heard them. Sitting in the growing light, on the veranda of his comfortable home, within which were sheltered his lovely children, and his clever, beautiful Dottie, all he could feel was gratitude. Not just that he had come back to them, but that they were still waiting for him, once he had returned. He owed it to them, to at least try this new job. He owed Arch too, for it must have cost him a fantastic amount, to consider sharing the business with him.

Down the end of the back yard, the chickens had begun to fret and flap, signalling that they wished to be allowed out of their house, into the run. Picking up his cane, Jack walked down to the chook pen and opened up the chicken house. As the chooks barrelled out, to scratch and search in the early morning sun, Jack entered the chicken house. In the gloom, where the smell of warm straw mingled with the earthy smells of the animals, Jack searched for eggs, his hand could still feel the warmth of the hens, in the straw of the laying boxes.

Suddenly, for the second time that morning, he was at the front, France this time and a newly abandoned farm house. He, and his men, were in a barn, sheltering until they could move more freely, under cover of darkness. They had lost their officer and he had taken charge, in his place. Here, in the scattered straw, what chickens remained had made their nests, all over the barn. They had scrabbled about, searching for the eggs and had eaten them raw, so great was their hunger. He had written a letter to Dottie, as he waited in the barn, his composure and steadiness, had calmed the men. He talked about the chickens, as if he had visited the farm, under less trying circumstances, pushing reality from himself for a few minutes. It was the last letter he had written to Dottie, before being wounded. That night, when he had got himself and his men back to the trenches, his captain said he would recommend him, for officer training. The next day he was wounded.

Jack stepped quickly out, into the chook run, the light and the familiar sights, allowing him to push the memories back where they belonged: into the darkness. Opening the door to the chook run, he stepped out onto the lawn. Looking up at the sky, he could see that the morning light had developed enough, to turn the sky blue, in the time he had stood in the chicken coop. The leaves of the eucalypts, were now reflecting silver, as they fluttered in the morning breeze. Like a school of small fish he had seen once, swimming before a dolphin. The magpies began calling, and kookaburras laughed, one following the other, until the gully behind the house, rang with their cheerful voices. The smell of eucalyptus smoke, so distinct and evocative, rose from the chimney, it had been one of the smells he had missed the most, while overseas. No smoke had smelt quite right, while he had been away. Just as the forests of England and France, had seemed as strange and alien to his eyes, as his beloved bush must have seemed to those first English men, who arrived in Sydney all those years ago. If he kept his mind on what was before his eyes, what was familiar and lovely to him, then perhaps, he could keep the memories that disturbed his sleep, and ambushed him when he was least prepared for them, where they belonged. For he felt certain, it was the idleness of the past few weeks, which allowed such disordered thoughts, to rise to the surface. Work would do him good, he felt sure of that, just as sure, as he was, that he did not wish to share his thoughts with Dottie. For Dottie had seen his distress, and had pressed him to know, what had drawn the colour from his face, and made him tremble, as if convulsed by a violent shock. But he would not say, not one word would he breathe, of that ugliness, to his dear Dottie. He would not contaminate her innocent, pure mind, with the mud and blood that spattered his own.

Looking towards the kitchen, Jack could hear the kettle whistling on the hob. He would go to work today, and tomorrow, and the day after that. Rebuilding his disturbed and splintered life, as his broken and fractured body, had been stitched and patched, leaving him scarred, but grateful.

Chapter Thirty five

Charlotte Joyce waited, as her daughter poured tea, her dark eyes flicking about the room, taking in all the changes, since her last visit. Jack's desk, had again become a site of activity, with papers and pens, strewn across its long neglected surface. The decanter of whisky on the sideboard, which had been newly filled last time she visited, was now nearly empty, only the slenderest dregs of amber could be seen at the bottom. Dottie too looked changed, though exactly how eluded Charlotte, as she returned her gaze to her daughter, and the cup of tea she offered.

"So Mum, what has been happening in the wide world this week?"

"You have heard about the California murder, I assume."

Dottie poured her own tea, and settled herself back into her chair. "A little, though I didn't know it was a murder."

"Oh, yes he died this morning. It looks like it will be a big trial. Killed for a diamond ring. Though what a man is doing wearing a diamond ring, I don't know. Was one for the ladies, so they say."

"Who is they, Mum?"

Charlotte demurred, gazing about the room with an airy expression, as if Dottie's question were not part of their agreed formula for these conversations, allowing her to show off her connections, without appearing to boast.

"Everyone, or more specifically, my cook's sister, who works as a maid up at The California. This really is good tea, where did you get it?"

"Jack brought it back with him. Bought nearly ten pounds of the stuff, when the hospital ship stopped off in Ceylon. So, tell me then, what happened?"

"Well, the way I heard it, George King, the murdered man, was innocently staying at the hotel, as he often did when he passed through. He was a regular and all the girls who worked there, knew him to be a charmer who spread tips about quite liberally. He was a well-liked man, up there. This trip had been no different to any other, except that over dinner, one of the other guests would not stop looking at Mister King. He was one of a set, of identical twins."

"This is the Shaw brothers, right?"

"Yes, apparently he just could not keep his eyes off this ring. I've heard he was a little bit simple. The other brother seemed normal, and took no notice of rings, but spent his time chatting, with a group of girls at the next table. Though that could have been a ruse to deflect suspicion.

"When dinner finished, the patrons went their separate ways. The whole hotel, including one of the Shaw brothers, went to bed with no presentiment of what would in a few short hours, befall them.

"In the middle of the night, screams woke everyone in that wing of the hotel, Keith Shaw, the slow one, had stolen into King's room, and had beaten him repeatedly about the head with a hammer. Frightful it was. He stole the ring and some money, but he did nothing to conceal his crime, and went back to his room afterwards. His bed was smeared with blood. Later that morning, he went out for a drive along the cliffs, said it would be his last chance to see them. I hear his brother is quite distressed. Though they sang to each other, like magpies, in the police cells."

"They'll hang the brother for sure," said Dottie. "I mean a murder like that, no provocation."

Charlotte lifted her tea from the tea-table and sipped it, holding the warm liquid a moment longer in her mouth, than usual. One of her molars was paining her, and as usual, she was delaying going to the dentist. Her fear of the dentist currently outweighing the pain in her mouth.

"That's what I think."

Looking at her mother, Dottie placed her cup on the table, and made to rise from her chair "Do you want some cloves to chew?"

"Why would I want that?"

"Because you have a crook tooth. I've got a jar in the pantry, it will only take a minute."

Charlotte placed a hand on Dottie's arm, forcing her back to her seat.

"I'm fine, I've been chewing the dammed things all morning. Don't fuss." Brightening Charlotte, refilled her cup, as Dottie settled back into her seat. "Did I tell you, Ferd is coming home?"

"No, when did that happen?"

"He just sent word. He fell down a flight of stairs, dislocated his collar bone and lost all the forward movement in his arm. So he is coming home."

"That is excellent news, though poor Ferd falling down the stairs. Jack could tell you how much that hurts."

"So, how is Jack settling into life again? Does he like his new job?"

"I think he finds it boring, he's usually finished by lunchtime, and comes home. His old job was a lot more challenging. But with the headaches and the pain he is in, he knows that he can't go back to something more difficult. He has good days and bad days, we never know which it will be."

"Was he very badly wounded?"

"All down his front is just a mess of scars. And then he has smaller, neater ones on his back, from where they took skin grafts. He can't bear to look at it. I want to weep when I see him, but that would upset him. Sometimes, I wake up in the night to the sound of him weeping, sometimes he's asleep, other times it's the pain that has woken him and he can't move for it, the poor dear."

Charlotte reached across, and lay her hand on Dottie's knee, blinking back the tears she could feel, prickling her eyes. Glancing at the empty decanter, she remembered her intention to have words with Dottie about Jack's drinking, in light of this new revelation however, such words could sound callous.

"I had no idea he was in such poor shape, he doesn't let on at all when we see him in town, or in church."

"He's proud and doesn't want to be pitied. It costs him though, when he gets home, he is so exhausted. He won't even tell his brother how poorly he is. Not that Arch is of a mind to hear such things."

"How have the children taken to him? Alfie seemed a bit hesitant at first."

"They've been really good with him. They talk to him and he tells them stories. They are so good when he is having a bad day, very quiet and careful not to disturb him. Alfie saw Jack crying in bed one day, and he gave him his teddy bear to try and cheer…"

Dottie broke off her words, as she heard a shuffling sound on the garden path, followed by slow, heavy tread on the veranda, and the scrape and creak of the front door opening.

"You're home early, Love," said Dottie, seeing Jack appear in the doorway. His face was pale and a frown played about his brow, though his mood was tranquil, a polite smile playing on his lips, as he looked at the two women.

"There wasn't much to do." Jack entered the room and placed his brief case on the floor, by his desk.

"Do you want some tea?"

Picking up the decanter, Jack poured the dregs into a glass, and sat down in his arm chair. "Later, I think I'll drink this and have a lie down before lunch."

"Mum was just telling me about Dad's plans to go out shooting, next weekend."

"Was I?"

"Yes, you were saying how much Dad was looking forward to Jack coming along."

"Yes I was," said Charlotte, trying to keep the confusion from her voice. Usually the leader in such subterfuges, she struggled to adlib a convincing second fiddle. "You know Harold is always most happy to have you join them."

"Thank you for the offer Mrs Joyce, but if it's all the same, I've rather had my fill of shooting." Jack swallowed the liquid in his glass. Rising from his seat, he moved back to his desk, opening his briefcase, he pulled out a fresh bottle of whisky. The women watched in silence, as Jack tore the foil from the lid, pouring himself a larger glass, shuffling back to his chair, and sitting heavily in it. "In fact, I was going to ask Mr Joyce, if he might take my shotguns and keep them with his. I don't really want them in the house anymore."

Rising from her seat, Dottie, busied herself transferring the whisky into the crystal decanter. Gathering up the torn foil, balling it into a hard shining pellet, as she moved back to her chair.

Charlotte, watching her daughter's nervous fidgeting, reached across and lay a hand on her daughter's wrist. Reassuring her, that the misstep with the shooting, was neither foreseeable, nor unrecoverable. Turning her honey eyes on Jack, she could see his head resting on his hand, and his eyes closed against the pain. "Of course. Harold is picking me up in a few minutes. He can take them today if you like."

"Thank you. Mr Joyce and I will have to think of something else to take an interest in together." Rising from his chair, Jack made to leave the room, turning back at the door, as a sudden thought struck him. "Dottie, you'll show your Dad where the guns are, won't you. The key is in my desk."

"Do you want anything to help you sleep?"

"I'll be right, let me know when lunch is ready."

Dottie listened, as Jack shuffled across the hall, closing the bedroom door behind him.

"Why did I mention shooting?" Dottie sank down into her chair, and buried her face in her hands.

Rising from her seat, crouching by Dottie's chair. Charlotte gently stroked her daughter's back. It made her think of when Dottie was a little girl, and would come to her, crying over some tiny tragedy or other, and she would gather her little girl up and rub her back. Reminding her that nothing was so hopeless, when there was someone to share it with.

"I don't think you upset him, Darling. He looked relieved that you reminded him about the guns."

"I'm just so worried that something will upset him, and he'll be back in bed for a week at a time. His health is so delicate." Dottie sniffed and blew her nose in her handkerchief.

"Have you been to see Doctor Allen?"

"He says there isn't much he can do. The doctors in England, proscribed heavy pain medicines for him, they have to be injected. So, Doctor Allen is teaching me how to give him those. He was ill for months after he was wounded, and you can't tell him this, but from what his records show, he has years rather than decades left."

"I'm so sorry Dottie." Charlotte sat back on her heels, clasping her well-manicured hands together, pressing them to her lips.

"He doesn't like to talk about the war. I don't want to press him, because he'd tell me if I needed to know. He has always been honest with me, even if it takes time."

It had taken over two years, but the other night, lying in the dark safety of their bed, he had confessed the fears that made him join up in the first place. Confessed his fear of becoming trapped again in this house, his fear of their future, and finding a new position. How he had hoped to improve his prospects, by joining up. He said he knew now that his fears were foolish. Bred out of his chaotic childhood, and the horrible things his father told him. Even in the dark, as he spoke in that warm rich voice that she so loved, Dottie could hear a new fear had crept in to his voice, replacing the old one: that he would fail her. That his health would fail completely, and that she and the children would be left without support. That he would leave her again, forcing her to grieve for him a second time.

"It's early days yet, I'm sure Jack will improve."

"Hmmm, he wants to be here, he fought for so long to be here. I can't imagine he'd give up." Dottie wiped her face, and rose from her chair. "Dad will be here any minute, I'd better get those guns out for him."

Listening to the sound of a motor car, pull up in the road outside, Charlotte raised herself, from her squatting position, smoothing out her crumpled dress. If Jack's return, was the miracle everyone said it was, then its character was not, what she imagined divine events to be. Then again, the gospels were silent on the second life, of Lazarus and his sisters.

Chapter Thirty six

Jack sat at the bar of the Harp and Fiddle, waiting for Billy's train to come in. It had been months since he had last seen Billy, as he had waved goodbye from the train, on the way to his own welcome home party. When Billy's letter arrived, suggesting a visit, Jack had welcomed it with some hesitation. Though he was curious, to find out what had become of his young friend, he found himself reluctant, to again endure the admiration and the moral certainty, that Billy seemed to embody.

Watching the door, Jack saw the local Push gather about, as they did every afternoon, begging beers from patrons and fighting drunks, for loose change. He didn't particularly like sitting in the pub, so close to closing time. The noise and chaos of the last couple of drinking hours, made him feel unsteady. Outside however, the sky threatened low and dark, promising either rain or snow. The idea of sitting at the station to wait, where the cold would sink into him, and make him ache, had not appealed either, so in the Pub he sat. The Lithgow train, had pulled in a few minutes ago, Jack watched the men entering the pub, for any sight of his friend.

Dressed in a new, but cheap suit, his hat worn low over the damaged side of his face, giving him a rakish air, Billy entered the pub, and looked about. Seeing Jack, for the first time in civilian attire, Billy was shocked. Jack wore a stylish and well cut suit, his hair, though worn on the longer side, was combed and dressed in a pre-war style. Across the table, lay an overcoat with a thick fur collar. Even Jack's cane had changed, a silver headed stick now rested against his chair, replacing the bare, but serviceable one from the hospital. Billy nodded in Jack's direction, and turned towards the bar. Turning towards Jack, beer in hand, Billy made his way across the crowded room to where he was sitting.

"It looks like it's gonna snow out there." Billy placed his beer on the table, and removed his hat and coat. "It started snowing back home, as I left, probably just a flurry, the big stuff will come tonight."

"So, how's life treating you?"

"Can't complain. Turns out, Cousin Henry quite fancies having a veteran working the till. Says he gets a lot more customers, with a 'Hero of the Western Front' selling his sausages. I was front page news, in the local paper, when I got back."

"Yeah, they did that to me too. The army told Dottie I'd died, so they called me: The miracle man." Jack curled his lip as he spoke, and immediately took a mouthful of beer, as if to rinse a bad taste from his mouth.

With almost equal distaste, Billy noted that on the pinkie finger of his right hand, Jack wore a large, silver signet ring.

"I heard about that. It was in the Lithgow paper too. I think it went round the country. M' family were dead impressed that I knew you. M' brothers all wanted to know what you were like, and even Dad said how lucky I was, to meet a real hero."

A sudden noise from outside, caused the men in the pub to look up and turn towards the big glass doors, watching, as two of the Push members, shouted lewd comments at a woman crossing the street.

Turning back to his companion, Jack swallowed the last of the beer in his glass. "How is your family?"

"They're well. M' brother Daniel tried signing up, but they knocked him back, 'cause he works in the mines. Mum gets upset when she looks at me, sometimes, but she's getting used to me now. She'd be really cross to see me in an Irish pub." Billy smiled, plunging into his beer, his veteran status having made it easier to buy beer, despite his age.

"You look well."

Billy looked across at Jack, and wished he could return the complement, but beneath the flashy clothes, his friend looked pale and strained. His face was drawn into the frown, of one who is in pain, and dark shadows hung beneath his eyes. His face was still gaunt, and his hands looked more like the bony feet of birds, than the hands of a young man.

"How's your family?"

"They're well. Edie and Alfie are used to me now. They were, understandably, a bit wary of me when I first arrived. We're expecting another, at the end of the year. My brother gave me a job in his office, he understands when I can't get in. I'm trying to avoid taking the pension. Dottie's…" Jack's words trailed off, as he struggled to find words to encompass how vital he found Dottie, to his continued life.

"I've got a girlfriend now. Gracie, she's my friend George's, sister." Leaning across the table, Billy added in a low voice. "You were right about the girls. From the beginning they hung off me, as if I had done something great and heroic. Mate, it almost makes the whole mess worthwhile."

"Finish your beer. I'll take you home, Dottie will have dinner ready soon."

Seeing Jack's eagerness to leave, Billy drained his half full glass, and rose from his chair.

Exiting the pub, Jack and Billy ran into the Push, who had by now managed to beg enough beer, to become more than just a pest. It wasn't yet five, but the sun was setting, and the streets growing dark and cold.

"Look 'ere, a bloke without a face," called one of the more inebriated young men, pointing at Billy.

"What 'appened to yer?" drawled the Push leader, pushing his bent nose into Billy's face.

"I dunno, what happened to you?" said Billy, shoving the

Push leader away.

"He shoved me," said the Push leader, in mock protest to his mates.

"I'll do more than that if you shove your ugly mug under m' hat again."

"What about your friend with the stick. What 'appened to 'im?" The Push leader walked before Jack, in an exaggerated imitation of his walk. Behind him, the Push laughed with drunken hilarity.

Jack watched the dumb show in silence, powerless to stop them, or raise a voice in protest.

"I don't see you doing any fighting," said Billy, directing the leader's attention, away from Jack.

"We fight all the time. We're bloody heroes!" laughed the leader, showing a mouth full of shining, white teeth.

"Really? You think fighting drunks and each other, is something to be proud of. You're just a pack of dogs. Fuck off, before I show you what a real fight is."

Behind him, the men from the pub gathered about, to watch the Push leader square off, against the hulking veteran, fresh off the Lithgow train.

"You think I'm afraid of you an' Limpie 'ere?" said the leader, dancing around like a prize fighter. The rest of the Push crowding round, jostling Jack and cheering their leader on.

Billy, who stood a full foot taller than the Push leader, removed his hat and coat with exaggerated care, handing them to the man behind him. Billy waited, stepping back from the jabs, the bouncing Push leader swung in his direction. Bringing his fits up at last, he threw a right jab to the solar plexus, and a left hook, catching the leader square in the jaw. The Push leader turned white and gasped, struggling to breathe, lying sprawled across the ground.

Turning back to the men from the pub, Billy retrieved his hat and coat, as the audience withdrew again, to the warmth of the bar.

The Push gathered around the fallen leader. Dazed and bleeding, the Push leader looked up at Billy.

"Yer got lucky." The Push leader spat out a mouthful of blood, and broken teeth, when at last he found his voice.

"I'll take my luck, over your, skill any day."

The Push, gathered up their fallen leader, and scurried like rats, towards Hudson's gully.

Turning to Jack, Billy saw his friend huddled on the ground, his arms over his head, rocking back and forth.

"Jack. Jack, are you alright Mate?" Billy crouched down beside Jack, placing a hand on his back.

Without lowering his arms, Jack turned his head, to look at Billy with wild eyes. "Has it stopped?"

Billy looked about the now deserted street. The cab rank across the road looked possible, if he could coax Jack to his feet again.

"Mate, we have to go over there," said Billy pointing towards the cab rank. "There's no more shelling, it's all quiet, we just have to walk across the road."

Jack shook his head, and clung to Billy's arm. Billy waved to the cabbie, parked nearest to him, across the street.

"Hey, cabbie! I got a Digger here who needs a lift. Come and get him," shouted Billy, using the words he had heard soldiers use, to hail the medics.

The cabbie, a young man, whose eyebrows gave his face a look of constant worry, jumped down from his seat and crossed the road.

"Shit, that's the boss. Wait, I'll bring the cab around," Smithy called, returning to his cab.

By the time Smithy had brought the cab across the street, Billy had coaxed Jack to his feet. Still Jack clung to his friend's arm, his fingers gripping not just the coat, but holding onto the man beneath, ready to pull him down to safety. As he had done before when bullets sparked hot on the pebbles of the dark beach, and the roar of guns shook the air. Smithy jumped down, helping Billy, get Jack inside the cab. Slamming the door, Smithy returned to his seat, driving the half mile to Jack's home.

***

"What happened?"

Billy's mum had always told him that Irish Catholics were devils, now standing before Archibald Kelly, he was inclined to believe her. This one stood before him, flaming hair and beard, even his eyes seemed red. All he wanted were horns, a tail and a pitch fork, to be old Lucifer himself, straight from the Sunday school textbook. He stood in the door way, his back to the hall, blocking the exit and listening to Dottie across the hall, try to soothe her husband and put him to bed.

"I'm afraid it's my fault, Mr Kelly," said Billy, standing in the front room. "We had a run in with your local Push. They wanted a fight, and in all the noise, I guess he just went back there."

"He was fighting?"

"No, I was fighting. I flattened their leader, they ran off like rats." Billy smiled, proud of his prowess as a street fighter. Glancing at Arch, the smile slid from his face. "We should have walked on. If I'd know he was a mental case, I would have walked on."

Behind Arch, the bedroom door closed softly, and Dottie stepped into the front room, sliding in behind Arch. Placing the dish she carried, containing wads of cotton, broken vials and a syringe onto the tea-table, Dottie sank down into her chair. Resting her head on one hand, she looked up at Billy.

Turning to look at Dottie, Billy had never seen such coldness in a look, before. If Jack's brother was a fiery devil, then his wife was something else entirely.

"Mrs Kelly, I had no idea he was…" Billy's words died in his mouth, as he endured Dottie's withering gaze. Helpless, as she rose from her seat, directing him towards the front door. When Dottie at last spoke, it was in the cool voice of a society hostess, and even more devastating to Billy's guilty conscious, than a roomful of screaming harridans could have managed.

"Thank you for bringing him home. He'll be all right now. I think the next Lithgow train will be here soon, you had better not miss it."

Billy could scarcely say, how he found himself standing on the door step. His coat and hat clutched in his arms, with the sound of the door slamming ringing in his ears.

Dottie, returning to the front room, sank back into her chair and buried her face in her hands.

"Damn." Dottie raised her head, and looked at Arch, now sitting on the sofa. "We had been so careful. In a few days the whole town will know. They'll say it's your mother coming out in him."

"Smithy's a good bloke, He won't tell anyone."

"And all the men in the pub, are they all good blokes?"

Arch looked away, and shuffled his feet on the carpet, he knew what Dottie said was true. Soon the whole town would know, and they would be as quick to judge, as that young fool Jack had thought a friend.

"Why didn't you tell me he was in such a bad way?"

"Jack didn't want to tell me. I only know, because I found him digging trenches instead of a vegetable garden. He was over a foot down, complaining that the subsoil would offer no protection, against shelling. I suspected something was wrong before that, but he was more worried about the pain he was in, so

I didn't like to bother him about it."

Arch looked at Dottie, her eyes glittered wetly. Tears had attached themselves to her thick dark lashes, but had not yet begun to make tracks down her face.

"The doctor says, rest and quiet should help. If he gets worse there are other options, rest homes for soldiers, but I don't want to send him away."

Chapter Thirty seven

Nights were the worst. The nightmares that snuck up on you, when you were at your most vulnerable. The daytime memories were one thing, a clean precise retelling of what he had been through, and although distressing they were endurable. The nightmares, on the other hand, were another order of torture entirely. In them, the war came home. It was his home, through which he searched, nightly. His wife, he found buried, beneath the fallen rubble. His children, dead in the fields. It was into the faces of friends, that he looked with pity, squeezing their hands, as they were walked past him on stretchers. And the men he saw fall through his gun sights, or on the end of his bayonet, all had the same face, the same horribly, familiar face of his brother. In the moment of recognition, he would wake into darkness. For it was always dark when he woke, sweating and trembling, his heart beating, as if from a ten mile run. And then there would be the rest of the night to get through.

If he were lucky, he would wake with a shout that woke Dottie. And in the darkness, he could hold her and feel her stroke his hair like a child, whispering to him in soothing sounds. He would listen for the clock, striking in the other room, while Dottie went to fetch his medicine. Measuring it out carefully, as the doctor had shown her, and giving him the injection. Then she would hide it away, careful that he not be able to find it, as the doctor had told her to do. By the time she had returned to their bed, he would be asleep.

The nights when he didn't cry out, and wake Dottie, were the worst. For those were the nights when he, came into the room. He, for he had no name and no voice, with which to identify himself, would stand always, within Jack's line of sight. If Jack lay on his side, he stood against the wall, opposite. If Jack lay on his back, he would be at the foot of the bed. Once Jack had tried facing his wife, but he followed Jack's gaze and stood menacingly, above the peacefully sleeping form of Dottie. Once he arrived, Jack knew that there was no option, but to wait the night out. Enduring for hours, the terrifying burning eyes, of that first man he had killed, in those dark dawn hours, on the ridges of Anzac cove. As the light grew, and the night faded into dawn, the figure too would fade, losing its apparent solidity, until as Dottie pulled back the curtains, it disappeared altogether. Then Dottie would notice Jack, and stroke his face, releasing him from the night's dark spell. Though exhausted, he would rise and wash off the terrors of the night.

Days were better, though they weren't without their own challenges. Work had gone after the big attack. He had tried for a few days, tried to work, with the clock ticking out the silence. The phone in the front of the office ringing, and the girl who answered it, chattering away. He had tried to make conversation with the men, as they came into the office, for breaks or to collect bookings. Tried to say the right thing, and hold his mind steady, as they spoke to him. But he could see, by the looks on their faces, that he had said the wrong thing, or looked strangely at them. Never had Arch said he wasn't to come in, but Jack could no longer face the looks, nor the conversations, that halted when he appeared. The whispers, which started behind his back. He could never quite, catch what they said, but several times, he had been certain that they had said the words, 'mad' and 'brothers' and 'murderer'. Though, it could have been a conversation about the Shaw brothers, one of whom was due to be hanged, for the murder at The California. The strain was too much. By the end of the week, the books were being delivered to the house, where he could work in peace.

Still, Jack found himself craving human contact. Leading him to join Dottie, as she ran errands in town. What had at first seemed a good idea, trailing along with Dottie as she shopped, quickly proved the opposite. The looks he received from passers-by, some filled with pity, some contempt, others still with anger. As if he were, personally, responsible for every boy who had not returned, made him shrink inside his clothes. In town, people had tried to engage him on the question of conscription, and Prime Minister Hughes' continued campaigning in its favour. Jack found that on more than on occasion, he had responded to such queries, by shouting. The violence of his response, almost as shocking, as his sentiments, which were a confused jumble of the images that ran about in his head, and his earlier opposition. That Dottie had to break off what she had been doing, to quiet him, left him open to looks of pity. Though it had become clear that the pity, was directed to his wife. They looked at her and then at him, the pity that escaped them, followed as their eyes slid back to Dottie. Pity that she had found herself lashed to him. Such an appalling wreck of a man, one who did not deserve such a lovely young family, after what he had become.

Church too had gone, after he found the pew he sat in, and the ones before and behind, were ranked up with men he had killed. Their awful dead faces, confirmation that to kill is a sin, and no clever exemptions Church officials gave to that simple command, thou shalt not kill, changed that fact. The cold, dead faces that looked at him, claimed him as one of their own, proving to him that, as he suspected, God was no longer listening.

Home was a much safer place to remain, here the sudden shocks and jolts of noise and activity in the outside world, could be avoided. Here too, the people who entered, could be trusted not to speak to the wider world, of what they saw of him. He could avoid them, without comment, and plead illness to retire from their company. Yet, even here, he knew that hushed conversations about him, continued behind his back. He knew Dottie talked to Arch about him. Knew that he had become a problem to be managed.

***

Sitting at his desk, Jack watched the rain, as it lashed the garden and battered against the windows, it had been raining for weeks, on and off. One of those wet winters, where it was impossible to get the washing dry, forcing Dottie to string it across the kitchen. Arch's books lay open on the desk before him. It helped most of the time, to keep his mind filled with something practical and useful, but not this morning.

Entering the front room with a cup of tea, which she placed on the desk, as she did every morning, Dottie bent down and kissed him on the crown of his head. "Are you alright, Love."

Jack shook his head, lifting the glass he held to take a drink. His hand trembled badly, forcing him to put the glass back down on the desk. He had almost done it, almost let his darkest thoughts become actions. Though to call them thoughts was to give the train of impulses, he had almost succumbed to that morning, more direction than they deserved. He had been shaving, no different to any morning, his face lathered ready for the stubble to fall beneath his razor blade. When he had found himself struck by the idea that all the suffering, all the pain that he was in, could be solved right now with one small cut. A few seconds, perhaps minutes, of pain and there would be an end to it. It seemed so easy. Though it would be Dottie or one of the children who would find him. Dottie who would be forced to explain, again suffering the grief of his dying. Though what was the alternative; to take them with him? Like the villain in a lurid newspaper serial, enticing them into the bathroom with him, one at a time and…The razor fell from his hands, onto the tiled floor, with a clatter. He had stopped himself there, right on the brink, before the awful impulse showed him images far worse than his nightmares.

Picking up the razor that he had let fall to the floor, Jack walked through the kitchen and out the back door, into the rain. Stepping across the back lawn, he looked towards the house, the rain blinding him as it beat down, soaking him through his pyjamas. Wiping the rain from his eyes, he threw the razor onto the roof, where it landed with a clatter, slid down the metal sheeting and lodged in the guttering.

Standing by the backdoor, Dottie watched as Jack slowly made his way across the slippery grass, mounting the steps to the back veranda. Picking up the edge of her apron, Dottie wiped the soap and the rain from Jack's face.

"You know there are easier ways to tell me you want to grow your beard, Love."

All morning, Jack had sat at his desk, staring at the columns of numbers, trying to makes sense of them. The numbers swam before his eyes, refusing to lie still in any coherent form. His head felt strange, as if some important part had stopped working, and the rest struggled to move in the haze that clogged his brain. One single thought obsessed him, and he worried at it like a dog: how close had he come to actually hurting those he loved. It was bad enough to live with this horrible confusion and panic, but to become a danger to Dottie and the children. He would have to go away to one of those homes, Dottie and Arch talked of in hushed tones, behind the kitchen door, when they thought he wasn't listening.

"I'll do the books, Jack. Why don't you get some rest?"

Jack rose from his chair, moving across the room, to lie on the sofa.

"I don't want to sleep." Jack patted the arm of Dottie's chair, beckoning her back across the room, to sit by him.

Pushing the chair she had been about to sit on, back under the desk. Dottie crossed the room and sat down in the chair, Jack offered.

Reaching out and taking her hand, Jack closed his eyes and took a deep breath. "Dottie, I've made a decision. You need a rest, you can't keep looking after me, the kids, and the house. You're exhausted and it's not good for you in your condition. I've been looking into it, and there are new Soldier's Homes. If I can get my head sorted out, then I can go back to work."

Leaning forward in the chair, so that she could run her fingers down the side of his face. Dottie smiled and shook her head. Shaking away words she did not wish to hear, as if they were so many flies pestering her.

"I'm not sending you away Jack. Doctor Allen says being at home will help you find your balance again."

"It's not forever Dottie, but I'm not getting better. If anything I'm getting worse." Jack pressed his free hand to his face, roughly wiping away tears with the heel of his palm.

"I've not told you how bad it is in my head. If I don't get a break from it, I don't know what I'll do."

"Alright Jack, I'll talk to Doctor Allen and I'll write some letters to the Repatriation Department. We'll sort something out."

***

Years later, when she ever dared to voice it, Dottie would say that it was the rejection letter from the Repatriation Department declaring Jack's illness hereditary and not the result of the war, that was the final straw for him. After that, he had ceased to struggle against whatever his mind threw up at him, sliding rapidly from the nervous tension caused by his nightmares and memories, to a numb and passive despair. Days, which had once been a time Jack filled with varying amounts of activity, slipped slowly into one with nights. As he sat in silence, his gaze fixed firmly inward, as his mood filled the room.

As Jack declined, Dottie and Arch wrote desperate letters, trying to find a suitable place for him to recover. All the while, fielding questions from concerned friends and acquaintances. Attempting to stem the flow of gossip, which had risen like flood waters around them, with assurances that it was merely physical ailments that kept Jack at home.

***

It was another cold wet afternoon, when Arch pushed open the back door and waited on the doorstep for Dottie to notice him. Wiping down the table and gathering the dough and flour into the skirt of her apron. Dottie looked up and forced her face into, what she hoped, was a smile.

"I've been making scones, my hands are all messy. Give me a moment and I'll put the kettle on." Stepping out the backdoor, past Arch, Dottie opened the skirt of her apron over the edge of the porch, letting the dough and flour rain onto the lawn. Turning back to face Arch, she felt him step towards her and wrap his arms about her, holding her, as she relaxed into his embrace.

Releasing Dottie, he led her to the bench beneath the kitchen window, and sat down.

"How're you going?"

"I felt the baby kick for the first time this morning. When I told Jack, he didn't react, it was as if I had told him that the milk had arrived. I thought the panic and the nightmares were bad, but I'd have them back in an instant rather than this. He's disappearing."

Arch wrapped an arm about Dottie's shoulders, drawing her close, so that he could rest his chin on the top of her head.

"I talked to Aunt Bette this morning, she said she's found Jack a place in a rest home." Beneath his arm Arch could feel Dottie's body respond to the news. The dejected posture lifting, as hope began to trickle in. "Problem is, it's down the South Coast, past Wollongong."

"I don't think we can wait for anything closer. He needs help now, it might be just the thing he needs to cheer him up."

"She said he can't get in for a couple of weeks, though."

Dottie leant forward, resting her elbows on her knees. How the news was broken, would be almost as important as the news itself. The vital thing was that there was a place, when and where that place would come, could wait. Knowing that the place was so far away, would not be good for him right now. The idea of being apart had been a possibility that Jack had considered before, but now, even trips to the shops left him fretting for her.

"Tell Jack that he's got a place, but don't be too specific, it needs to be tiny steps or he'll panic."

"Don't worry Dot I know how to deal with skittish horses. Is he in bed?" Arch rose from the bench, opening the back door.

"He's in the front room. Take some wood in with you, he'll have let the fire go out."

Picking up the wood basket, Arch stepped inside. Dottie listened as the back door banged, and Arch's footsteps faded into the house.

***

"How're you goin' Jack?"

Receiving no reply from his brother seated by the fire, Arch entered the front room, and sat down opposite him. Placing the basket on the floor, Arch saw that just as Dottie had guessed,

Jack had let the fire die down to coals. Adding a couple of logs to the fire, Arch watched as the coals glowed, then began sending out tongues of flame to lick at the fresh wood.

"Dot said you'd be here."

"Go away, Arch," said Jack, trying to shield his face and the fact that he was crying from his elder brother.

"You have to talk Jack. You have to share what is in your head."

"No. I don't." Jack threw a fierce look at Arch.

"It'll get better."

"No it won't. I'll just get worse and worse, until you and Dottie have to send me away. But that will be all right. I'm the one who doesn't fit anymore. I had everything, then I threw it away for an adventure," said Jack, his tone hollow, as he gazed at the fire.

Suddenly, the idea of finding a place in a rest home, no longer seemed the good news he and Dottie had hoped it would be. To be sent away seemed another form of punishment. A final indignity to crown his failure to adapt to civilian life, as he was meant.

"Jack you have to leave the war behind. You have a life here, now with Dot and your children."

Jack closed his eyes resting his head on his hand.

"We were all right, after Mum died. You'll be fine without me."

Arch looked at his brother, he had seen the eerie calmness that spread across Jack's face, as he spoke those words, before. It was the look on the face of every jumper he had rejected, in his life as a cabbie. Worse than that, it was the look on their mother's face that last morning, as he left the house to spend a day in the stables. Never had Jack looked so like their mother than he did at that moment, and it horrified him.

"No, we weren't. After Mum died, Dad changed. After Mum

died, I was angry with her, for not letting me try to show her how much she was needed. I was angry that she didn't love me enough to stay."

"I can't do this Arch. I'm not sad. I'm dead. You don't need me. I can't love you. I can't love Dottie or our children. Everything is just black and empty. I don't want to live like this. I look at you and I see that you are upset, but I can't feel it. I can't feel anything. I'm dead inside. Arch, all I see is death. Everywhere I go I see dead things. I look at you, I look at Dottie and my children and I feel nothing. I see men I've killed, and it doesn't matter what they say, I can't get rid of that. I can't live like this."

Arch looked at Jack. He wanted to gather him up in his arms and hold him, as he did when they were children. He wanted to make it better. To take out the suffering part of him and throw it into the fire, so that it could be consumed and melt away. He felt sure that this fit would pass, just as the others had. It was just a matter of making Jack see that there was hope.

"Dot and I love you, Jack. Your children love you. You have medals and ribbons for bravery, you didn't do anything wrong."

Grasping his head in his hands, Jack gripped his hair, as if he wished to tear it out in handfuls. "I killed! Each time I killed, another piece of my soul got torn away. It's all been ripped away and dragged down to Hell."

"It was war, Jack. God doesn't hold that against you."

"They say not, but He does. There isn't any forgiveness. There is just Hell."

Jack looked up at Arch, his eyes red and swollen from weeping, and gave him a withering look.

"Go away Arch."

Still Running

He is a man running. A man so caked in dust, he looks like a statue. He is an armed man running. His arms and legs ache with fatigue, yet he cannot stop. He can feel the sweat running down his face, bleeding tracks of living colour back into it, as the dust turns to mud. He cannot stop. On his heels, another man, clad as he is, pursues him. His chest is burning. Every breath he takes is painful. Above him tower the walls of the city, around which he runs. Three times, he will run around these walls, before he halts his flight. He is man-killing Hector and today his fate will be decided.

It was one of those clear crisp mountain days, where winter seems to have placed itself on hold for a few hours, granting a brief reprieve to the inhabitants of the towns clinging to the ridges overlooking the valleys. At this time of year, the cloudless sky looked cobalt blue, above the sapphire mountains and valleys. It was a day for activity, as gardeners taking advantage of the mild conditions pruned fruit trees and ornamentals. The century old custom, of imposing gardens of European favourites on the thin fragile soils of the sandstone ridges, first begun when homesick colonists and convicts alike stepped off their ships in Sydney harbour. Another blue jewel in this unfamiliar land. Here the mountain ridges bore the brunt of the southerly winds causing the wanton eucalypts to dance a wild jig, but tearing down far more staid oaks and pines. Today there was no wind. Today the gardeners' waste material ascended to the heavens in orderly columns, while slow combustion stoves fuelled by local eucalyptus, perfumed the air, so that one at once recognised the smell of home and warmth.

Jack wasn't sure what had brought him to this exact spot. It was not the most convenient spot for what he had in mind, not with all the sightseers flocking around the viewing platform like a noisy gaggle of geese. Pointing and exclaiming, some holding guide books, trying to name the cliffs, which rose from the valley floor like ridges along a dragon's backbone. Women in white dresses, clung to the rope at the edge, as they looked down to the valley floor, invisible beneath the thick canopy of eucalyptus, coach wood and sassafras.

Sitting down on a bench, Jack placed both his hands over the handle of his walking stick. Leaning forward he rested his forehead against his hands, closing his eyes. Perhaps, if he wished hard enough, they would all go away. He was too old to believe in wishes anymore. He felt so old, like he had lived more lifetimes than he could count, yet at the same time it had not been enough. The same way, that one can sleep for eight or nine hours and still wake up feeling exhausted. Hell, he would be thankful for three or four hours, of uninterrupted sleep.

Raising his head, he rested his chin against his hands, watching the tourists walk to and fro.

"Mummy, that man is crying!"

Turning to look, Jack saw a small boy, having broken away from the crowd gazing at the view. He stood staring at Jack, as if he were far more interesting a sight than the mountains that the boy had in fact come to see. Turning away, Jack swiped at the tears with the back of his hand. Helpless to stop their flow, he squared his jaw and stared back at the boy, making further ineffectual swipes at his face. Until the boy had seen him, he hadn't even noticed that he was crying. Things like this happened all too often these days.

"George, come here! Leave that poor man alone," called one of the women, standing by the edge.

The boy turned his head towards the voice with a look of irritation, acknowledging that it was his mother who had spoken to him, but remained fixed to the spot.

"George, don't make me come over there!"

Hearing this too common threat, the boy turned and ran back to his mother. Jack watched, returning the child's gaze as he twisted his head round to watch the crying man. Jack once again attempted to dry his face, before accepting the futility of such action, resting his forehead against his hands, watching as big salty tears dripped from his nose, and splashed onto the dry sand between his feet.

As the afternoon drew to a close, the constant stream of sightseers dwindled and the warmth of the day died, bringing with it hardness, as the temperature dropped rapidly. With no cloud cover, the temperature would fall below freezing tonight, and tomorrow morning would wake to a thick layer of frost. Jack shivered in his coat, as he watched the sun disappear behind Narrow Neck. Already the moon shone in the darkening sky.

Alone now, Jack rose from the bench he had occupied, all afternoon. His movements were slow and uncertain. He leant on his walking stick, dragging his left leg, which had grown stiff and sore with cold and hours seated in the same position. As he made his way, across the viewing platform, to the ropes strung above the drop.

The two dozen steps from bench to the edge had exhausted him. He leant against the ropes, looking over into the gathering gloom, which hid the forest from sight. This was it, the end. He had travelled this far and would go no further. He had walked these forests as a boy, not so many years ago, though it felt like centuries. It was fitting that he should return to them. Here, he could find the peace, which no green and pleasant countryside had given him.

Behind him, he heard the sound of a cab roaring down the road. The wheels scattered gravel, as the driver brought the car to a sudden halt. Mustering all his energy, Jack swung his left leg over the rope. He paused a moment, gathering his strength, one leg planted on the ground, the other dangling over the valley floor, waiting.

***

Elizabeth Ebsworth, opened the suitcase that she had placed on the bed, and began to unpack it. Trailing her into the room, her nephew sat beside the case, on the bed. The room was simple, but attractively so. It was certainly not the prison like asylum, he had been imagining, as they travelled down on the train. In his mind he had seen padded cells and straightjackets, being locked away in the dark, like so much rubbish. Here the white walls and furniture offered a clean and fresh quality to the room, aided by the large window, which gave a view of the garden. The locks on the window and the outside of the door, the only things differentiating it, from a room in a nice guest house.

"It's not such a bad place, is it?" Elizabeth opened the top draw of the dresser, filling it with pyjamas and underclothes. "It's very progressive, they offer the best treatments available. They have lovely food, fresh sea food every night, you'll like that. They have a reading room and a piano. You can see the sea from the dining room."

"When can Dottie come visit?"

"Soon, but not until you have settled in." Elizabeth sat down next to Jack, feeling him lay his head against her shoulder. "Your job is to get better. There are other soldiers here, other people who know what you went through. The harder you work, the sooner you can go home again. I've rented a cottage for a month from now, it'll be spring, and lovely and warm. I'll bring Dorothy and the children down to visit with you."

Jack lifted his head from his aunt's shoulder, and rose from the bed, moving to look out of the window. Elizabeth returned to unpacking, putting away Jack's clothes and belongings. Once she was finished, she placed the empty case under the bed.

"Mrs Ebsworth," said a nurse appearing at the door. "I'm afraid visiting hours are over, could you say goodbye, please."

"Well Jack, you'll be okay here, won't you?"

Jack nodded, without turning away from the window. The sun hung low on the horizon, in a few minutes it would vanish entirely, but at the moment it dyed the clouds a vivid and startling orange and pink, while the darkening sky seemed almost violet.

Moving to stand beside Jack in the golden light, Elizabeth reached for his hand, feeling him squeeze it tightly. "I'll come tomorrow and see how you are settling in."

Releasing his aunt's hand, Jack listened, as her footsteps left the room and echoed down the hall.

Alone now, Jack moved to the bed. Sitting down, he took off his shoes and slid them across the floor, away from the bed. Lying on the bed, watching as the setting sun filled the room with gold. Spreading long shadows from the nearby eucalypts, across the curtains and bedspread, patterning them with leaves. He waited.

Tell it Again

Sitting in her air conditioned office, in the humanities block at the university, Meredith Butler looked out the window at the students, wilting on the browned off lawn. Checking her mobile, she saw that there was still half an hour before she was due to give her first lecture. 20th century Australian History for the fresh faced, first years. Every year they were getting younger, or perhaps it was she, who was getting older.

Turing her attention away from the window, to the blinking cursor on her computer screen, Meredith knew that she ought to use the next half hour working on her conference paper. She would be flying to Melbourne in the Easter break to give a talk: Heterodiegetic narrators and the suppression of the Other in popular Australian history narratives. She had been inspired to write it, after yet another fat, unreflective book, celebrating the achievements of straight white men who built the nation, had appeared in the bookshops. Just in time for the centenary of Anzac. Despite the air conditioned office, today was not the day for work, outside where the students sprawled the temperature must be nearly forty degrees. The pressure in her head, told her that a storm was brewing.

Opening her desk draw, Meredith took out a couple of aspirin, swallowing them down, with the dregs from the bottle of water, beside the computer. She would have to get a new one, from the machine, before she entered the lecture hall. Hopefully, the aspirin would allow her to get home tonight, before the migraine she could feel building struck.

"Professor Butler?"

The voice belonged to Nadir, a tall slim young man with a thick black beard. Today he was wearing a turban of brilliant blue, above a pair of rumpled cargo shorts and a tee-shirt, for one of the many bands that she had never heard of. Under one arm he held a package.

"Hi." Meredith spun around in her chair to face the open door.

"I've come to drop off my latest draft of my thesis," said Nadir, fishing in one of his voluminous pockets, for a thumb drive.

Taking the thumb drive, Meredith placed it on her desk. "Thanks, I'll read it and we'll discuss it on Friday. What's in the box?"

"Oh, it's for you, the office gave it to me when I asked if you were in." Nadir placed the box on the desk. "I'm off to the library, so I'll leave you to it."

"Thanks."

Turning her attention to the box, Meredith slit the tape, opening the box. Lifting the contents carefully wrapped in plastic packaging, how she hated plastic packaging, she placed it on her desk. Opening the plastic, the package contained, a photograph of a young man in a First World War AIF uniform, a box containing service medals, a diary, and a pile of letters tied up with ribbon. Underneath these, lay an envelope.

Picking up the envelope, Meredith glanced again at her phone, twenty minutes until her lecture: plenty of time.

Dear Professor Butler,

My name is Sarah Kelly, I heard you on the radio last week, talking about the need for a more nuanced understanding of Australian History, and the need to recognise alternative narratives. Your discussion of the book you are working on, examining the connections between the soldiers of the First World War and the family on the home front, made me think of the box of relics that I was given by the nursing home, after my great grandfather passed away.

The man in the photo is, John Michael Kelly, my great grandfather's great uncle. Family history tells me, that Jack Kelly was the younger of two brothers at the time of the First World War. The elder brother, Archibald was married to a woman with German ancestry, and they had three children. Jack Kelly was a solicitor when the war broke out, and signed up on the first day. He was in the first wave of men who landed at Gallipoli, fought at Lone Pine and Poziers, where he was killed. The diary, although rather damaged, was sent back with his effects, after his death. The letters are addressed, both to his brother Archibald and to his brother's wife, whom he calls Dottie. Jack wasn't talked of much in our family, and we suspect that it might be his closeness to his brother's wife which caused this.

Apparently, Dorothy Kelly was very active in the anti-conscription campaigns, and the whole family has taken a pacifist stance, in relation to subsequent wars over the years. In light of this, the presence of an original Anzac, seems to have been a cause of embarrassment, rather than the usual patriotic pride.

I hope that this might prove useful for your research and that you might be able to find a home for these relics at the university.

Sincerely,

Sarah Kelly.

P.S. I am sorry to send the photo in a frame, but the photo appears to be stuck and cannot be removed from it without causing damage.